SIREN'S SONG

SIREN'S SONG

Legion of Angels: Book 3

www.ellasummers.com/sirens-song

ISBN 978-1-5455-6063-1

SIREN'S SONG

Legion of Angels: Book 3

Ella Summers

Books by Ella Summers

Legion of Angels

1   Vampire's Kiss

2   Witch's Cauldron

3   Siren's Song

4   Dragon's Storm

Dragon Born Serafina

1   Mercenary Magic

2   Magic Games

3   Magic Nights

4   Rival Magic

Dragon Born Shadow World

The Complete Trilogy

Dragon Born Alexandria

1   Magic Edge

2   Blood Magic

3   Magic Kingdom

4   Shadow Magic [2017]

Dragon Born Awakening

1   Fairy Magic

2   Spirit Magic [2017]

More Books by Ella Summers

Sorcery & Science
Coming soon…

Read more at
www.ellasummers.com

Chapters

CHAPTER ONE

War of Willpower

"STASH, GIVE ME another one," I said, clunking my shot glass down on the counter with fervor. It was two o'clock in the afternoon, and this party was just getting started.

Now, any reasonable person might have wondered what I was doing at the Magic Formula, a witch bar in New York City, taking shots of glowing alcohol mixed with magic at this early hour. It wasn't depression, a broken heart, or lamentations of a wretched life that had brought me here. It was my training with the Legion of Angels, an elite unit of supernatural soldiers with powers gifted to them by the gods themselves.

Stash looked at me, stroking the dark stubble of his two-day beard in thoughtful silence, like he was considering cutting me off. Instead, he poured me another shot of magic-tinted pink alcohol.

"Smart man," I said.

He snorted.

"I can handle it," I assured him, throwing back the shot. It burned like lighter fluid on the way down, just like it was supposed to.

His eyes followed the shot glass as I set it daintily back on the counter. My hand didn't even shake. Compared to what I was used to, this fizzy pink stuff was child's play.

"I have no doubt of that, sweetness. You eat poison for breakfast."

Stash was right. Nectar, the drink of the gods, was essentially poison, a magical substance that either killed you or leveled up your magic. That's what they gave us at the Legion of Angels when we were up for a promotion, a do-or-die sort of test. The Legion was big on do-or-die.

He leaned his elbows on the counter, the corners of his mouth lifting. "So, what is a girl like you doing in a place like this?"

I laughed at his feigned attempt to flirt. Outside of my family and the Legion, Stash was probably the closest thing I had to a friend. A shifter who'd gotten kicked out of one of the city packs, he now did odd jobs for other supernaturals in the city. We'd met in a fairy bar a few months ago. He'd been earning money arm-wrestling the bar's patrons. He hadn't counted on my Legion status, that I was stronger than most supernaturals, even a big, tough shifter like him.

"Sorry, buddy, this visit is strictly business," I told him, turning my head toward the stage where a live band was playing under a turning light show of artificial colors.

On cue, a vampire burst out of the bathroom and streaked naked across the stage, zigzagging around instruments and band members, red and green light bouncing off his pale, naked ass. Laughter and cheers rose up from the crowd as all across the bar, people lifted their drinks in salute, a thank-you to the vampire for that brief moment of amusement.

They were thanking the wrong person. The vampire hadn't come up with the brilliant idea to give these people something to cheer about. That had been all me. I'd put the idea into his head—literally, with magic. It had many names: compulsion, enchantment, charisma, the siren's song. It was a tricky beast of a spell, and I'd been spending the past four months practicing it nonstop. This was necessary training for the next Legion level.

"Pretty good, right?" I said, turning to look at Jace.

"You convinced a drunk male vampire to part with his clothes. Bravo," he replied drily.

Jace had been my practice partner over these four months. He was a Legion 'brat', an endearing term for a Legion soldier with an angel parent. They had all the magic, discipline, and arrogance you'd expect from people with their esteemed heritage, but Jace wasn't so bad once you got a few drinks into him. Real drinks, laced with drops of Nectar. These witchy shots and cocktails didn't seem to affect him at all.

"It doesn't matter. I was successful, so you have to drink," I told him.

Jace drank his fizzy blue shot, then set the glass down in front of Stash.

"Oh, yes, I can see you're working real hard, Leda," the werewolf said to me.

I grinned at him. "Work and play. Killing two birds with one stone, my friend."

"Just how many stones are you planning on throwing in here, sweetness?"

"Until the birds start throwing back."

Eventually, it would happen. I'd run out of steam or I'd pick the wrong target, someone strong enough to resist my still-weak magic. Compelling people was hard work, so I'd had the idea to bring it to a bar and make a drinking game of it. Every time either Jace or I successfully compelled someone, the other had to take a shot. I hadn't counted on my opponent in this game being immune to alcohol.

I looked at Jace. "Your turn."

His eyes panned across the club, finally settling on a female fairy with a pixie cut of bubblegum-pink hair. Putting down her drink, she slid her hand down to the leather strap of knives fastened to her thigh. It was common practice to go to a supernatural bar armed to the teeth. The fairy's fingers danced across the knives, throwing them in quick succession at the opposite wall. Even though the crowd was as thick as molasses in winter, she hadn't hit a single person. What she had done was spell out 'Jace' on the wall with her knives.

"Good one," I told him, laughing. I took a shot from the glass Stash already had waiting for me.

"This is the most bizarre drinking game I've ever seen," the werewolf told me. "And I have seen a lot of weird shit."

A vampire on the other end of the bar was staring at me, his mesmerized eyes locked on my pale hair. He was looking at it like he wanted nothing more than to stain my platinum ponytail with my blood. Vampires had a thing for my hair. I'd never understood why, but something about it made them want to bite me, sparking hunger in even the most satiated vampire.

The vampire rose, his silver-blue eyes glowing with savage need. He was about to lose it. If he went for my neck, I'd have to shoot him, and I really didn't want to do that. It wasn't his fault my weird hair was a trigger for bloodlust in vampires.

I'd just have to put his energy to better use. I concentrated on his mind, on that spark of consciousness buried beneath a firestorm of instinct—and I grabbed onto it with everything I had. His consciousness retreated further, seeking refuge in the depths of his mind. I didn't let it go. I poured my own will into him. I didn't have a lot of magic, but what I did have was enough to get me in. And once I was in, his mind was mine. Compulsion was a game of mental gymnastics, a war of willpower. And there were few people who could match me in raw stubbornness.

The vampire stopped in front of me, the silver-blue sheen of his eyes fading out. He stared down at me, a blank slate. I gave him a big smile. In a burst of supernatural speed, he was suddenly on the bar, cartwheeling across the countertop in a series of stunts that would have made a top-tier gymnast green with envy.

"You really are the bringer of chaos," Stash told me, then he ran after the cartwheeling vampire, trying to knock him off the bar.

I drew another mark under my name on the napkin Jace and I were using to keep score.

"That was…showy," Jace said.

"You're one to talk. You had a fairy spell out your name in knives on the wall."

"That was a test of precision mind control."

"Yeah, yeah, tell that to the scoreboard." I showed him the napkin. "I'm ahead, goldilocks."

"The people you picked are drunk, so they'd do anything you tell them anyway. With the way you're dressed, it doesn't take much convincing."

I was wearing a dark red minidress and knee-high black boots, so he might have had a point.

I smirked at him. "Was there a compliment buried somewhere in that excuse?"

"Gods, no. I know better than to hit on Colonel Windstriker's girlfriend."

"I'm not his girlfriend."

He gave me an indulgent look. "You keep telling yourself that, Leda."

"We haven't even gone on a date yet."

"*Yet*," Jace repeated with emphasis.

"Ok, yes. He asked me out, but he's been out of the office more than he's been in lately, so we haven't actually been on a date."

"That hasn't stopped you from making out with him in the library."

How could he possibly know about that? Nero had found me in the library, reaching for a book on the reading list he'd given me to prepare for my next Legion level. The bookcases in the Legion's library were too high, obviously built with angels in mind. That created problems for those of us with our feet stuck on the ground.

Nero had plucked the book from the high shelf for me. One thing had led to another, and before I knew it, I was tackling him against the bookshelves, books raining down around us.

A sigh escaped my mouth. Kissing Nero was a dangerous pastime—an addiction, a gateway to dark and deadly seductions. And I was already in too deep.

"When is the last time you saw him?" Jace asked me.

"That day in the library last month."

And that little rendezvous had certainly left its mark. He'd kissed me like I was the only woman in the world, and then he'd just left. That angel was playing a game with me, a game I didn't even know the rules to, a game I was beginning to realize I'd lost before it had even begun.

"You've got it bad, Leda," Jace said, chuckling.

"Oh, shut up." I tossed a piece of popcorn at him. "You're one to talk. Rumor has it you and Mina are getting pretty cozy lately."

The smile wilted from his lips. "Mina and I are just friends."

"You just keep telling yourself that."

He clenched his jaw. "We should get back to practice."

"Then, by all means, impress me."

"Compelling someone is about controlling them, inside and out, body and mind, every sliver of self-control, every thought. There." He pointed at two groups of men facing each other down. They looked a hair's breadth away from breaking out in a fight. "What do you see?"

"Shifters versus witches, the epic showdown."

He didn't laugh. "It's one thing to convince someone to do something they might do anyway. The true challenge is in convincing them to do something they don't want to do."

The shifters and witches suddenly stopped, eight men completely frozen in time. A moment later, they clapped their hands, the synchronized pop echoing over a lull in the music. A stomp followed. A turn. A twist. They broke out into a coordinated dance, like they were caught in a musical. Spinning, spiraling, circling, lifting. On and on they moved, not enemies but partners. Pivoting, prancing, snapping, tapping.

"That was cool," I said to Jace as the shifters and witches finished their musical number. Their faces red, their eyes turned away, they parted ways too embarrassed to fight. "So much control. Every step was perfect. You should do shows."

"Siren's Song isn't a party trick. It's an important skill. It helps the Legion rally its troops. It diffuses problems. And learning this ability builds up a soldier's resistance to mental control."

"Did you swallow the Legion handbook?" I asked him.

He shot me a perplexed look. "You're doing that thing you do again."

"What thing?"

"Teasing."

"And that's a bad thing?"

"I…can't really decide if I like it."

"So growing up, you and your family didn't tease one another."

"My father doesn't tease. He disciplines you for your own good."

I snorted. "He sounds like your typical angel. I take it that speech about Siren's Song was a quote from him."

"Yes."

I added another mark to the napkin under his name. "Well, I think I've proven that we can work on this important skill and have fun at the same time."

I caught the arm of a passing vampire. She paused, her eyes taking on that distinctive hungry sheen as they slid down my hair, dipping to my neck. Her mouth curled back, exposing her fangs.

"My, my, what long teeth you have," I said, taking hold of her mind.

The vampire kicked off the floor, sliding with silky grace over the bar.

"Hey, you can't be back here," Stash told her as she

hopped down beside him.

The vampire batted her glittered eyelashes with false modesty. Then she grabbed Stash and kissed him hard on the lips. Her fingers, tipped with dark red polish, clawed through his hair, scraping down his stubbled jaw. Stash was kissing her back, and he wasn't being gentle about it either. I guess he'd decided she could be back there after all.

"Are you done yet?" Jace asked me.

I chuckled. "They're doing it on their own now."

Surprise flashed in his eyes. He looked from the kissing couple to me.

"Pretty good, huh? The compulsion became ingrained, not just when I was actively controlling her."

"It's hardly surprising," he said, recovering. "She is a vampire after all."

I sighed. "What will it take to impress you?"

Jace glanced across the dance floor. "There," he said, indicating the witch sitting on a sofa set atop a raised platform, looking down over everyone and everything like he was the king. "Enchant him. Convince him to sing 'In the Moonlight', and then I'll be impressed."

"That's a shifter song," I told him.

'In the Moonlight' was the shifters' anthem, their theme song. It's what they sang before getting furry and howling at the moon. Convincing a witch to sing it was about as easy as convincing a vampire to go on a no-blood diet. Nowadays, the shifters and witches of New York were getting along about as well as pickles and chocolate.

"Well, if you're afraid of failing…" Jace allowed his voice to trail off.

"I'm afraid of nothing, least of all a witch wearing a purple wig and a gold suit."

I poured myself another shot and drank it down. The witch king had bodyguards, two big witches who looked like they'd fallen off the pages of a bodybuilding magazine. I threw back another shot.

"If you're not scared, then why do you need so many drinks?" Jace asked me.

"Just boosting up my magic."

Which was kind of the truth. Witchy drinks had a hint of magic in them. Certainly nothing akin to Nectar, but you could only get Nectar drops in Legion bars. It was, after all, poison, so the fatality rate was pretty shocking. And killing your customers simply wasn't good for business.

"He's a leader," I said, glancing at the witch king tucked safely behind his wall of bodyguards. "Leaders are harder to compel. The qualities that make others want to follow them also make them resistant to mental attacks."

"That's why it's called a challenge," replied Jace. "Don't you want to push yourself?"

I did. Like everyone else, I had my reasons for joining the Legion. Some just wanted a place to fit in, others were hungry for power—or desperate for the magic that the gods' gifts bestowed. That was me. Desperate. After my brother Zane went missing without a trace six months ago, I'd gone to the Legion with the intention of blasting through the ranks to gain the magic I needed to find him. The catch? The magic that would allow me to link to him, something called Ghost's Whisper, was a ninth level Legion ability. I had a long way to go, assuming I even survived. This training was what I needed. I *had* to push myself.

The Legion was doing a good job of pushing me too. Thanks to the First Angel, I was on the fast track, an accelerated path of intensely brutal training. And I wasn't the only one.

"Ivy told me there are dozens of us across all Legion offices in this fast track program," I said.

"How does she know that?"

I shrugged. "She talks to people. And you know Ivy. People tell her everything."

"Maybe she could convince the witch king to sing 'In the Moonlight'."

"I'll do it. Just give me a moment." I traced my finger across the lip of my empty shot glass.

Jace's brows lifted. "Need another?"

"I think I can manage without," I said, tapping my fingertips atop the counter. "So many of us being pushed to grow our magic faster. The Legion must be preparing for something."

"You ask too many questions. That's what gets you into trouble."

"Has your father told you anything?"

"This is exactly what I'm talking about," he replied, frowning. "Trouble."

I smirked at him.

Jace sighed. "No, he hasn't told me anything. Colonel Fireswift is not big on sharing."

"Just like an angel," I commented, rolling back my shoulders as I stood. "Ok, I think I've procrastinated long enough."

I cut around the dance floor, keeping some distance between me and the hot scent of sweaty armpits and raging hormones. Sometimes possessing the heightened senses of a vampire was more of a burden than a boon. I strutted straight for the witch king's stage, my eyes raised with confidence, my heels clicking hard against the floor.

Attitude was everything, a little tip I'd learned in my bounty hunter years.

I'd made it to the wall of hired muscle. The witch king waved his bodyguards aside. Obviously, he was impressed by my attitude. Either that or my red minidress.

"Come here," he purred richly, patting the empty seat to his right. The spot to his left was already occupied by a raven-haired witch covered in a tiny piece of lacy black lingerie masquerading as a dress.

"I think I'll stand. I have the perfect view of your lovely companion's panties from here."

Silence filled the space between the witch king and me. The seconds dripped by. Then, suddenly, he threw back his head and laughed.

"Fantastic." He pulled out an embroidered handkerchief and wiped the tears of mirth from his eyes, careful not to smear his eyeliner. "You are perfect. Too perfect. Did Constantine send you?"

"Constantine Wildman?" I asked. He was the only witch named Constantine I'd ever met.

"Yes. He's always sending his minions to try to recruit me into his coven. After the last one, I told him that his next messenger had better be a pretty girl, or I wasn't listening."

"I'm not one of his minions."

He braided his fingers together. "Then to what do I owe the pleasure of this visit?"

"You sound like a man with a spectacular singing voice."

His smile grew wider. "Go on, you silver-tongued siren."

"I was hoping you'd honor us all with a song tonight." I

reached for the threads of his mind. "Something emotional. Something deep."

"What did you have in mind?"

This was the moment of truth. How much of the siren's magic was already in me? "In the Moonlight."

His smile soured. Anger flashing in his eyes, he jumped up. Chants—or were they curses?—spilled out of his mouth. He snatched a vial from his belt and threw it at my feet. An invisible weight pressed down on my shoulders. I felt like I was caught inside an airtight bottle, slowly suffocating on my own breath. Something hard slammed into me, and the witch's spell hurled me off the platform. My back hit the dance floor with a dry crack. I rolled over, gasping for breath, pushing myself up on my shaking arms.

One of the big bodyguards was waiting for me. His fist slammed down like a hammer. I slid out of the way— barely—and his hand broke through the floorboards. He shook off the splintered wood fragments and tried again. I rolled away, bouncing back to my feet. The bodyguard grabbed the closest table and pulled up so hard that the screws bolting the legs to the floor popped out. Then the friendly fellow hurled it at me.

I ducked. "That's not nice," I told him.

There was a strange, subtle glow to his body, some kind of spell. A strength-enhancing spell, I realized. He'd sprinkled the glittery gold powder all over himself. I ducked a second flying table. One of my witchcraft books had mentioned how to counter this spell. How did it go again?

I reached into my pouches, mixing together Wildflower and Unicorn Dust. Then I tossed the resulting pink-white powder at him. He froze, suspended in time. It wasn't the spell I was looking for, but it would do for now. I was about to go find a chair to finish the job when a cloud of sparkling midnight blue powder hit him in the back. His mouth puckered up into a surprised O, and he hit the ground, revealing Jace behind him.

"I thought you could use a hand," he said, looking down at the unconscious witch.

"I was doing all right."

He looked around the club pointedly. It was open warfare season. The shifters and witches were fighting, and the vampires had taken chase, hunting down the fleeing fairies.

"Ok, so maybe it could have gone better," I said.

A thunderous boom shook the building. Everyone stopped. The boom repeated. The staircase shuddered. Pictures tumbled off the walls, the glass front shattering against the quaking ground. What was going on?

"Uh-oh," Jace said, his voice low.

"What is it? A monster? A demon?"

He shook his head. "No, an angel."

The door to the club flung open, and golden streams of sunlight poured inside the dark room, lighting up a winged silhouette in a halo. He stepped inside, flaming cinders sprinkling off of him like burning rain.

"You're in trouble now," Jace whispered.

I met the green fire burning in the angel's eyes, a fire that threatened to consume me. It was like time had stopped. I couldn't help but stare at the angel moving toward me—or appreciate the muscled physique crafted over centuries of hard training. He moved like satin over steel.

His skin seemed to shine from within with the gods' light. And those wings! He'd spread them wide, showcasing the darkly beautiful tapestry of black, blue, and green feathers. He'd obviously done it to get our attention. Well, he had it, one hundred percent. I couldn't have looked away if I'd wanted to—and I definitely didn't want to. I wet my mouth, my tongue sliding slowly across my lips. His gaze dipped to my mouth, and something dangerous sparked in his eyes.

"Leave us," he said with a wave of his hand.

And just like that, the club emptied. His face impassive, the angel stopped in front of me and Jace.

"Nero," I began.

"Why am I not surprised to find you at the center of this chaos?"

Nero had an aura that toppled mountains and froze hurricanes. He moved like he owned every room, like he owned *you*—and you just wanted to please him, to make him look at you, to notice you. A hot sweat broke out across my skin, fear and excitement swirling inside of me.

"We were training," I said weakly.

Nero's hard eyes turned on Jace. "Training is over. Go back to the office. Your father is waiting for you there."

"Yes, Colonel." Swallowing hard, Jace trod across the floor and left the club. He must have known his father's visit wasn't about father-son bonding time.

Nero watched him leave, then his eyes snapped back to me. "Is there any point in lecturing you about proper decorum?"

"Probably not." I leaned my back against the bar.

"It was foolish of you to try to compel Orsin Wildman."

I didn't ask how he knew what had gone down here. He'd probably lifted it from the minds of the partiers. Nero was an accomplished telepath.

"It was Jace's idea."

"The witch was wearing an amulet to ward against compulsion," Nero said. "You will need to gain a lot more magic before you can break through a spell like that."

"An amulet? So that's what that glitzy necklace was."

"You need to read more of the books I assigned you," he replied with practiced patience.

"I *am* reading them. There are just so many to get through."

His brow arched. "An excuse?"

"A fact," I retorted.

"Being a soldier in the Legion of Angels is a constant struggle to improve yourself, to grow every skill, even the ones you think you've mastered. I'm trying to help you."

"I know, and I'm trying." I sighed. "I'll try harder."

"I didn't come here to lecture you, Leda."

"Then why did you come?" A smile tugged at my lips. "Want to make out behind the bar?"

Nero's eyes flickered toward the bar. Silver sparked in them for a brief moment before sinking into the emerald depths. I winked at him.

"You live dangerously, Pandora." His eyes dipped down, sliding across my body like molten honey.

"I love it when you call me Pandora." That was his nickname for me, the bringer of chaos.

His hand brushed down my arm, his touch featherlight. Goosebumps prickled up across my skin, like I'd been zapped by lightning. And not in a bad way.

"I came to tell you about our new mission." He lifted his hand to my neck, brushing back my hair.

"Our? As in you're going too?"

"Yes."

"And what mission has finally brought the illustrious Colonel Windstriker back to us?"

"I wanted to come back sooner."

"Oh? Missing the days of torturing new initiates?"

"I missed *you*, you smart ass."

I chuckled. "Tell me about this mission."

"We'll be guiding a group of Pilgrims across the Black Plains."

The Black Plains was a scorched expanse that was home to hundreds of different monster varieties. The only people who went there were the criminal and the insane—and soldiers of the Legion because angels like Nero thought fighting off human-eating monsters built character.

"The Pilgrims are going on a holy pilgrimage to the battleground site of the final showdown between gods and demons two hundred years ago."

"So I take it our job is to protect them from being eaten by monsters?"

"Yes."

"How romantic."

"Leda, I've assigned you to this mission because you know the area, not because I have any ulterior motives."

"Of course not." I kept my face perfectly serious. "Because that would be completely inappropriate."

"Exactly."

Ok, fine. Professional. I could do professional.

"When do we leave?" I asked.

"In half an hour."

CHAPTER TWO

Monsters and Outlaws

THE LOBBY OF the New York office of the Legion of Angels was busy today. Two Legion soldiers dragged a handcuffed fairy with floppy blue hair between them. A third soldier walked in front of them, carrying an oversized bag marked 'evidence'. Beyond the clear plastic front, simmering particles of rainbow-colored dust swirled in tiny cyclones. Pixie dust. It was a drug that made supernaturals lose control and hallucinate. And these weren't hallucinations of the sunshine-and-daffodils variety. Pixie dust made people paranoid and murderous. Usually, the Legion left drug cases to the paranormal police. This fairy must have dealt to the wrong people.

Nero and I passed by a trio of soldiers armed to the teeth with guns and knives. Their expressions were as deadly as their weaponry. These were hard, cold killers, the sort of soldiers the Legion sent in to take down the really nasty criminals.

"Where are they going?" I asked Nero.

"West. On a joint operation between us and the Los Angeles office."

"Monsters?"

"Outlaws," he replied. "They've left a trail of destruction from the east coast to the west."

"And them?" I asked.

Nero followed my gaze to a group of five soldiers dressed in thick winter wear. "They're going after a rogue band of shifters hiding out at the north end of the Wilds. These shifters stole Legion property."

That was a generic term the Legion applied often and generously. It could mean any number of things.

The door past the reception desk whooshed open, and a fourth group of soldiers walked into the overcrowded lobby. Of the four, I knew one of them. We'd gone on a few missions together over the past month. Sergeant Lavender Kane. She and her three companions were on the fast track to level four, and today was the day they headed out to special training. She'd been really excited about it when she'd told me. That same excitement sparkled in her eyes now. She looked from Nero to me, then gave me a conspiring wink.

"Why has Nyx put so many of us into accelerated training?" I asked Nero.

"I can't say anything about it."

Of course not. "Her new mystery plan has something to do with where you've been these past few months, doesn't it?"

He'd left shortly after we'd saved the witches' airship from being blown to pieces, after he'd asked me to go out with him. That was nearly four months ago, and since then he'd only returned here once a month for a few days at a time. Suffice it to say, there hadn't been any time for dates.

Not that I had time for dates anyway. I didn't even have

time for sleep—not between my usual work, the extra training Nyx assigned me, and tackling the never-ending reading list from Nero. Never-ending because he was adding on new books faster than I could read them.

In Nero's absence, Captain Somerset had been running things here. Now that he was back with a mission, though, maybe things would get back to normal—or at least as normal as things could be for soldiers of the gods' army. Hey, who knew? Maybe we'd even finally get around to going on that date.

"Be in the garage in fifteen minutes, Pandora," Nero told me, then he headed down the hallway that led to his office.

I leaned my elbow against the reception counter and let out a sigh. Encounters with angels were kind of hit and miss. It's like they were twenty different people, and you never knew which one you'd get. Today I'd gotten professional Nero. I swiped a donut from the box on the counter. Being professional sucked. I much preferred making-out-in-the-library Nero.

"What's it like to kiss him?" Cocoa, the secretary, asked me.

"He tastes like Nectar."

Cocoa blinked, obviously confused on how to respond to my statement. Nectar was a poison that either blessed you with new magic or killed you.

My donut in hand, I headed for my apartment on the second floor, a three-bedroom suite I shared with my friends Ivy and Drake. Neither one was at home right now. I went straight to my bedroom to change. The soldiers heading to the Wilds up north might be facing the harsh winds of winter, but right now the Black Plains were basking in the heat of summer. In February. I didn't question it. No one did. Magic had changed the Black Plains and the nearby Frontier. The weather rarely made sense. You could have a week of scorching heat followed by a week of blizzards.

I shrugged out of my long winter coat, tossing it onto my bed. I traded my club clothing for a tank top, shorts, and hiking boots. Ivy and Drake entered the apartment as I finished braiding my hair back. I was carrying two swords today. They were freakishly sharp, and I had no intention of slicing my hair off by mistake. Legion soldiers were expected to be ambidextrous, flexible, and fast—and I hadn't quite gotten the knack of it yet.

Ivy's infectious laugh jingled over the click of the apartment door. I grabbed my donut, then headed into the living room.

"Hey, Leda," she said, setting down her phone on the coffee table. Her long red hair bounced against her back as she moved. "What's this I hear about you going out drinking with Jace instead of with me?"

"It was training." I smirked at her. "It didn't mean anything, honest."

She snorted. "So, how long do you think you'll be stuck training with him?"

"Until one of us dies, I guess." I devoured my donut in four bites. "But he's not all that bad."

"I'll forgive that comment because you're obviously inebriated."

I licked the icing from my fingers. "My head is perfectly clear." That was one of the benefits of a turbo-charged supernatural metabolism.

The door opened again, and Drake entered the

apartment. He wore a muscle t-shirt, cargo pants, and heavy hiking boots. His dark hair was cut short and brushed up into spiky peaks. He looked ready to kick ass and break hearts.

Drake was a frontline fighter, someone you brought in when you had a nasty job that needed to be done. He'd been doing a lot of tough missions lately. Captain Somerset liked to use him because he bulldozed through anything in his path.

"Ladies," Drake said with a suave smile.

Ivy fanned herself. "Someone call the doctor."

Drake winked at her. "Should I carry you to the medical ward, honey?"

Ivy and Drake had been best friends since birth. They were also totally into each other, though neither one seemed to realize it. They were each dating someone else right now.

"On second thought, no." Ivy plopped down on the sofa. "I spent the whole day in there. I never want to hear that stupid Sandy Marine song ever again."

"I thought you liked that song," I said.

"I did before last month. But they play it over and over again, hour after hour, day after day." She dragged her fingers through her hair. "It's enough to make anyone go mad. If this is the gods' testing me, I'd rather just take the Nectar and be done with it."

Drake and Ivy had been promoted to level two in last month's ceremony. Witch's Cauldron was a mental ability, and some of the Legion brats hadn't thought my friends had it in them to be brainy. But Drake was an avid reader, and Ivy had turned out to have quite a knack for potions. She was working in the medical ward now, trying to find her true calling.

"Did Leda tell you about the mission we're going on?" Drake asked her.

I turned to him. "You're going too?"

"Yep."

"Oh, I feel left out," said Ivy.

"We're guiding Pilgrims across the Black Plains," Drake told her.

"The monster-infested wilderness?" She grabbed a piece of chocolate from the bowl on the coffee table. "On second thought, I'd rather stay here, even if it means listening to that wretched song over and over again."

"Well, have fun with that." Drake grabbed his jacket and pre-packed bag. "I need to help load up the truck. I'll see you later." He blew Ivy a kiss, which she caught in her hand.

"You going to hold onto that for a while?" I asked her when Drake was gone.

She looked down at her clenched fist. Her hand uncurled slowly, as though she could still feel the weight of his kiss in her palm.

"Air kisses aren't as fun as the real thing," I said, grinning.

"What?" She looked up at me, distracted.

"Never mind. I have to be going too. If I'm late, I'll incur the wrath of New York's favorite angel."

"He's back? When did this happen? Did he come to see you yet? Did you kiss?" The questions spilled off her tongue so fast that I could hardly follow.

"Yes, he's back. I don't know when he got in. He came to see me about a half hour ago when I was training with Jace. And, no, we didn't get around to kissing."

23

"But you expect there to be kissing?"

I shrugged. "I don't know. He's leading the mission to the Black Plains, but I think we'll be too busy fighting monsters to make out."

"Don't be so sure, Leda. He was at the office all of five minutes last month, and he still found time to make out with you in the library."

"I shouldn't have told you about that," I said, frowning.

"You didn't."

"Oh, right."

Ivy had a talent for always knowing everything that was going on in the Legion. Hell, she even knew things about Legion soldiers she'd never met in offices she'd never visited.

"See you later." I swung my pack over my back. "Try to stay out of trouble while I'm gone."

"You too, Pandora." She winked at me.

Chuckling, I left the apartment and headed for the staircase. The halls were busy like always, people coming and going between work and their tiny piece of privacy in an office of over a thousand soldiers.

Everyone I passed stared at me. I was neither popular nor unpopular at the Legion. Some people liked me, others disliked me, but everyone knew who I was. They knew me for my unparalleled ability to attract trouble wherever I went—and for Nero's unspoken promise to make me his lover. Mayhem and sex, the perfect recipe for gossip.

"Leda," Jace said, sliding into step beside me. "I hear you're headed to the Black Plains with Colonel Windstriker."

"News travels fast. It looks like you're headed out yourself." I glanced sidelong at him, noting his fitted jacket and pants, the Legion-approved uniform for sub-zero missions. Wherever he was headed, it was someplace cold. "I take it your meeting with your father went well."

"As well as a meeting with him can go," he said grimly. "He's recruited me to join his latest mission."

"Your father heads the Chicago office, right? Is it common to recruit a soldier from another Legion office to join a mission?"

"Not common, but it does happen if the soldier you want has special skills critical to the mission's success."

"And what are your special, mission-critical skills?"

"That I'm his son."

"Ah."

"We're tracking down Osiris Wardbreaker. He's part of Nyx's inner circle, one of the first soldiers she trained to be an angel."

"He's gone missing?" I asked.

A dark look crossed Jace's face. "He's gone rogue. This is bad news, Leda. He's the first angel to go dark in a long time. If he joins the demons, we're all in a lot of trouble. We have to stop him." He fell silent, not speaking again until we were on the stairs. "My father put me on this mission so I could prove myself to the First Angel."

"I'm sure you will."

"Why are you being so nice? Don't you understand?" he demanded, frustration pulsing through his voice. "It's hard to beat what you did, saving an airship full of witches. Capturing a rogue angel is about as big as it gets. He wants me to upstage you."

I laughed. "And?"

"You are my biggest competition, and an angel—my father—is helping me. Don't you think that's really unfair?"

"You want to beat me in a fair game," I said.

"Yes."

"I have an angel helping me too," I pointed out. "So I think it's about as fair as it's going to get."

"You have a point," he said, a thoughtful look sliding across his face.

"But this doesn't have to be a competition, you know," I told him.

"Tell that to my father."

I set my hand on his shoulder. "Your father does not control you, Jace. He does not define who you are."

"You don't know him."

"No, but I *do* know you. And when you're not trying to be the person your father wants you to be, you're a great guy." I smiled at him. "A great friend. Remember that."

I turned toward the garage.

"Leda, wait."

I looked over my shoulder.

"Watch your back out there on the Black Plains, in the Lost City," he said. "Some say the phantoms of the past still linger there, waiting to be released. Others say that the place holds a gateway that leads straight to hell."

"I'm actually more worried about monsters than phantoms, but thanks for the warning. And good luck."

"Thanks. I'll need it. My father's plan to distinguish me just might kill me instead." Then he turned and walked back down the hall.

CHAPTER THREE

Playing Legion

AN HOUR LATER, I and eleven other soldiers were on a train headed for Purgatory. No, that's not Legion humor. Purgatory was the name of my hometown, a tiny pocket of civilization at the edge of the Frontier, the gateway to the plains of monsters. It was where criminals went to disappear into the Black Plains—and where soldiers and bounty hunters went to track them down.

The train that traveled between New York and Purgatory had a carriage reserved for soldiers from the Legion of Angels. The seat cushions were an opulent red velvet, the floors were solid wood, and the snack corner was well-stocked. Someone had decided that chandeliers were the epitome of fanciness and had placed one at the center of our carriage, neglecting to take the low ceiling into account.

The bundle of bells above the door jingled, and Drake came down the aisle, carefully avoiding the swaying crystal branches of the chandelier.

"The cargo is all secure. What did I miss?" he asked, sitting down beside me on the cushioned bench.

"Grass, trees, a few ponds, some wildflowers." There wasn't much else out here.

He glanced out the window. Outside, the countryside whisked by at five hundred miles an hour. He was breathing normally, and he hadn't broken a sweat moving the enormous crates stuffed with supplies for the Legion office in Purgatory.

"Do you miss home?" he asked me.

"Every day." I sighed. Though I was closer to home than I'd been in months, I felt further away than ever before. I would be right there in my hometown, and I might not even get to see my family. "Do you ever regret joining the Legion?"

"No," he replied immediately, like he didn't even need to think about it. "Ivy needed me, and I was not going to leave her to face this life alone. That's not what friends do."

Drake and Ivy had joined the Legion at the same time I had. Everyone had their own reasons for joining the Legion: power, the need to prove themselves, desperation. Drake had joined to be there for his best friend Ivy. She'd joined to gain the power to heal her mother, but her mother already had a plan of her own, a plan that meant making a deal with demons. Those deals never worked out. Ivy's mother, the reason Ivy had come to the Legion, was dead now, and it was too late for Ivy to leave. The Legion of Angels was a lifetime commitment, and that was a long time for an immortal.

I knew Drake had been a star athlete at a university before he joined the Legion. He had vampires and shifters in his family, but the powers never came to him. Like many of us with supernatural blood but no magic, he was a bit stronger and faster than normal humans. Ok, maybe more than just a bit in his case.

They'd called him 'the Dragon' on the football field—the strong, powerful force that could go through anyone. He'd had a future, a long list of professional teams who wanted him after he graduated. He could have been on one of those teams now, in the spotlight, signing autographs, on commercials, on billboards, his image projected on the buildings of New York City. On the buildings of every major city in the world.

Instead he was a relative unknown in the Legion, working his way up like everyone else, eating danger for dinner, and death for dessert. Risking himself every day. He had given all that up for Ivy. And he truly didn't regret it. I saw it in his eyes.

"There's a group of paranormal soldiers in the next carriage," Drake told me.

They must have been the replacement forces for Purgatory. The paranormal soldiers never stayed on the Frontier for long, rarely more than six months. As a child, I'd watched them come and go from Purgatory, standing guard on the wall, the barrier that separated civilization from the savage lands of monsters.

"They're playing Legion," he continued, amused.

Legion was a card game roughly based on the Legion of Angels. And I do mean roughly because no card game could come close to the blood, sweat, and tears of the real thing. The paranormal soldiers' training wasn't easy, but they didn't find half of their initiation class dead before the training had even begun. They had no idea of what we went through.

Some people in Purgatory romanticized the paranormal soldiers. My sister Tessa was one of them. I'd never understood why she was so enamored with them, why she considered them heroic and brave. A vampire had once beaten me bloody right in front of them, and they hadn't lifted a finger to help. They'd never lifted a finger to help anyone else in town either. They were cowards.

At least that was what I'd always thought. Now that I was a soldier myself, I found myself revisiting my previous prejudice. Like soldiers of the Legion, they weren't allowed to interfere. They were supposed to follow orders to the letter, and getting mixed up in local affairs was not part of that.

"Back when I was a kid living on the streets, I used to play pranks on the paranormal soldiers," I told Drake.

"Oh?" He didn't look the least bit surprised. "What kind of pranks?"

"Mostly I just stole their food, but sometimes I'd steal their guns and plant them on their comrades."

"Oh, really?" His brows lifted in challenge.

"You want me to prank them now?"

"I'm daring you to do it."

"Sure, why not?" I rose from my seat. "We have some time to kill."

I slipped off my jacket, evidence of my affiliation with the Legion. This wasn't going to work if they weren't at ease —and a soldier of the Legion would not put them at ease. Captain Somerset, seated at the other end of the carriage, watched me strip out of my jacket with great amusement. Beside her, Nero didn't look amused. He didn't look much of anything, in fact. His face was a mask of hard marble. The other eight soldiers didn't even look up from their own card game.

I waved my hand in front of the sensor to open the

door and stepped into the paranormal soldiers' carriage. Twelve clean-cut men in well-ironed uniforms looked up as I entered. Their eyes started at my crop top, sliding down to my fitted shorts, then back up again. This was going to be too easy.

"Hey, boys," I said with a little wave. I wasn't a first class flirt like my sister Tessa, but I'd found in my years as a bounty hunter, that the words coming out of my mouth were far less important than what I was wearing. "You think I could join you?"

"Of course," one of them said as they all shifted around to make space for me.

"Thanks," I said, smiling as I took a seat.

"You know how to play Legion, peaches?" a man with a phoenix tattoo on his neck asked, dealing me ten cards.

More than you do. I've survived the real thing, pumpkin. But I just kept smiling. "I think I can figure it out."

"Just let me know if you need a hand." He winked at me.

"Or a sword."

They laughed.

Har, har. I hope you're all better at playing cards than at making innuendoes.

Phoenix Tattoo opened the game with the vampire card. I let the first round play out before bringing out the real magic.

"Stop," I said, and they all froze, their eyes blank. "Set your cards on the table, face up."

They obeyed. My gaze panned across their cards. There was no reason I couldn't prank the soldiers and practice compulsion at the same time.

"Actually, I don't need a sword," I told the man who'd

so generously offered to loan me his sword. "But I will take your angel."

I snatched a card with a half-nude angel on it. With her long black hair and shimmery pale skin, she bore an uncanny resemblance to Nyx—but I'd never seen the First Angel straddling a motorcycle in her lingerie. Who the hell had designed this deck?

I gave him my monster card in exchange, then directed my attention to the other players' cards. One of them had an angel too, which I immediately nabbed for myself. This angel was the spitting image of Nero, though I'd never seen Nero carrying a fire sword as tall as he was. I turned the card, trying to figure out how you'd even swing a sword that big. I decided it was impossible, even for an angel.

The soldier got my initiate, a fellow with a weak willpower stat, so he probably wouldn't make it far anyway. I couldn't help but feel bad for the two-dimensional drawing on the card. Just like in real life, he'd never had a chance.

My exchanges complete, I looked at the soldiers and said, "Resume."

They picked up their cards and began to play like nothing had happened. The two guys I'd traded with squinted at their cards, confused. They must have been wondering where their angels had gone—or if they'd ever really had them or just imagined it.

I glanced back at the door between the cars. Drake stood there, looking through the glass window, struggling to contain his amusement.

"You're cheating," one of the soldiers growled, drawing my attention back to the game. But he wasn't looking at me. His angry eyes were focused on the man to his right.

"That blue fairy card you played was mine. I had it in my hand just a moment ago."

To spice things up, I'd rearranged some of the soldiers' cards. That was even more fun than pilfering them for myself.

"Well, that witch coven leader card was mine," he shot back.

"Where's my werewolf?"

"My healing potions are gone!"

The soldiers were shouting now, each one louder than the last. Cards flew across the table, mixing together into a sloppy heap. I looked at the door again, expecting to find Drake laughing his ass off. What I found instead made my heart stutter in alarm.

Nero stepped through the door into the carriage, his eyes burning as cold as an Arctic storm. That was the look he always got right before he punished me. The paranormal soldiers froze when they saw the angel, scrambling to their feet to salute him. Paranormal soldiers revered the Legion of Angels nearly as much as they feared it.

"We apologize for disturbing you, Colonel," Phoenix Tattoo said, bowing his head. "And we submit ourselves to your holy judgment."

I choked down a laugh. Nero's head snapped around at the noise, those cold eyes locking onto me.

"Corporal Pierce, come with me."

I knew I was in trouble when he didn't call me Leda or even his favorite nickname Pandora. I took a deep breath and followed him. The paranormal soldiers gaped at me in shock.

"It was nice hanging out with you guys. We should play again sometime," I told them, winking.

They looked at me, horrified, like they were swearing to themselves that they'd never hit on a woman again in case she turned out to be a soldier of the Legion.

I followed Nero through the cargo carriage and then into the driver's car.

"Leave us," he told the driver.

The man took one look at the cold fire burning in Nero's eyes, then scrambled out of there so fast that he nearly slammed into the door.

"Well, that's nice," I said to Nero when we were alone. "Now who's going to drive the train?"

"These things drive themselves. The train can survive without him for a few minutes."

"A few minutes? I think you are underestimating how long your lectures take."

Nero gave me a cool look. "I am very aware of how long they take."

"Oh, have them timed, do you?" I asked, my sass getting the better of me. Again.

"That would be impossible. You defy every law I know, Pandora, including the laws of time."

I smirked at him. "That must be frustrating."

"Yes." His icy expression cracked, revealing frustration, like he didn't know what to do with me. Nero rarely showed his emotions, but when he did, this expression was a frequent visitor. "What were you doing with those paranormal soldiers?"

"Practicing compulsion."

His mouth thinned into a hard line. "You were playing pranks on them."

"I can multitask." I grinned at him. "I was just trying to pass the time."

"If you're bored, I can find things to fill the time."

The smile died on my lips. Nero's idea of 'filling time' involved running laps and punching a hard metal wall over and over again to build up your pain threshold. But we were on a train, so neither of those things were practical at the moment. *Unless* he was thinking of making me run across the tops of the train cars as it sped along at five hundred miles per hour. But that wasn't even possible.

Nero's mouth quirked up, like he'd heard my thoughts again. Damn it. The look in his eyes was daring me to say it was impossible. Soldiers of the Legion defied the impossible. We weren't supposed to even contemplate the meaning of the word.

Time to take this in a different direction. "Pass the time, you say?" I arched my brows with deliberate slowness. "What did you have in mind?"

Nero's gaze followed my hands as they brushed out a wrinkle in my shorts. He went eerily still, fighting temptation.

"You know what? Just forget it." I shrugged. "I'll just find some more soldiers to annoy."

"Leda, wait. Stop."

The command in his voice made me pause, more out of the desire to know what he was going to say than the urge to obey.

"Your power has grown in the last month. You had those soldiers completely enchanted."

"Maybe it was my magic, or maybe they were just enchanted by my lack of underwear."

His gaze dipped to my skintight shorts. The lower half of the Legion's wilderness uniform looked an awful lot like hot pants.

I smirked at him. "I can't stand panty lines."

"Is that all?" His voice going lower, darker. "Is that the real reason?"

My throat tightened under the intensity of his stare. "Yes, of course."

He stepped toward me, filling the shrinking distance between us. "I've missed you. Every hour I've been away from you, I've thought of little else but you."

The blunt statement caught me off guard, derailing the smart ass comment I'd had ready to go. "Where have you been?"

"It's not your place to question an angel." His whispered words fell against my ear like silk kisses.

"Yeah, well…" I cleared my throat. "You know I'm not good at following orders."

"No, you're not."

He grabbed me roughly, pivoting me around. One hand was on my hip; the other traced my neck. Pulling back my braid, he dipped his mouth to my throat, teasing the throbbing, pulsing vein between his teeth. A soft moan broke my lips.

"I and the other angels in North America have been training with Nyx," he said against my neck.

I leaned against him, his chest hard against my back, his hand locked around my hip. "Angels still have to train?"

"Of course. The training isn't over until you're dead. And I'm half-convinced Nyx designed the training to kill us."

I laughed softly.

Nero spun me around. "You have such a perfect laugh." His fingertip touched my lips. "The perfect blend of good and wicked."

He'd said that before, that I was a perfect balance of light and dark.

"Warm, rich, soft." His kisses traced my jaw. "Like coffee."

"I thought you didn't drink coffee. Caffeine is a weakness," I teased.

"*You* are my weakness, Leda. My temptation, the siren's song that I would willingly follow to my own demise."

My pulse popped against my skin like a bubbling volcano, building, brewing. I lifted my gaze, meeting the green fire in his eyes.

He kissed me slowly, softly. "I wish to take you to dinner."

"I already agreed," I reminded him. "Against my better judgment, I might add."

I took his lower lip between my teeth, drawing it out slowly. A deep, low moan rumbled his chest, buzzing against my skin, bringing my tired, overworked body back to life.

"I didn't anticipate Nyx would put us through that training so soon after I asked you to dinner," he said. "I regret the delay. If you would allow, I plan to make it up to you."

His voice was laden with unspoken things. It tasted of sweet seductions and wicked promises. My skin tingled with the magic of that promise, the promise of an angel who never went back on his word. He traced a trail of wildfire down my arm.

"How can I refuse an offer like that?" I said, my voice breaking.

He gave me a satisfied smile. He knew he had me. I could see it in his eyes, that arrogance tinted with a touch of naked vulnerability. Like I could penetrate the marble mask of the angel, like I could wound him with a single word. But I didn't want to hurt him. I wanted to see those eyes burn with pleasure, not pain.

He kissed me again, his mouth coming down hard on mine. He wasn't being gentle this time. He didn't tease or taste; he devoured. Heat flashed through my body, a cascade of feverish sensations and hard, raw need. I grabbed his collar, pulling him against me.

Far too soon, he pulled back. "All in good time." His hand lingered on my cheek for a final moment before he withdrew it too. "We have a job to do."

His face had grown serious, cold. It was like a switch had flipped inside of him. The passionate lover was gone, leaving only the colonel.

"Get back to the others," he said. "The train is coming up on Purgatory now."

CHAPTER FOUR
Cowboy Royalty

DRAKE GAVE ME an amused look when I got back to the Legion's carriage. "Did your boyfriend scold you?"

Several of our teammates snickered. I stuck my tongue out at them. I was mature like that.

"Colonel Windstriker sure was in a fury," Monique Park commented, lifting her bag off the floor.

"I wonder why that is." Claudia Vance winked at me, twirling the tip of her long blonde braid around her finger. It was a rather coy gesture from the Battle Maiden of New York, as some called her. Sergeant Vance was an interesting dichotomy, voluptuous curves and battle-hardened muscle all wrapped up into one person.

"He's mad because I compelled the paranormal soldiers in the next carriage to give me all their angel cards," I said.

"Those boys are playing Legion, are they?"

"Yes." I reached down and pulled my new Nero card out of my boot.

Claudia looked at it, laughing. "The artist sure does know how to make an angel," she purred, her tongue sliding slowly across her lips, her eyes tracing the illustration of Nero in a suit of sleek black leather.

"You going to screw him already or what, Leda?" Alec Morrows asked me.

Sergeant Morrows was one of the heavy hitters like Drake. Just last week, the two of them had taken on a whole pack of werewolves who'd broken the gods' laws. Morrows was freakishly strong and tough as nails, but that didn't mean I was going to let him tease me without retaliation.

I was just thinking up a juicy comeback when Lieutenant Lawrence said, "Don't encourage the poor girl, Morrows. She has no idea what she's in for. Remember the shit storm that went down the last time Nero took a lover." She simpered, her lips curling with vicious delight. "He left the poor girl a mess. She was so heartbroken that she transferred to Europe."

The train coasted to a stop, and the doors slid open. Overhead, the chandelier crystals jingled in celebration of our arrival.

"I'm reminded of why I never liked that woman," I whispered to Drake as Lieutenant Lawrence walked off the train.

"She's just bitter. She spent years trying to get Colonel Windstriker's attention with all kinds of crazy stunts, but he never gave her the time of day." Claudia wrapped her arm around me, leading me toward the door. "And then you came along and had him wrapped around your finger by the end of the first day."

"I wouldn't say I have him wrapped around my finger." If I had, I'd have been able to sweet-talk my way out of all those extra laps and pushups he liked to assign me when I gave him lip.

"Yes, there *are* better places to have an angel wrapped around you," she said with a wink, then hurried ahead to walk beside her best friend Captain Somerset.

Drake and I were the last to step off the train. Well, I hadn't seen Nero leave, but maybe he could teleport or at least make himself invisible. The spells of the higher angel echelons were a mystery to me—and to pretty much everyone else who wasn't an angel.

Together with the others, Drake and I carried the Legion's cargo off the train and loaded it into the big truck waiting in front of the station. By the time we were done, the truck was so full that there wasn't space for any of us. We walked through the town, drawing stares and whispers as we made our way to the Legion office.

It had been five months since I'd been back home, but it felt like years. And not just because I was homesick. Something had happened to Purgatory in that half year, a decay, a corrosion that should have taken years rather than months. A trio of shady men, automatic rifles hidden away beneath their huge trench coats, stood outside the Witch's Watering Hole. That was the last bar I'd gone to before leaving for New York. Purgatory was on the Frontier, so people had always walked around town with guns and knives. But not so many guns and knives—and not ones like those. They weren't armed to defend themselves; they were armed to destroy life. I recognized the dark brown leather trench coats, heavy boots, and fedoras. These fellows belonged to Prince, one of the town's district lords who fancied himself cowboy royalty.

They weren't alone. I saw thugs from five distinct district lords. They were everywhere, more of them than ever before. They were in the restaurants, shops, and bars.

Walking the streets like they owned them. There was a strange smell to the town, the smell of overpriced cologne, a deep musk lathered on to cover the stench of fear bleeding down the streets. But there was no scent, no matter how potent, that could cover fear. Fear was the basest of instincts, the strongest of scents. It permeated everything, a sickly sweat scent of overripe fruit spoiling in the summer sun.

"The town feels different," I said quietly to Drake.

"Things change, Leda. It's a natural part of life."

"This change is for the worse. The town was never luxurious or shiny, but it was comforting. Like an old security blanket stained by twenty years of tears and sweat."

"Security blanket? I prefer something with a bit more kick." He tapped his crossbow. "I used this baby to clear Sapphire Point of winged serpent monsters."

"That exact one?"

"The one and same. Fifty-two fiends, two hours, one man. A battle that will go down in the history books," he declared, his eyes lifted in triumph, his voice soaring with nostalgia.

I grinned at him. "That's just beautiful. Kind of sounds like the start of one of those horror movies Ivy likes."

"Oh, no. This was better. Much better," he replied seriously.

We stopped outside the Pilgrims' temple of worship. The town's Legion office was just a room inside that temple.

"File in," Nero said, emerging from the doorway.

How had he gotten here so fast? Maybe he really could teleport. Or maybe I'd just been slow, distracted by the epidemic of corruption consuming my town.

We followed Nero into a small office down the hall.

Seven Pilgrims waited inside. They weren't dressed in the usual robes of the clergy but instead in cargo pants and t-shirts. I might have mistaken them for regular people, if not for the distinguished way they folded their hands together, palms out. It was a Pilgrim gesture, one that broadcasted their wish to pass along the gods' message.

"Our mission," Nero said when we were all there. "Is to guide and protect the Pilgrims in their journey to the holy battle site at the Lost City, which sits at the middle of the Black Plains."

Centuries ago, monsters had overwhelmed the Earth. The Book of the Gods tells us that the gods came down to our world, pushing back the beasts and saving humanity from certain destruction. The truth was a tad more complicated—ok, a lot more complicated. So complicated, in fact, that no one knew exactly what had happened all those years ago.

We did know that the gods had helped us build walls to separate humanity from the monsters. We knew they'd formed the Legion of Angels, a new breed of soldiers to fight the war against demons and monsters. The Pilgrims had risen from the ashes of humanity at our worst hour. They worshipped the gods, building temples in their honor. Just as the Legion represented the hand of the gods, the Pilgrims represented their voice.

"Valiant tells me that objects of great power lay buried beneath the Lost City," Nero said, indicating the Pilgrim standing to his right.

Valiant. His name meant he was a higher member of the Pilgrims, someone the gods had distinguished by blessing with long life for their service. They all held honorary titles named after virtues.

"It is absolutely essential that we recover these precious historical relics before thieves or mercenaries get their hands on them," Valiant said, his voice trembling with emotion.

If the artifacts were from the time of the final battle, they'd been in the Lost City for centuries. Either relic hunters had long since found them, or they were buried so deep that no one ever would.

"We must head out immediately," Valiant declared.

"That would be unwise," I told him.

Everyone looked at me.

"The Black Plains aren't safe at night," I continued. "The worst beasts come out after dark."

Nero watched me, as though he were debating whether or not to punish me for speaking out of turn. "She's right," he finally said, much to Lieutenant Lawrence's dismay. "We'll sleep here in the temple tonight and head out tomorrow at first light." He waved his hand at the door, and it swung open, revealing a Pilgrim in a plain dress.

She bowed to us. "Please allow me to show you to your rooms." She looked so young, no older than my seventeen-year-old sisters.

I was about to follow when Nero said, "Pandora, a word."

My comrades followed the girl, and the Pilgrims followed, shutting the door behind them. Leaving me alone with the stony-faced angel, who from the looks of it hadn't appreciated my desire to speak my mind.

"You're going to punish me, aren't you?" I said with a heavy sigh.

"I fear it won't do any good."

"That never stopped you before."

A hint of amusement broke past his granite mask.

"Admit it," I said, grinning. "You appreciate my sharp wit."

"In private perhaps, but not in front of my soldiers. And most certainly not in front of outsiders."

"All right." I sighed again. "Give it to me."

"When we get back, an additional twenty miles every morning for a week."

As far as Nero's punishments went, it was pretty lenient.

"Feeling magnanimous today?" I asked.

He shot me a hard look. "I can make it fifty miles instead."

"No, twenty should be fine. Thank you. I'm already feeling very repentant." I should have stopped there, but then I'd never known what was good for me. "Will you still punish me with extra laps when I'm an angel?" I asked him. I just couldn't help myself.

"Do you think I'll still need to punish you with extra laps when you're an angel?"

"Probably," I admitted.

A small smile touched his lips. "I hope so."

"Oh? And why is that? Because you enjoy punishing me that much?"

"No, because it means you managed to become an angel without changing who you are." He brushed his hand against mine. "I didn't ask you to stay just so I could punish you."

"Nero, I'm not going to make out with you in this tiny office. It doesn't even have a proper lock. Anyone could walk in at any time."

He laughed out loud. "You made out with me in the library. There wasn't even a door."

Heat rushed to my cheeks—and a few other places.

He lifted my hand to his lips, kissing my fingertips. "I didn't ask you to stay here for that either. I just wanted to inform you about the unfortunate shortage of beds at the temple."

"And this is where you generously offer to share your bed with me?"

He snorted. "That is one option, of course. But I was going to propose you go stay with your family."

The sass sizzled out inside of me, washed away by an overwhelming surge of gratitude. "Really?"

"It is an appropriate solution to the problem."

"Thank you." I threw my arms around him. "Thank you so much."

"I expect to see you here tomorrow at a quarter to six. Don't be late."

"I won't be," I promised, giving him a second hug before heading for the door.

"And Leda."

I turned my head to look at him.

"I know it's difficult for you to see the changes in this town since you left, but I must remind you not to interfere in local affairs. You are a soldier of the Legion now, sworn to uphold the gods' justice. If you forget that, even I cannot save you from the gods' wrath."

"I know." I drew in a deep breath. "I'll remember."

"Sleep well."

I smiled at him. "You too."

There was nothing better in life than dinner with your family. Being away from them for so long had reminded me of that one simple truth. Calli and the girls, Tessa and Gin, were there. The New York University of Witchcraft was closed between semesters, so Bella was home too. The only person missing to make this family dinner complete was Zane. I glanced at my brother's empty chair, and a twinge of melancholy burned in my heart, a single black spot on this otherwise perfect evening.

"You will find him," Bella said from beside me. She squeezed my hand. "We all believe in you, Leda."

Calli lifted her glass to me. My sisters mimicked the gesture. We were only drinking water tonight, but I appreciated it all the same.

"So, how's school?" I asked Bella as I shoveled sweet potato fries onto my plate. "Anything interesting happening?"

"Well, there's no way I could beat the adventure we had, Leda, but I did score the top marks in my class on the semester finals."

"That's awesome," I told her. "I knew you could do it."

"That's cool and all," Tessa said, grabbing the bowl of corn. "But what I'm interested in is hearing about this 'adventure' you and Leda had."

"Oh, it was no biggie. Bella and I just stopped a conspiracy from tearing New York's witch community apart." I looked at the bowl in front of Tessa. "Could you pass the green beans?"

"That doesn't sound like no biggie to me," Tessa commented, looking from me to Bella.

"You give me far too much credit," Bella told me. "I merely played a small role in a larger plot that you and Colonel Windstriker unravelled."

"Colonel Nero Windstriker, as in the hot angel from

New York?" Tessa asked.

"Don't talk with your mouth full, dear," Calli chided her.

Tessa swallowed, then looked at me with hungry eyes. "And? Don't leave me hanging here!"

"I'm the one left hanging. I'm still waiting on those green beans," I reminded her.

She passed the bowl to me. Her lips trembled with a hundred followup questions just waiting to be launched.

"Yes, *that* Nero Windstriker," I told my suffering sister. "How do you even know who he is?"

An expression of pure teenage horror flashed across her face. "Are you serious? Of course I know who he is. *Everyone* knows who he is. Haven't you seen his Legion trading card?"

I hadn't known who Nero was when we'd met, but then I didn't collect Legion trading cards. Well, at least I hadn't until today. I pulled the Nero card out of my boot and slapped it down on the table.

"You mean this card?" I asked Tessa.

An impish smile twisted her lips. "Gods, Leda, did you just pull that out of your boot?"

"Yeah. And?"

Tessa's eyes darted to Gin. "She keeps his picture in her boot. That's like the Legion's equivalent of a locker."

"Do you keep that card on you at all times?" Gin asked me.

"Ever since I nabbed it off some paranormal soldiers on the train an hour ago."

Tessa crossed her hands in front of her heart. "How romantic."

"If you say so."

Tessa caressed the outer edge of the playing card. "Are his muscles that big in real life?"

"Oh, much bigger. They're like, totally enormous," I told her, taking the thick slice of turkey Calli had cut for me.

"Really?" Tessa wet her lips.

"Yeah, so big he was always bursting out of his uniform, so now he just goes around the Legion office naked."

A pout displaced the euphoric smile on her face. "You're mocking me."

"Just having fun with you, little sis." I glanced at Bella. "So, when we're back in New York, we should go out to celebrate your academic triumph. How about cheesecake?"

"That sounds divine."

"You know what else is divine? Angels," Tessa said with a smirk. "Tell us more about your angel, Leda."

"There's nothing to tell. How about you tell us about school? What's new?"

"I won the Winter Queen pageant," she said. "And I'm in charge of the prom committee. Dani Wilkinson wanted the theme to be Witches, but we already did that for homecoming three years ago. I mean, seriously, what would these people do without me to keep track of these things? I told her we're doing Angels this year, and of course everyone loved it. Who doesn't love angels?"

No one apparently.

"How are classes?" I asked Gin.

"I got an A in Steam Tech," she said, smiling.

Calli beamed at her. "Gin has been helping me in the garage. Remember that old motorcycle we found last year in the Junkyard just outside of town, Leda? She managed to get it working."

"That's fantastic," I told Gin. She was really gifted. People just didn't see it because she was living in Tessa's shadow.

"It really is," Tessa said. She might have been an attention hog, but she did love Gin. "All the guys at the wall were really impressed. I think that cute one with the dragon tattoo is going to ask you out."

Gin blushed a lovely shade of pink.

"And how is your paranormal soldier, the one whose name you wanted to tattoo into your skin?" I asked Tessa.

Tessa pushed out her lower lip. "Don't even mention his name."

"I think you're safe there. I don't even remember his name." It was impossible to keep up with Tessa's revolving door of boyfriends.

"He left town when his time was up. He said he'd write to Tessa, but he never did," Gin told me.

"Whatever. I met someone who is ten times the man he will ever be," Tessa declared.

"Oh, really. Who is this wonderful fellow?"

"Uh-uh. I'm not telling." Tessa zipped her fingers across her mouth.

"Why not?"

"Because I can tell from the look in your eyes that as soon as I do, you'll go find him and give him a speech about staying away from your little sister."

"Unfortunately, little sister, I don't have time to play hot potato with paranormal soldiers right now." I sighed, looking at Calli. "What's happening here? The town feels different."

"The government cut funding to the sheriff's offices in several Frontier towns, ours included. The resources are being diverted into the Legion, the wall, and the fight against the beasts. Sheriff Wilder didn't have the money to keep paying us bounty hunters to track down criminals."

"You're not working?" I asked.

"We're working, just not enough. Many of the local bounty hunters have moved on, but even with just a few of us left, there's not enough work to go around. And your friend Jinx has made a habit of letting us do all the work, then snatching our marks out from under us."

I gritted my teeth. "Where is he?"

"Don't even think about going after him. I know the Legion has rules about interfering in local affairs."

"The man is a vulture," I growled.

"He's a lot worse than that, but most of all, he's not worth it, kid. Leave it be. Thanks to you, we're getting along all right." She met my eyes. "You didn't have to send us so much money."

"After what you said, I'm wishing I'd sent more."

"It's your money, Leda."

"The Legion feeds and houses me, and I don't have the time to spend money anyway."

"I could help you with that," Tessa offered.

Calli gave her a hard look.

"What? I was offering to do her shopping for her."

"After Sheriff Wilder lost his funding, he took drastic measures to keep crime in check, didn't he?" I asked Calli.

"Yes, he accepted the district lords' help. The common criminals are all but gone, but now we have organized crime in its place."

I clenched my fists. "It wasn't a good trade. He shouldn't have made a deal with the district lords. He knew that their help came at a price. They are the police now.

They are the ones running this town."

"He didn't have much of a choice, Leda," Calli told me. "He tried to hold out, but as soon as the criminals learned the sheriff didn't have the manpower to keep them out, they flocked here in droves. I tried to help him. So did a few others. But it wasn't enough. He had to make the deal or watch the town burn to the ground, its people murdered, their houses stripped bare."

Two pieces of warped metal hit my plate. I looked down at my hand to find I'd broken my fork in half. I knew I wasn't allowed to interfere. As long as the district lords did nothing against the gods' will, as long as they continued to make donations to the Legion and to the Pilgrims, my hands were tied.

"Come on, Leda. Let's not speak of these unhappy things," Calli said. "There's nothing we can do to change them. We'll survive just as we always have. The tides will turn, and we'll get our chance to right this wrong."

"Do you really think so?"

"Of course."

"Yes," Bella agreed. "Hope is a powerful magic, Leda. Don't forget that. We'll save this town. And we'll save Zane. Tell them what you told me, about how you saw him."

"You saw him?" Gin said, her eyes going wide. "Where?"

"I didn't see him in person. I caught a passing glimpse of him. He's safe. For now."

"How did you see him?" Tessa asked me. "I thought you wouldn't gain that kind of magic until you became an angel."

"I don't have that magic. I...borrowed it for a short time. It wasn't enough to track him down, but at least I got to see that he's all right."

"So the dark angels of hell don't have him?" Gin asked.

"Neither gods nor demons have him. He is someplace where he feels safe. That's all I know."

"How did you borrow this magic?" Tessa asked. "Could you do it again so we can all see Zane?"

I shook my head. "It doesn't work that way."

"Then how does it work?"

I hesitated.

"You performed a blood exchange with an angel, didn't you?" Calli asked.

Tessa's jaw dropped.

"And with not just any angel," Calli continued. "With Nero Windstriker."

"Yes." The word hung over the table, filling the silence.

"Leda." Calli sighed. "He's an angel. When push comes to shove, he will choose the Legion over your brother. You can't trust him."

"He's not like that. He's...different."

"I thought you knew better, but you're still just as naive as Tessa."

"Hey!" Tessa exclaimed in protest.

"Nero knew about Zane. I didn't tell him. He came to me, offering his help. He's been training me, helping me get stronger."

"And you never wondered why?"

"Because he's a good person."

"He's not a person, Leda. He's an angel. He might look like us. He might even talk like us, but he is not like us. None of them are. The gods' Nectar has changed them. They're no longer human."

"Neither am I!" I shouted, jumping up. "I've drunk the

gods' Nectar, and I will do it again many more times before this is over. To find Zane and bring him back to us, I will become an angel, the very thing you hate."

"I don't hate the angels." Calli rose to her feet. "I just want you to be wary of trusting them."

"Will you trust me when I'm an angel."

"Always." She set her hands on my cheeks, pressing her forehead to mine. "Because I know you will always be you. You're stronger than the Nectar. It won't change you. You are too good."

I set my hands over hers. "Nero is good too. I can feel it in his magic, in his blood."

Calli's brows drew together. "There is darkness in that angel."

"There's darkness in me too." Darkness wasn't evil. And light wasn't goodness. Darkness and light were just two sides of the same magic. "Please, Calli...Mom. You need to trust me."

"Always." She squeezed my hands. Her expression lightened. "Though I do reserve the right to warn you about getting involved with an angel like Nero Windstriker. Mother's prerogative."

I laughed. "Of course."

Calli lifted the cover off a glass dish. The delicious aroma of baked apple and cinnamon rose up. It was the sweetest smell in the world—because it smelled like home.

"We get to tease you about Nero Windstriker, you know. Sisters' prerogative." Tessa said, heaping steaming cinnamon apples onto her plate. "What's it like to kiss an angel?"

"I see you're starting with the easy questions right off the bat," I commented.

She smiled at me. "Spill. I want to know all about that angel's lips."

"It's classified."

"His lips are classified?"

"Yep."

"Come on, Leda. I'm dying here. You have to give me *something*."

"Fine. Nero asked me out on a date."

Her eyes sparkled in delight. "And how was it?"

"I don't know. It hasn't happened yet. We've both been too busy the past four months."

"He asked you out four months ago, and you still haven't gone on a date?"

"Pretty much."

"But you have kissed him right? And exchanged blood with him? What was it like?"

Not for your ears, little sister. I stretched out my arms and yawned loudly. "Wow, would you look at the time! I have to get up really early tomorrow, so I'd best be going to bed now."

"Coward," Tessa muttered.

"I'm going to go to bed too," Bella said, following me into the bathroom.

After we'd brushed our teeth, we headed into the bedroom we'd shared since we were kids. Our old bed waited for us. We dove in and pulled the blanket over our chins.

"You disappointed Tessa," Bella told me, her mouth twitching.

"When you want to know everything there is to know in the world, you're going to be disappointed now and again." I hugged my sister to me. "I did want to ask you something, though."

"Oh?"

"It's about the gods' Nectar."

"I think you know more about Nectar than I do, Leda. The offices and buildings of the Legion are the only places on Earth you can find it. We witches don't have access to Nectar."

"But you do have access to knowledge. You must have read about Nectar," I said.

"A little. I know it's a poison, more powerful than any poison on Earth. That's why Legion soldiers can't be poisoned. Your bodies have already survived the strongest poison known to man—and it changed you, bestowing you with powerful magical gifts."

"What do you know about what happens when someone drinks the Nectar?" I asked her.

"If the person is uninitiated, the Nectar either kills them or it unlocks their magical potential. The initiates train and then drink the Nectar again, this time in a less diluted form. Those who survive, gain the gods' first gift. With each new level, each new ability, you drink a stronger, less diluted Nectar. If you haven't trained hard enough—if you haven't gained at least a hint of the next level's magic— you die. I've heard it's an agonizing ordeal."

"Yes," I said, remembering the faces of everyone I ever saw drink the Nectar in a promotion ceremony. "It's agonizing. For them. But not for me. Nectar doesn't hurt me. It makes me drunk."

Bella went very still. "I remember reading a case of someone who had that reaction. Both his parents were angels."

"Nero has the same reaction to Nectar, and both of his

parents are angels. He's the only person I know of with two angel parents, in fact. Maybe you read about him."

"Maybe. The study didn't list names."

"Bella, do you think it means… Do you think it means both my parents were angels too? That I'm a brat of the highest tier?"

"A brat?" she asked, amused.

"It's what Legion soldiers call the recruits with an angel parent."

"I see." Bella paused. "Leda, I can't tell you if both your parents are angels, but it might explain your reaction to the Nectar."

"Do you recall the title of that book?" I asked her.

"Poisons and Potions."

"Thanks." It looked like I would be adding another book to my reading list when I got back to New York.

"I'm glad you're here," she whispered in the dark. "It's been too long."

"Yes, it has."

We closed our eyes, holding to each other, two sisters, two friends. Just like the old days. Things had been so much easier back then, so much more peaceful. I fell asleep, expecting the sweet dreams of those happy golden years.

Instead, I dreamt I stood back-to-back with Nero on the Black Plains, fighting off the horde of monsters closing in on us. It was a long battle, a hard battle, but we were finally victorious. We celebrated our survival by having sex on the back of Nero's motorcycle.

Yeah, my life had definitely changed. And there was no going back.

CHAPTER FIVE
Law of the Gods

THE NEXT MORNING, I woke to darkness. It was so early that not even the birds were chirping yet. It was the quietest hour of the day, before the early risers opened their eyes and after the party animals and drunks had gone home to their beds—or passed out cold on the streets.

The window was open, letting the air in. It was warm, even before the sun broke the horizon. The heat and humidity hung in the air like a fleece blanket, hot and smothering. I couldn't help but marvel at the bizarre February weather. I should have looked outside to see ice-laden trees and snowy sidewalks—not this.

I put on my wilderness wear, thankful for the shorts and tank top. My black leather Legion uniform would have been unbearable in this heat. Even in my light clothing, a hot layer of sweat coated my skin. And it was only going to get hotter from here.

As I stuffed my night clothes into my backpack, I watched Bella sleep. She was so quiet, so peaceful. I kissed her gently on the forehead, then left the room, closing the door behind me.

The house was dark, and I didn't turn on any lights. I crept along with softened steps, not wanting to wake anyone. I paused in front of Zane's open door, taking a moment to send him a silent promise that I would find him. I doubted he could hear me, but just in case he could, I wanted him to know I was looking for him.

"Leda."

I spun around, drawing one of my swords as I moved. I stopped when I saw it was only Calli. I must have been so caught up thinking about Zane that I hadn't heard her approach. Nero would have chided me for being sloppy, and he was right. I had the heightened senses of a vampire. There was no excuse to let anyone sneak up on me. Well, except for angels. I swear they came with built-in silencers. You couldn't even hear them breathe.

"You're up early," I said to Calli.

"Same as every day."

Calli always had been an early riser. Back in the old days, she'd used those quiet hours to work in the garage, make breakfast, and to do all those small things that otherwise didn't seem to ever get done in a household of kids who played as hard as we fought. I'd known she woke up long before us, but I hadn't realized until today just how early her day began because I was *not* an early riser. As a teenager, I could have slept until noon every day of the week. I'd given up my lazy mornings and late breakfasts the day I'd joined the Legion of Angels. It was one of the things I missed—just not as much as I missed my family.

Calli looked through the open door to Zane's room. Everything was exactly as it had been the day Zane was taken. It was waiting for his return.

"He'll be back," I told her, setting my hand on her

shoulder.

"Of course he will. He's a fighter." She turned and went into the kitchen. "His mother was a fighter too."

I grabbed a roll from the bread bowl. "You knew her?" Calli had never told me about Zane's birth mother.

"Yes, back from my days with the League."

The League was the world's largest bounty-hunting company. Calli had worked there before coming to Purgatory, before raising us. Every so often, we met one of her old friends from the League, but I didn't actually know much about the time she'd spent there.

"Her name was Cora. I hadn't seen her in years, not since the League. She left the year before I did. I never found out why until the night she showed up on my doorstep with a young boy. Her son."

"Zane," I said. "He was hunted even then?"

Calli nodded, stirring her tea. "Cora begged me to take him in. She was crying hysterically, but between her pleas and sobs, I managed to piece together what was going on. The gods had learned her son was a ghost."

Ghosts, people with telepathic powers, were very rare and highly prized. The strongest telepaths could do so much more than just read thoughts; they could see things and track people across great distances. Even angels with telepathic magic could not do this; they could only link to those they loved.

Only a handful of telepaths were born into each generation. Both the gods and the demons hunted down every one they could find to test, drug, and use as spies, as a window into their enemies' camps.

"The gods sent the Legion of Angels to hunt down Zane and his mother," Calli said. "They'd traveled from far away to get to me. But we all know that no place on Earth is truly safe from gods and demons." She wiped a tear from her cheek. "She knew the Legion would chase her to the ends of the Earth to find her son, so she left him with me. I saw the look in her eyes as she left, Leda. It was as if a part of her had been ripped out. She gave up her son to save him."

"What happened to her?" I asked, my throat growing hoarse. I feared I already knew the answer.

"Cora caught a train west. The Legion wasn't far behind her. She was trying to lead them as far as possible from Zane. So she went out on the Western Wilderness. She knew she was going to her death, but it was the best chance her son had. They found her body one week later. She'd managed to survive the monsters long enough to lead them on a wild goose chase across the Western Wilderness. To give her son a chance at life," Calli finished, her voice shaking with emotion.

I stood there for a minute, trying to think of what to say. Cora had known the Legion had magic that could break any mind, even hers, and she'd chosen death over giving up her son's location. There were no words to describe the harrowing beauty of that mother's sacrifice for her son.

"Calli, why are you telling me this now after all these years?" I asked her.

"Because I know you feel guilty about what happened to Zane."

"He went missing on my job, helping me, saving my life. He exposed himself—his power—to save me. I have every reason to feel guilty. This is my fault."

Calli was quiet for a few moments, watching me.

Finally, she said, "I taught Zane how to use his power and how to hide it, when to use it and when to hide it." She paused. "Zane chose to save your life that day, Leda, and I would have expected nothing less of him. Of any of you. You are fantastic and giving individuals, every one of you, and I'm proud to have raised you."

"Calli—"

"But you have to let go of this guilt. Zane knew what he was doing."

"Just as I know what I'm doing. It's my turn to save him."

"That's why you joined the Legion. That's why you said it had to be you. Of all of you, you always were the one to get into the most trouble," Calli said. "More than all the others combined, in fact." She chuckled. "And you always insisted on getting yourself out of it too."

"Of course. The one who made the mess should fix it. That's orderly."

Calli gave me a strange look I couldn't decipher. "You are more like your Colonel Windstriker than you think."

I didn't bother to argue with her about 'your angel'. I'd argued the point with my sisters and friends, but not with Calli. She'd always been able to see right through my bullshit. And truth be told, all pretending aside, my heart did lose a beat whenever someone called him mine or said that I was his. I tried not to think about that too much, about what that meant, because, honestly, it scared me shitless—even more than the thought of trekking to the heart of the monster-ridden Black Plains.

So I merely said, "You don't even know Nero. How can you say we're alike?"

"I know he's an angel. And that's how angels think.

Cleaning up messes. Restoring order to chaos. Like you."

Nero called me the bringer of chaos, and he was right. But so was Calli. I did feel the need to restore order after unleashing that chaos. It was a weird dichotomy that lived inside of me. A split. That's what I was—perpetually caught, constantly tugged between order and chaos.

"Also I read about him," Calli continued.

"Oh, really?" I imagined Calli, my badass mother, flipping through the latest tabloid column, and I couldn't help but laugh at the image.

"I felt it prudent to know what you were getting yourself into," she said. "Leda, he's an angel nearly two hundred years old, so I don't need to tell you how dangerous he is. You know the Legion of Angels doesn't have its soldiers do the right thing, just the lawful thing. The law of the gods. This might be our world, but it's their playground. And their rules."

"I know, Calli. And you know I never wanted any of this. I never wanted this life. I wanted to be here with all of you, together."

Calli set her hand on mine. "This life was never meant for you, Leda. I always knew it, deep down. I wouldn't admit it to myself, even after you left to join the Legion. But it is the truth. You were meant for great things. You were meant to join the Legion of Angels."

Nero had once told me something just like that. He'd told me that my path would eventually lead me to the Legion.

"Do you believe in destiny?" I asked Calli.

"For most of my life, I'd have said no. But now…" She shook her head. "I'm just not sure anymore."

I'd never seen Calli so indecisive. It was unsettling. Calli was our rock and our glue. She'd always known what to do, no matter what problem we'd had.

"Do you know anything about my past?" I asked her, then took a bite of my roll. I was running out of time.

"Nothing before your days of living on the streets. I once looked up your previous foster mother, but I couldn't find anything about a witch named Julianna Mather."

"Thanks," I said, disappointed but not surprised. I pushed back from the counter. "I have to go now."

I walked down the dark streets of Purgatory. The town was waking up, people hurrying from one place to another, as though afraid to be caught outside in the dark. They watched me from their windows, hope in their eyes. They thought I was here to save them from the atrocities that plagued the town. My throat constricted with guilt. I wasn't their savior.

"Come on, honey," a male voice cooed. "Don't go doing that now."

I snapped my head around, looking for the man who owned that voice. I found him in the shadows of an old building. He and his buddy were wearing black trench coats. That meant they were Royal's men.

"What is that she's carrying?" the other man asked.

"A taser. Magitech. The boss says civilians aren't allowed to carry weapons in town."

A shadow beyond them shook. As I moved in closer, I saw that shadow was a woman. Trembling, she held the taser before her body. The first man smacked the weapon from her hands. It slid across the cobbled street and clinked against the stone building on the other side. The temple. Those fiends were doing this just outside the Pilgrims' temple.

"Don't even think about it." The first man moved with her, blocking her from reaching the weapon. "Don't move, or I'll cut up that pretty face of yours."

I hurried forward, my steps fueled by pure anger. I didn't care that I wasn't allowed to interfere. I didn't even think about what would happen to me if I did. All I could see was that poor woman, those two thugs, and the end of my sword.

A hand locked around my arm like an iron clamp. I spun around to punch whoever had the gall to stand in my way of helping that woman. Nero caught my fist mid-air.

"Let me go," I growled.

"You will not interfere in local affairs."

I gritted my teeth, pushing against his hold. I couldn't budge him an inch. I was stuck.

"Stop, Leda."

I kicked him in the shin.

"This is your last warning."

I pushed with every shred of supernatural strength I had, but I might as well have been trying to move a mountain. Nero's hand jerked sideways. I heard my wrist snap a moment before the pain tore through my nerves. I swallowed my agony and didn't stop fighting. I pushed and pulled and kicked.

"The Legion will punish you if you attack those men," he told me calmly.

"I don't care," I spat.

"Attacking them might save her, but it won't save anyone else here."

I aimed another kick at him, but he deflected it. His kick broke my leg.

"How can you be so cold?" I demanded, trembling with

anger and pain.

"The Legion will never let you come back here, Leda. You might never see your family again. And you'll ruin your chances of gaining the magic you need to save Zane."

The sound of my brother's name made me stop—or maybe it was the firestorm of agony rushing through my body, dragging me under. I blinked my eyes, trying to stay conscious. The next thing I knew, Captain Somerset was carrying me down the hallway of the temple. Nero was nowhere in sight.

"You just can't stay out of trouble, can you, Pandora?" she said, setting me down on a chair inside the Legion office.

Nine pairs of eyes turned to stare at me. It looked like everyone was here—everyone except Nero. And the Pilgrims.

"Take this." Captain Somerset handed me a potion. She added in a lowered voice, "No one can make a clean break like Nero. Your injuries will heal in a few minutes. Try not to break anything else in the meantime." Then she walked over to our comrades.

"What happened to you?" Drake whispered as he sat down beside me.

I used my good hand to pop the potion, drinking it down in a single gulp. "An angel happened to me."

"Colonel Windstriker did this to you?" Surprise flashed in his eyes. "Why?"

"The district lords—crime lords really—run this town now. People are scared, Drake. They're hurting. I was going to stop two of the district lord Royal's thugs from hurting a woman." I frowned. "Nero stopped me from interfering in local affairs." I looked for something to kick—then remembered my leg was still broken. "What is the point of all this, of being strong, if we can't help the weak? If we can't right the world's wrongs?"

"There are a lot of wrongs in the world. So much evil," Drake said. "The Legion cannot correct every wrong or banish every evil."

"Evil doesn't come only in ugly, monster-shaped packages. It hides behind human smiles and behind the false platitudes we tell ourselves so that we can sleep at night. I could have stopped those men, Drake."

"But not all the others, and not the system that created them. At least not in a day." He set his hand on my arm. "That is a longer war, the war against the evil that lies within us all."

"Can we ever win that war?"

"Yes," he said immediately.

"How can you be sure?"

"Not everything the gods do is kind, and not everything we Legion soldiers have to do is pretty, but I truly believe we're making the world a better place. You have to have faith, Leda, that it will happen. Faith, hope, love—those are the things that keep us going. The things that keep us fighting for what really matters."

"You sound like the Pilgrims," I said.

"Do I?" His eyes twinkled. "I spoke with them last night. They are doing what we do, fighting evil and preserving what is good in this world. Humanity has lost so much since the monsters overran the Earth. But we have gained a lot too. You should talk to the Pilgrims, Leda. They can help you remember that."

I hadn't had good experiences talking with Pilgrims, at least not the ones who handed out pamphlets on the street corners of Purgatory. They were selling blind faith, and I had a knack for questioning everything.

"Pandora, Football, do you think you could grace us with your presence?" Captain Somerset called out.

I tested my leg. When I discovered I could move it without agonizing pain, I rose to my feet. I didn't collapse, which was a good sign. My wrist felt fine too. Whatever potion Captain Somerset had given me was top notch.

"We're taking two trucks. Pandora, you'll be in the first truck to show us the fastest path to the Lost City," Captain Somerset said. "Park, you haven't crashed Legion property lately, so you're driving."

Morrows snickered.

Captain Somerset snapped her head around to him. "Morrows, you always crash everything, so you're not to go near the wheel."

"What if everyone else is dead?" he asked solemnly.

"If everyone else is dead, then fine. Knock yourself out. But until that point, I'm going to put your talents to better use. You have first shift with the cannon. Shoot down every monster that threatens the trucks."

Morrows grinned like his birthday had come early.

"Norman, Football, and I will also be in the first truck," Captain Somerset continued. "Lawrence, you'll drive Colonel Windstriker's truck."

Lieutenant Lawrence sneered across the room at me.

"Vance, you take the cannon. Silvershield, Greer, Cupcake, you're in the second truck too."

"I wonder why only some of us have nicknames," I whispered to Drake.

"I guess only the good ones stick."

"It's hard to beat Cupcake." I glanced at Maton

Chambers, aka Cupcake. I actually felt bad for him. He was a really nice guy.

The door to the office opened, and Nero stepped inside with the seven Pilgrims. He nodded to Captain Somerset.

She returned the nod. "All right, get moving. The sun will be up in just a few minutes. It might feel like summer, but the days are still short this time of year, and we need to use every daylight hour."

We headed down the hall toward the garage. I ignored Nero along the way—or ignored the back of his head anyway since he was ahead of me. I didn't mind the broken bones; I'd had plenty of them since joining the Legion. But I was pissed off as all hell that he'd broken them to stop me from saving that woman. It was my choice whether I wanted to get myself in trouble, not his. There was this pesky little thing called freewill that he regularly forgot existed. Just like an angel. Maybe Calli was right. Maybe Nero wasn't as different as I'd thought.

I climbed into the truck, sitting between Drake and Captain Somerset. I was so glad that Nero was in the other truck. I didn't think I could hold my tongue all the way to the Lost City if I'd had him sitting next to me.

The trucks pulled out of the garage. As they turned around the temple to drive toward the wall, a flicker of light caught my eyes. Two bodies hung from the temple's chimney, swinging in the wind. Royal's men. Their throats were slit in cold, merciless strokes. They were killed quickly, before they could fight back. There wasn't a single other scratch on them. This wasn't an act of anger or malice; it was an execution.

I looked at the truck driving beside us. Nero met my gaze, his eyes devoid of emotion. He'd killed those men. I knew he had.

"I think he left them there for you," Drake said, wide-eyed.

"That is one strong signal, Pandora," Captain Somerset commented.

"But he said we're not allowed to interfere in local affairs."

"Technically, that's true," Captain Somerset said. "But Nero always took it upon himself to learn the rules to the letter. Because when you know the rules inside and out, you can find all the loopholes. Legion soldiers may not interfere in local criminal activity, *unless* it pertains to the mission or it takes place on the gods' property. Such as the grounds of a Legion office or a Pilgrim temple."

"They weren't on the gods' property." They'd been across the street from the temple.

"I bet they were standing on the gods' property when Nero executed them."

She was right. Nero was a stickler for the rules. He'd probably lured them onto the Legion side of the border—and then killed them for their crime.

"Loophole," I muttered.

"Proposition."

I looked at Captain Somerset. "Sorry?"

"Nero has it bad for you. I thought a little fun could cure him, but it seems he only wants one cure. You. And now he's stringing up dead criminals to let you know." She shook her head. "Why couldn't he have gone with chocolate?"

"Because he's an angel, that's why," Morrows said from his seat behind the cannon. "And you know chocolate isn't the same. Not at all."

"Chocolate is less complicated."

I felt like I was missing part of the conversation—a conversation about my love life that now involved everyone in the truck except for me. I glanced at Drake, who shrugged. Well, at least I wasn't the only one who didn't get it.

"It is a fine line between loopholes and the path to self-destruction. What game are you playing?" Captain Somerset demanded.

"I'm not playing any game."

Captain Somerset gave me a critical look. "This is how angels fall. And you just might be the catalyst to his downfall. I like you, Pandora, but if you ruin Nero, I will kill you."

I could see it in her eyes that she meant every word. With Harker gone, she was Nero's best friend, and she was fiercely loyal to him.

"I haven't done anything," I told her.

She continued to glare.

"What would you have me do?" I demanded.

"Honey, I think you know what you need to do to make him stop stringing up dead bodies."

I returned her glare. I was not going to have sex with Nero just so Captain Somerset would stop sharpening her knives—literally. She had her weapon out and was sharpening the blade. Ok, so it wasn't a knife. It was a sword. Which was even worse, actually.

"So, what kind of sword is that?" I asked her, trying to change the subject.

"A fire sword." Flames burst to life, sliding in silken waves across the blade. "A fine weapon. They're sharp and cut through flesh easily, especially when they're nice and hot."

I had a feeling she was talking about my flesh. "I'd better go guide our driver." Before this conversation turned any further downhill.

CHAPTER SIX

The Lost City

I STARED OUT across the Black Plains, the expanse of scorched earth where nothing natural grew. There were plenty of unnatural things growing, though, products of magic gone wrong. We passed a forest of black trees, their trunks shining like hot bubbling oil. From their alien branches, crunchy leaves rustled in the wind, creaking like an old staircase.

Ten minutes into our journey, a giant beast that looked an awful lot like a tyrannosaurus rex tore out of the forest, hurling splintered tree trunks aside. Two of the Pilgrims in our truck began to shout hysterically, like they'd not actually expected to be attacked by monsters on the plains of monsters. Actually, I was surprised. I'd heard the beasts' numbers were growing, that they were venturing closer to the wall, but this close? It looked like the rise of the crime lords was just one of the problems Purgatory was facing.

The truck's cannon roared, and Morrows laughed with glee as he shot the red beast full of ammunition designed to penetrate tanks and the scales of giant dinosaur-like monsters that shook the earth as they ran. The dinosaur went down, but there were three more already closing in on us—and even our Magitech-powered trucks weren't fast enough to outrun them.

The green tyrannosaurus rex crouched into its legs, its muscles tightening. It sprang up, then came down with a resounding thud right behind us. I looked back. The second truck screeched as it swerved to avoid the beast's swinging tail. Ben, the Pilgrim sitting behind me, fainted. Morrows turned the cannon toward the monster and shot a magic bullet right through its chest. Greenie tipped and hit the ground like an earthquake, missing our truck by mere inches.

The third dinosaur leapt over the fallen beast. Another of the Pilgrims peed his pants as its giant jaws snapped at the truck. Not that I blamed him. I might have peed my pants too if I'd thought it would have done any good.

The monster spun, going for the other truck. Claudia was behind their cannon. Our shooter Morrows preferred the brute force attack: shoot the target as many times as possible until it went down. Claudia preferred a more efficient method. She hit the beast where it hurt. And if it truly did hurt, she shot it there again.

"That is one sexy woman," Morrows commented as the beast hit the dirt.

I smirked at him. "The dinosaur?"

"No, you smart ass. Sergeant Vance. I love a woman who knows how to handle a big cannon."

"I really did *not* need to hear that."

"None of us did," Captain Somerset said. "Morrows, keep your hobbies to yourself. And your cannon too."

I snorted.

"Hey, wasn't there another monster?" Drake said,

looking around.

A heavy object dropped out of the sky. It landed with a sickening crunch inside a deep ditch to the side of the dilapidated road we were driving on.

"Never mind," said Drake.

"What happened to it?" I asked.

"Colonel Windstriker happened to it," Captain Somerset said as Nero coasted down from the sky and landed in the other truck. "Or, more specifically, one of his telekinetic bursts."

"I think your angel left you another present, sweetheart," Morrows told me.

Lovely.

"I bet the Colonel appreciates a woman who knows how to handle a big cannon too," Morrows added.

"Oh, shut up."

He chuckled.

"Is everyone all right?" Drake asked the Pilgrims in the truck.

"We're just fine, dear, thank you," replied Grace, a woman who appeared to be in her early sixties.

Drake had been talking to her before the monsters attacked. She was actually over a hundred years old, one of the Pilgrims the gods' had gifted with long life. Her great act had happened late in her mortal life. She'd recovered the Diamond Heart, a necklace that belonged to the goddess Kiara, from the Wilds. So braving monsters and hunting down ancient magical relics were nothing new to her.

"The beasts that live on the plains of monsters have grown bold of late," Valiant said. "And big. We saw only a few small fire lizards during my journey across the Western Wilderness last summer. I've never seen a dinosaur before.

And certainly not four of them together."

"As you venture deeper into the wild lands, the beasts grow nastier and more abundant," I told him.

"Those dinosaurs attacked us within twenty miles of the wall," he replied. "It sounds like they are the ones venturing. Just like in the early days, the days before the wall."

He stroked his hand across his smooth chin. He looked like he was in his twenties, but his eyes were older. Much older. They'd seen horrors the rest of us could only dream of.

"Were you there before the wall was built?" I asked him.

"Yes. I saw the monsters consume the Earth, destroying towns, toppling cities."

"Oh, now you've gotten Gramps started," Grace teased me.

I almost laughed at hearing the elderly lady call him Gramps, a man who looked young enough to be her grandson.

"You were made immortal very early in life. You must have done something very important," I said to him.

"It was the days before the wall. I was part of a group of volunteers that drew the beasts away from our town, buying the witches the time they needed to activate the magic wall. Over two hundred of us went. Only I returned. For my service, the gods made me immortal. I survived for a reason: to protect humanity from the monsters that plague our world. The holy relics are objects of great power. This isn't just about the thrill of locating relics that have been missing for centuries. It's about saving the world." He smiled at me. "And we can only do this together."

"Wow, that's a great motivational speech."

"He does excel at that," commented Grace. "And that's why we're all here, seven pilgrims from seven cities."

"That's a great line for the memoir."

Soft, kind wrinkles crinkled her brow as she smiled. "It really is."

We had to park outside the Lost City. Over the past two hundred years since the end of the war, sections of the crumbling city ruins had sunk into the ground. There was no road that led into the city, at least not one our trucks could drive on.

So we approached the city on foot. The ruins glowed eerily, reflecting the light show of mixed colors dancing across the sky. It was as though magic were brewing and blending up in that supernatural kitchen in the sky. A clash of heaven and hell. Ice and fire. Sun and smoke. It sure had made things hot down here. The temperature had risen at least ten degrees since I'd woken up this morning. Sweet beaded up on my body, saturating my clothes, pasting them to my skin.

We passed the husks of old buildings blast apart two hundred years ago in the battle to decide the fate of the Earth. Time had slowly eaten away at what was left, corroding, decaying, corrupting. The streets were split open, their dirty guts exposed. At least what was left of the streets. The ground had swallowed up most of the city's paved surfaces. We sidestepped potholes and craters. We walked across sunken rooftops. We balanced atop toppled bridges, those fallen giants that had once spanned raging rivers lost to the ages.

The Lost City hummed with magic, a resonance that buzzed against my skin like the air after a lightning storm. I paused to inhale. A stale, broken scent permeated the ruins —the smell of utter desolation and ultimate defeat. Just standing here, this tale of woe and despair being whispered into my ear, almost made me too depressed to continue.

I shook myself. *Whoa, what was that all about?*

The city had lain dormant for centuries. It was not alive. It did not think or feel. And it was certainly not whispering to me.

Then why could I hear a quiet battle hymn playing in the distance, a song of ancient battles and earth-shattering, unimaginable magic? Why did I hear gunfire hammering, swords clashing, magic blasting? Why did the final dying shouts of the soldiers echo in my ears? The closer we got to the city center, the louder this symphony of sounds pounded in my head.

"Pandora."

I jumped at Captain Somerset's voice. She was looking at me as though I'd lost my mind. Maybe I had. No one else seemed to be hearing voices in their head.

"Looking to take a swim?" Her lip twitched.

I looked down at the bubbling pool of thick mystery goo that I'd nearly stepped in. I needed to get my head in the game. This was no time to lose my mind. I fortified my mental shields, a skill I'd built up to block my thoughts from eavesdropping angels, and the sounds of battle faded. Maybe hearing voices from the past was another weird ability I had, along with my unusual reaction to Nectar. They had to be linked, right? The alternative was I was crazy, which sounded way less appealing than cool magic powers.

"The Pilgrims have reason to believe the holy relics are in the sunken sections of the city," Nero announced. "Get ready to make the descent."

"Is something wrong, Leda?" Valiant asked me. "You're not afraid of heights, are you?"

"No."

He looked down into the chasm before us. "I am." He gave me a sheepish look.

"I'll be right here beside you." I attached his rope into the hook in the rock. "Ok?" I smiled at him.

He smiled back. "Ok."

We took the descent slow.

"How long have you been searching for the relics?" I asked him, trying to keep his mind off the dark abyss beneath us.

"Since I was made immortal. I heard of these objects of power that had the magic to turn day to night and darkness to light."

"What does that mean?"

"It means they possess great magic, and that magic can be used for good or evil."

"Like most objects of power," I commented.

Excitement shone in his eyes. "These relics are our salvation. With them, we will drive the monsters from this Earth and reclaim our home."

"I can't even imagine a world without monsters. But I do wish I will live to see it."

"If we are successful, you will get your wish. Ever since the monsters overran our world, I've dreamt of this day."

"Even through all that, all the horrible things, you kept hope? How did you do that? How did you know things would get better?"

"Faith," he said, echoing Drake's words from earlier when I'd spoken of the crime lords taking over my town. "You must believe. You must never give up looking for the spark of light in the dark. Speaking of which, I believe we've reached the bottom. It appears that I will in fact live to see another day."

We disconnected ourselves from the ropes.

"How will the relics destroy the monsters?" I asked him as we walked through this sunken section of the city. The buildings and roads were almost perfectly preserved, in far better shape than the ones above ground.

"I haven't figured that out quite yet. I've had to piece this all together from dozens of sources, many of them contradicting one another."

"So even if we find the relics, we might not be able to use them?"

"Not right away," he said quickly. "But with time, perhaps."

I sighed. "I guess I might be waiting awhile on that monster-free world."

"This isn't only about using the relics against the monsters. It's about keeping the relics away from scavengers, from the fiends of hell, from anyone who would use them for evil." He pointed at a tower of steel and glass. "Look there. The Spiral Tower. We're getting close to the Treasury."

"The Treasury?"

"According to my research, the holy relics were kept in a Treasury of magical objects not far from the Spiral Tower. The Treasury is guarded by magic as ancient as the gods."

"So how do we get through this magic?"

"Well, it's not—"

A deep roar cut through his words like sharpened steel. The sound bounced off the rocky sky, echoing through the buildings. I saw a flash of movement on the Spiral Tower, then dark shadows jumped down, landing on the street.

"What the hell?" Morrows muttered from in front of me.

I couldn't see anything over his big head, so I shifted to the side to look between him and Drake. The shadows were monsters, but they didn't look like any monsters I'd ever seen. A messy meld of plant and animal parts, the beasts were shaped like lions, but instead of fur, they had shimmering green scales. And in place of a mane, a wreath of tangled vines and leaves had grown out of each monster's neck.

The monsters were about the size of a large dog. But there were a lot of them, at least fifty by my count. And they didn't look like herbivores.

"Snap dragons," Nero said. "Watch out, they spit."

One of the beasts chose that moment to leap at Nero. A glob of mucous-colored goo shot out of its mouth. Nero darted out of the way. Instead of hitting him in the face, the steaming goo smacked against the street. A patch of pavement split and sank, leaving a pineapple-sized pothole.

Drake and Morrows drew their guns and shot at the snap dragons. The bullets bounced off their hard scales. They switched to swords, but their blades didn't penetrate the beasts' armor. And one of them retaliated by spitting fire.

"They spit fire and venom. *And* they're immune to guns and swords? How are we supposed to kill these things?" Morrows demanded.

Claudia tossed a grenade into the pack. The magical cocktail exploded, igniting the spell that turned six snap dragons to stone. She pulled out her gun and shot the beasts in quick succession, shattering their petrified bodies.

"Hey, Vance, what kind of bullets are you using?" Morrows asked her.

Her lips curled back. "Big ones." She hurled her second grenade.

"I love that woman," Morrows laughed, shooting the new monsters she'd left petrified.

The rest of us followed suit. Except Nero. He charged at the monsters, drawing them away from the Pilgrims. Monsters were drawn to magic. The stronger the magic, the more they wanted to consume it. Nero's angel magic must have looked like an all-you-can-eat buffet to them. Telekinetic waves pulsed out of him, gluing the monsters to the ground as he unleashed a thunderstorm upon them. Tendrils of lightning licked at their scaled bodies, slowly, stubbornly. He was cracking their armor like a nut.

Snap dragons streamed out of the buildings in an angry river. There were so many I couldn't even count them all. Hundreds and hundreds.

"The floodgates have opened. It looks like that first group was just the welcoming party," I commented.

"How many petrifying grenades do you have left?" Drake asked me.

"This is my last one," I said as I threw it.

"I'm out too."

A quick look around told me the rest of our team was out too. And the tsunami of snap dragons wasn't showing any signs of letting up. Where had they all come from?

Captain Somerset ran forward, swinging her sword.

Flames burst to life on the blade, which she sank into the beast's body. She hadn't been kidding earlier when she'd said her fire sword could cut through anything.

She kicked the dead monster off her sword. "Lawrence!"

Lieutenant Lawrence's sword caught on fire too. Together, she and Captain Somerset stood against the wave of monsters, hacking them apart.

The pack turned away from Nero, drawn to the combined magic of the two fire swords. They overwhelmed Lieutenant Lawrence, and she stumbled, the sword falling out of her hand. Her eyes darted to the sword still burning on the ground, as though she were considering going after it. But the monsters were too close. She lashed out with her electric whip. She was good, hitting her target with every snap of the magic-charged coil: the soft flesh of the beasts' noses.

I dug into my potion pack, looking for something useful. I settled on a corrosive potion. Maybe it would be strong enough to break through the beasts' armor. Holding my breath, I tossed the pale orange powder at one of the snap dragons. Dark smoke rose from the monster's scales. It squealed and ran off. Ok, so maybe that wasn't as spectacular as I'd hoped for, but at least it did *something*, which was better than pretty much every other one of our weapons.

Two snap dragons slammed into Captain Somerset, knocking the fire sword from her hand. It disappeared into the pack of monsters. She kept fighting, tossing corrosive powder at them like the rest of the team was doing by now. Minus Nero. He was splitting them open with telekinetic slashes, then setting them on fire.

I caught a glimpse of the two fire swords amidst the monsters. They weren't too far from me. I had to get to them. They worked better than any weapon we had except for Nero. The flames were still going strong, but for how long? I had to act fast. I didn't have the magic to relight them. That required elemental magic, a level four spell.

The snap dragons were packed too closely. I'd never make it through if I didn't thin the herd, but I was all out of corrosive powder. Hmm. I grabbed a vial of sticky potion, uncorked it, and tossed it at the monsters in my path. Then I grabbed my magic flare gun and fired. I knew it wouldn't penetrate the beasts' armor, but that wasn't the point.

The flare, bewitched by witches, was a beacon of magical energy, designed to attract the attention of monsters. We sometimes used them in the wild lands; if you shot one into the distance, the monsters sometimes chased the flare instead of you. Sometimes. The more magic you yourself had, the less likely the monsters were to run after the decoy, which is why Legion soldiers didn't carry them around.

The flare did its job today, though. It stuck to the monster's rear end, held to the scaly hind by the sticky potion I'd thrown at it. Immediately, the snap dragons around it turned, attracted to the flare's magic. The beast let out a yelp of alarm, then ran off, trailing a stream of ignited magic after it. Its pack mates took chase.

"Not too bright, are they?" Drake commented.

"Well, what do you expect when you combine a reptile with a garden plant?" I replied, grinning.

My path clear, I grabbed the two fire swords off the ground. There were still more than enough monsters to go around, and I had not one but two flaming weapons. I slashed at the nearest beast, my right sword cutting right through it. I thrust up with my left sword, skewering the snap dragon that had tried to jump me. Both blades crackled in fiery appreciation. Cool.

I cut and hacked, breaking through the monsters. I moved fast, tirelessly. As long as the spells on the swords held, I wasn't going to stop.

A shrill human scream wailed over the sizzle of the fire swords, and I did stop. I looked around, searching for the source. I found them: three Pilgrims besieged by a fiend. But the fiend wasn't a monster; it was a man in a hood, his face concealed, his sword drawn.

I turned away from the snap dragons, sprinting straight for the man in the hood. He stepped aside with fluid ease, moving faster than anyone I'd ever seen. Like he was the wind. My sword cut through empty air. I thrust with my second sword. He caught my arm, holding it there for a moment. I pushed against his grip, but I might as well have been encased in stone. He released me, dancing back. The fire on both my swords went out. Oh, shit.

He struck fast and hard, throwing me at the three Pilgrims. I looked up, jumping to my feet, but he was gone, without a trace. Well, almost. I had a sizable bump on my head that could attest to his existence. Still, I had to ask…

I glanced at the Pilgrims. "Did you see that man in the hood?"

"Of course," Grace replied.

Yay for me not imagining things that weren't there. At least not this time.

"Where did he go? Why didn't you stop him?" Valiant demanded, hurrying toward us. Behind him, the ground was a thick carpet of dead monsters.

"Does anyone require medical attention?" Nero asked.

"Leda does," Claudia sang with a smirk, adding in a whisper to me, "You're welcome."

Nero moved forward, his eyes flickering up to the wound on my forehead.

"I'm fine, Nero," I told him, brushing his hand aside. "But Grace is bleeding."

His gaze slid to the cut on her finger. He uncorked a healing potion.

"I'm all right. It's just a scratch."

"Magic isn't the only thing that attracts monsters," I told her as Nero poured a drop of potion on her cut. "Many of them are drawn to the smell of blood."

"Oh, of course. I should have remembered that," she said, blushing. "It's been ages since I've been this close to monsters."

"Oh, yes. Monsters. How frightening. But we have far bigger problems!" Valiant exclaimed, his mouth trembling. "Where is that hooded bandit?"

"Bandit?" I asked.

"Yes, bandit. He stole my research notebook. He must have been following us all along, just waiting to rob me."

"Calm down, Valiant," Grace said in a soothing voice.

"Calm down? That notebook contains everything. All my notes on the relics, all my research."

"You mean *our* research," said one of the Pilgrims.

"We're teetering at the precipice of disaster, but, yes, by all means let's argue semantics," Valiant snapped.

"How essential is this notebook?" Nero asked.

"Weren't you listening? I said it contained *all* of my research!"

"Our research."

Nero looked at Grace.

"Losing the notebook is bad, but not catastrophic," she told him. "Valiant has backups of his research."

"Where?" Nero asked him.

"In New York."

"I'll have it sent over."

Valiant sighed. "No need. I have it memorized."

"The whole notebook?" I asked, impressed.

"Yes. But we have a bigger problem. Remember how I was telling you about keeping the relics safe from those who would use them to do evil? Well, one of those evil fiends just got his hands on my notebook."

"How do you know he's an evil fiend?" Claudia asked him.

"I'm going to go with Valiant on this one. That guy hit like an evil fiend." I rubbed my forehead.

"Well, even with the notebook, it will take this 'fiend' some time to decipher it," Grace said.

"You wrote it in code?" Nero asked Valiant.

"Yes, a precautionary measure in case it was stolen. I didn't actually expect anyone to steal it, especially not with the Legion guarding us. You need to go after the hooded bandit and get my notebook back before he deciphers it," he told Nero.

Nero gave him a cool look. "No. The sun will be setting soon. We'll head back to town, then return here in the morning."

"The bandit's trail will be cold by then," Valiant protested.

"If he's after the relics, he's not going far. And he will return here. My first priority is your safety. The Black Plains are even more perilous by night than they are during the day, especially in recent weeks. I will not take the chance that you and your colleagues will be killed."

"I'm willing to take that risk," Valiant insisted.

"This isn't up for discussion. We will return to town and come back here tomorrow."

Valiant seemed ready to plant his feet in the ground and refuse to go, but the cold fire in Nero's eyes must have reminded him that Nero was an angel—and that angels had no problem hurting you to keep you safe.

We made it back to town without being eaten by monsters. Considering the day that I'd just had, I was counting that as a victory. Valiant was feeling notably less victorious.

"I'll go out there alone. No one else will be in danger," he said to Nero when we were all back in the Legion office inside the temple.

"This matter is closed."

"I disagree."

"Disagree all you want. It won't change anything," Nero said icily.

"Valiant, do show some restraint," Grace said gently. "Colonel Windstriker is an angel."

"He is being unreasonable."

The other Pilgrims looked appropriately shocked by his mild complaint. I'd never seen a Pilgrim argue with Nero. They were always too busy revering angels to disagree with them.

"The man in the hood was probably just a common thief," one of the Pilgrims said. "The Lost Relics have been missing for centuries. A thief like that wouldn't even know they exist."

"Lost Relics?" I asked. "I think I've read about them. Is that what we're after?"

Valiant frowned at his colleague. "Nice going."

"From what I remember, the Lost Relics were made by gods," Captain Somerset said.

"Yes, made by gods for angels," said Nero. "It is said that these are the most powerful weapons the Earth has ever seen."

"What do they do?" I asked.

"They can kill an angel in a single strike."

CHAPTER SEVEN

Dark Delights

KILLING AN ANGEL wasn't an easy feat. So many doses of gods' Nectar, so much magic, so much training—altogether it made angels nearly unkillable. It was scary to think there was a weapon that could kill an angel in a single strike. It was even scarier to know that weapon was out there now, just waiting to be found.

It all made sense now, why the gods had granted the Pilgrims' special assistance from the Legion, including that of an angel like Nero. But the gods had still left Nero in charge of this mission, and he was right. There *might* be a weapon beneath the Lost City with the power to kill angels, but there *definitely* were monsters out there right now on the Black Plains with more than enough power to kill anyone crazy enough to be caught outside at night.

The magic tides of the world were changing. We'd just been through more monster attacks during the day than I'd ever experienced, even at night. Going out there right now was suicide and I said it.

Nero nodded in approval, but Valiant frowned at me like I'd just fallen a few notches in his esteem.

"I'm not going to lie to you," I told him. "I've lived out here at the edge of the Black Plains my whole life, and I've never seen so many monsters. This is bad. Really bad."

Nero looked worried. Well, at least as worried as he could look. There was a tiny crinkle between his eyes, but the rest of his face was as hard as marble, as unfeeling as stone. Perhaps it was that hard, unfeeling expression that told me he was worried, that he wanted to go back out there and secure the Lost Relics as much as Valiant did.

"We will depart at first light," Nero told us. "I'm ordering you all to eat and then go to bed. I expect tomorrow will be at least as eventful as today, and I need you all fed and rested so you'll be at full power."

My stomach rumbled, and I wondered what Calli was making for dinner. I hoped she'd cooked enough to feed an army because I was famished.

"Leda," Nero said.

Everyone else had left while I'd been standing there, fantasizing about dinner. Nero closed the door. Uh-oh.

"Is this about the fire swords? I know I didn't exactly ask permission to use them. Are Captain Somerset and Lieutenant Lawrence upset?"

"Lieutenant Lawrence detailed her grievances to me on the drive back to town."

Figured. She was probably happy to have an excuse to talk to him—and to complain about me.

"Captain Somerset was amused."

"Amused?" I asked.

"Yes."

"Hmm."

"She did express her concern that if your technique did not improve, next time you might set your hair on fire."

"She was laughing when she said that, wasn't she?"

"Yes," he confirmed. "But this isn't about the fire swords."

"The flare guns?"

"Those guns are not standard issue for soldiers of the Legion."

"I know. I borrowed it from my mom. We used to bring them with us when we traveled across the Black Plains, so I thought it might be useful to carry one. The flares are made by witches, a brew of concentrated magic designed to—"

"I know what they're used for."

I smirked at him. "Do you? Even though they're not standard Legion issue?"

"Careful." He folded his arms across his chest.

I mimicked the gesture, but I had the feeling it looked less badass on me. "Always."

He arched a single eyebrow, daring me to tease him further. For once, I behaved myself.

"Next time you wish to bring along an unsanctioned weapon, discuss it with me first. Flare guns are a fire hazard."

I nearly laughed in his face. "Almost every weapon in the Legion's armory is a fire hazard, including each and every soldier level four or higher."

He watched me with mild amusement.

"You're teasing me."

"How could you tell?"

"I don't know. Must have been the sudden outburst of unfettered emotion," I said, sarcasm dripping from every word.

He didn't take the bait, even though I'd left it right out

there for him.

"So about those flare guns," he said instead of something, well, I don't know, romantic. Only Morrows thought guns were romantic.

"We're still talking about the flare gun?"

"You set a snap dragon's ass on fire with a magic flare, Leda. Of course we're still talking about this."

I couldn't tell if he was serious or amused. Probably both. I seemed to bring out conflicted emotions in people.

"Did my unorthodox battle strategy upset your prim and proper angel sensibilities?" I asked him.

"There was a strategy to that madness?"

"Sure, you just said it: to set a snap dragon's ass on fire with a magic flare." I smiled with satisfaction. "I bet the fiend never saw it coming."

"Yes, that's typically what happens when you shoot someone from behind." He even managed to say it with a straight face.

We stared at each other for a few seconds, his hard eyes against my smiling ones. It was a real struggle not to look away from the swirling storm of gold and silver magic in his eyes.

"So, I take it from your stony silence that you want to analyze my actions in the snap dragon fight," I finally said.

"You fought well."

I blinked in surprise. I hadn't expected that. "You always deconstruct my fights."

"Not this time."

"Oh?"

A slight smile touched his lips. "Disappointed?"

"Of course. I love analyzing my inadequacies one-by-one after the fact."

"Go to dinner with me," he said suddenly.

I stared at him.

"You aren't inadequate, not even a bit," he added.

"You're just saying that so I'll go out with you."

"You already agreed to go out with me."

"I guess you've got me there."

"Yes, I do," he replied, his voice seductive, possessive.

"Go easy on the compulsion there, angel," I said against the heat rising under my skin.

He shrugged. "You're immune." He leaned in closer, his lips brushing against mine as he said, "As your continued resistance to following orders proves."

Not completely immune. "Hey, I'll have you know that I haven't disobeyed an order in at least a week."

"Somehow, I seriously doubt that, Pandora."

"Ok, so maybe I did disobey Lieutenant Ripley last week when he told me to use Saintly Suds to wash the truck, but in my defense, that was a really stupid idea. Everyone knows that Blessed Bubbles are the superior product. Anyway, I didn't see it as an order so much as a suggestion."

"How many times do you tell yourself that before you get ready to disobey something I've ordered you to do?"

"Hardly ever. I typically only think about that afterwards."

"Stop." His hands slid down my cheeks in a gentle caress. "Don't confess your sins to me, or I'll be forced to discipline you."

"Are you really sure you want me to stop? I know how much you love assigning me pushups."

"And how much you enjoy doing them, especially when I'm on top of you."

Of course, he'd meant sitting on me as he sometimes did to make the pushups harder, but he'd chosen the words purposefully. He *always* chose his words carefully, every one placed exactly as he wanted. The innuendo was as thick as heavy whipping cream—and just as deliciously unhealthy. That's one of the benefits of leveling up your magic in the Legion. You could survive all kinds of deliciously unhealthy things. Like angels.

I took a moment to collect myself so that when I did speak, I didn't stutter like a fool. "I'm surprised that you want to have our date now of all times."

"It will never be the right time, so it might as well be now."

I liked that argument. I liked it a lot.

As Nero and I walked through the town, I listened to the night. The Black Plains were wailing tonight. The moon was nearly full, and magic was in full bloom. Dark, sinister magic that made me want to curl up in my bed until morning.

"It isn't safe out there," I said quietly.

"The monsters are hungry tonight. Restless."

"So are the thugs," I commented, glancing at the two men in trench coats who'd been following us from the other side of the street for the last two blocks.

Nero turned to face them. "Leave," he said, that single word chilling the humid evening air.

The thugs spun around and ran the other way.

"Now, *I* am hungry."

"You used a lot of magic today," I said.

"As did you."

"Nah, I mostly just shot off my flare gun and stole other people's fire swords off the ground." I stopped in front of the restaurant. "We're here."

"The Jolly Joint?" Nero read the sign with a dubious slant to his mouth. "Is that Frontier humor?"

"Trust me. It's awesome." I reached for the door, but he got there first.

"Allow me." He held the door for me.

"Oh, so this is like a real date?" I grinned at him as I entered the restaurant.

He slid into step beside me, glancing around at the rustic interior. "We'll manage the best we can."

The Jolly Joint wasn't a fancy place, but it had some of the best food in town. The furniture looked like it was from the last century, antique as in 'old', not as in overpriced collectibles. The tables were small, nicked, and in dire need of a good sanding. The fabric of the seats was stained, and some of the stitching was unraveling. They smelled like they'd absorbed the scents of all the meals that had come before this one. I loved every popped stitch and wobbly leg because they meant this place had a history, a personality that hadn't been scrubbed, sanded, and whitewashed away.

Arlo, our waiter, set down a large bread basket between us, his gaze lowered to Nero's jacket. The reverence in his eyes said he knew what Nero's rank meant—that there was an angel in their midst. His back still bowed over, the waiter left us alone at our table. Nero took a bite of a roll. He quickly finished it off.

"I knew you would like this place," I said as he started on his second roll.

"The place is rough around the edges, but it only makes

it more charming."

From the way he was looking at me, he wasn't talking about just the food. He was talking about me too.

"Yes, it is," I agreed. "And at least it's away from the prying eyes of the Legion."

"You shouldn't allow yourself to be bothered by their gossip."

I traced my finger across marks in the table, where someone had carved 'Heather loves James' into the wood with a steak knife.

"To which gossip are you referring?" I asked him, abandoning the table graffiti to take a sesame roll from the basket. "Perhaps the rumor that you decided to make me your lover the moment I sped off across the Black Plains to save you from a nest of nasty vampires? Or everyone's insistence that I don't even have a choice in the matter because Nero Windstriker always gets what he wants?"

"They're bored and need a way to fill the time between battles and getting high. You shouldn't believe everything you hear."

"So it's not true?"

"No. Of course not," he said. "I didn't decide I would make you my lover after you rescued me from the Black Ruins. That only reenforced what I knew about you."

"Meaning?"

"I decided I would make you my lover the moment I met you." Danger sparked in his eyes—danger that tasted like cherries dripped in dark chocolate. "And you always had a choice, Leda. I'm just making it my mission to convince you. Because, yes, I do usually get what I want."

Our waiter chose that moment to return to take our orders. He turned to Nero. Usually, it went ladies first, but it was angels first above all.

"You will take my lovely companion's order first," Nero said.

Surprise flashed in Arlo's eyes. Angels enjoyed privileges, and they always came first.

"Of course," Arlo said, recovering. "What can I get you, my lady?"

My lady? I thought about reminding him that we'd gone to school together, but what was the fun in that?

"I'll have the Jolly Platter and a pineapple juice," I told him.

Nero peered over his menu at me. The table was so small that as he turned the page, his hand brushed past mine. Then it retreated, so close and yet so far away. Nero was playing with me. Or was he? Maybe I was getting myself wound up over nothing. He was just flipping through a menu, for crying out loud. And yet he'd been looking at me the whole time, not at the menu

"The Spring Chicken and an Angelfire spring water." His eyes didn't leave me even as he placed his order.

I braided my fingers together, looking into his eyes, wondering what secrets lay beneath his armor. A shadow hovered over my shoulder.

"What is it, Arlo?" I asked him impatiently, keeping my eyes on Nero.

"Your menu, Leda," he whispered.

I slid my elbow off my closed menu. "Take it."

I heard the rustle of leather and pressed cotton, and then he was gone with the menus. Nero's hand slid over mine, and though his touch only brushed the surface, a river of liquid fire burned through my veins, enveloping my entire body, consuming me. I didn't want to lose this staring contest, whatever game it was that angels played. But I just couldn't look anymore. The look in Nero's eyes should have scared me, but it didn't. It excited me. And *that* scared me.

I could feel everyone's eyes on us. When I turned to meet their stares, they hastily looked away. But I knew they were still watching us out of the corner of their eyes.

"We might be away from the prying eyes and gossiping mouths of the Legion, but we are under the spotlight of the town," I said, taking a sip of the pineapple juice Arlo had just set down. "And the denizens of Purgatory don't have monster battles and getting high on Nectar to fill the boring hours. We are their entertainment."

"You sure are worrying a lot about others. The only eyes you should be thinking about right now are mine. The only mouth that you need to worry about is mine."

Another innuendo. This had to be some kind of record for him.

"This is our date," he continued. "Not theirs."

"You're right. I'm sorry."

"If it makes this easier…" He gave his hand a little wave, and as if by magic, the people in the room all looked away.

"You compelled them?"

"Every single one of them," he said without a shred of shame.

I chuckled. "So, do you really think those relics are under the city?"

He gave me a hard look.

"What? You've got them all oblivious to us, right?"

"All but the waiter. He's been compelled to bring us our dinner as soon as possible."

"I don't think you needed to do that. Your wings are a pretty compelling argument on their own."

"I haven't shown my wings here."

"It doesn't matter. Arlo knows they're there."

"How do you know our waiter?"

"We went to school together," I said with a shrug. "We didn't hang out in the same circles, though."

"And what circles did you hang out in?"

"Just with my sister Bella mostly—when I wasn't hunting down criminals to turn in for cash."

"You've led an interesting life."

"It's gotten more interesting recently," I said, stirring my juice.

His hand closed over mine. "So has mine. For better or for worse."

"Do you think we'll find the relics?"

"Nyx thinks we will." His thumb traced small, slow circles into my hand. "I called her on the drive back. She confirmed that she'd known all along about what the Pilgrims were after. She's keeping too many secrets."

"Well, she is an angel."

"What do you think I am keeping from you?"

"A lot, I'm sure. The Legion guards its secrets well."

Disappointment flickered in his eyes, and he dropped his hand.

"I'm not asking you to tell me," I said.

He watched me for a long, silent second, then he replied, "You are too good."

"For the Legion?"

"To survive this world." He brushed his hand against mine. The spark of heat returned, taking on a life of its own, waking me up as though from a dream, from a life I'd never truly been living.

Arlo came with our dinner, and we unlinked hands.

"So, what was it like growing up as the only known child of two angels?" I asked Nero. "Did you always have powers, even as a child?"

"From an early age, yes. I couldn't control those powers very well, but they were there."

"Do the children of angels always have these powers before they join the Legion?"

He finished chewing the piece of chicken he'd cut off, then said, "You're wondering if you are the child of two angels."

"The thought did cross my mind. I don't react to Nectar like other people. I react like you do."

"In response to your question, yes. All children with an angel parent manifest at least some powers, even early on. Did you ever manifest any powers?"

"No." And there went my theory.

"There is something different about you," Nero said. "Something special. That's why Nyx put you on the Legion fast track."

"There are a lot of people on the fast track now. Why? What is the Legion gearing up to do? Fight?"

Nero took a long, slow sip from his glass. "Asking questions like these will get you into trouble."

"So you've warned me before. And so has Captain Somerset. In fact, she's warned me about more than just that."

"What do you mean?"

"She is scary sometimes, you know. I'm getting the feeling that she's going to skewer me with her swords if I don't sleep with you. Or if I do sleep with you. I don't think she's decided yet."

Nero's face was impassive.

"I think you really need to teach me to use a fire sword. Just in case."

"I take it from that statement that you don't plan on sleeping with me."

"Well…I…um…"

A deep, low noise rumbled in Nero's chest.

"Are you laughing at me?" I demanded.

"Yes."

I glowered at him. "That wasn't funny."

"Firstly, it was very funny. And secondly, I told you not to glare at me like that until you have the magic to back it up. You don't, Pandora."

"Yet."

A slight smile touched his lips. "Yet," he agreed.

"So about those fire swords," I began.

"What about them?"

"I need you to teach me how to wield them. I want to be able to do more than just spin them around while trying not to burn myself."

"Not burning yourself is an important first step."

"I'm serious, Nero. I want to master them."

"I'm not sure I want to help you set things on fire. You're dangerous enough already."

"Very funny."

"When you gain the power of elemental magic, you'll be able to set more than swords on fire. Clothes lines, sticks, ropes, everything in your vicinity that you want to misuse as a weapon."

I stuck my tongue out at him.

"Very scary, Pandora." Nero slipped a vial out of his

jacket.

"Nectar?" I whispered, recognizing the liquid flowing like shimmering rainbow lava inside the tiny bottle.

"Just the drops."

Nectar drops were the diluted form of Nectar, the drug of choice of the Legion's soldiers. A drop or two added to a drink made us happy, high, and really relaxed, the perfect combination after a long and grueling day.

"Would you like some?" he asked me.

I hesitated, even as my tongue darted out to slide across my lips. "Are you sure that's a good idea?"

"I think it's a very good idea." Under the table, his leg brushed against mine, causing me to jump a little in my seat. "You're way too tense." He poured a drop into each of our drinks. "Here, we'll do it together."

"How can I refuse an offer like that?"

We lifted our glasses and drank. The Nectar danced across the pineapple flavor, enhancing it. Making it richer, sweeter. The hot river of magic poured down my throat, setting off a cascade reaction, a dozen tiny explosions of ecstasy. My muscles, tense from a day of fighting monsters and hiking through ruins, grew liquid. I hadn't felt this relaxed since, well, the last time I'd had Nectar. The spa trip with Ivy last month, while fun, couldn't even compete with this.

I gazed across the table at Nero. A pale ethereal light glowed around him, that soft angelic halo contrasting with the wicked fire burning in his eyes. My gaze slid across the smooth fabric of his shirt. There wasn't a single wrinkle—or a single bead of sweat—on it. It was perfectly pristine, as though it had been ironed onto him. Or melted on. I wondered if he was as hot as I was—or if angels even sweat.

"You are making this all too easy, Pandora."

"Making what too easy?"

He leaned in, the hard muscles of his chest shifting against his shirt. "Seducing you."

He captured my lips with his mouth. His kiss was slow, searing—and ruthlessly erotic.

"Would you like to skip to dessert?" His words fell against my jaw, dipping to my throat.

Did he even have to ask? A hard, base hunger had taken root deep inside of me. If we didn't get out of here now, I was going to do something that broke every rule in the Legion's decorum rulebook.

"Yes," I said. My top felt like a straightjacket against my swelling breasts.

His smile was pure sin, the retreating whisper of his final kiss an unspoken promise of dark delights. "We're ready to order dessert."

I blinked, my mind unable to process his words. I looked up to find our ever-attentive waiter standing beside our table. Oh, *that* dessert.

"What would you like?" Nero asked me casually.

"I…"

"Do you need a moment?"

He was right. He really didn't want me to gain the power to set things—and wicked angels—on fire.

"I'll have a slice of apple pie."

Arlo looked at Nero.

"Same," he said.

Arlo bowed and left. Nero continued to stare at me, his eyes alight with mischievous delight.

"You enjoyed that," I growled at him.

"I will. Dessert is an indulgence but one worth every

bite."

"Not the dessert. Confounding me."

"I am merely upholding my promise," he replied calmly, clearly unbothered by the looping mental fantasy of setting his hair on fire that I was broadcasting to him loud and clear. When I gained elemental magic, he was in for trouble. "You wished for us to have dinner someplace public. I get the feeling you're still not certain you want to be involved with me."

"I know I want to be with you. It's the other guy I'm not sure about."

"What other guy?"

"The angel."

"I am the angel."

"Not always."

He mulled that over for a moment, then said, "If you want to be with me, the 'other guy' is part of the package."

I sighed. "I know."

"Leda, *you* want to be an angel. That means spending a lot of time with other angels."

I smirked at him. "It's a sacrifice I'm willing to make."

He leaned in, capturing my lower lip between his teeth. "Careful, Pandora. There's a fine line between foreplay and insubordination."

His fangs broke the surface of my lip. A drop of blood rose slowly, pulsing, burning, shooting my senses into overdrive. I was suddenly hyperaware of everything. Every beat of his heart. Of mine. Every whisper, every breath. The thick, rich aroma of his scent caressed my senses, potent and pure. The taste of an angel. Of *my* angel. I tilted my neck, brushing my hair aside.

Nero's eyes flickered to my naked throat. "Stop," he

whispered, his voice rough with need.

I smiled. "Stop what?"

I slid my hand down my neck, tracing the line of my pulse throbbing beneath my skin. With my other hand, I reached for his hand, but he withdrew it. I slid my leg against his, and a low, masculine noise buzzed in his throat.

"You are making it exceedingly difficult for me to hold to your conditions of this date," he said, each word perfectly articulated, as though he were struggling to maintain control.

I arched my brows at him. "What if I were to remove those conditions?"

"Are you?" he asked cautiously.

"What would you do if I said yes?"

"The things I would do to you I cannot speak of here."

My inner thighs clenched together, shaking, quivering. I swallowed down the rising tide of excruciating lust, and stuck a sassy smile over it. "I never took you for the modest type."

His voice dropped to a rough, ragged whisper. "Do not challenge me, Pandora. I have no qualms about burning off all your clothes and taking you here and now on this table." His hand traced up my thigh, teasing the bottom hem of my shorts.

My head spinning, my heart hammering like a runaway train, I arched my back in silent, sensual invitation. My entire body, head to toe, peak to valley, was burning for him like I had never truly been alive before this moment.

"In front of all these people?" My voice was a raw rasp.

"I never took you for the modest type," he repeated my earlier words back at me. They sounded so much sexier sliding off his tongue.

"Very funny."

"I can compel them all to leave if you wish." His fangs traced the soft, sensitive flesh of my throat.

"Bite me," I said, caught somewhere between desperate plea and rough demand.

He pulled back, meeting my eyes. "Do you wish to be alone with me, Leda?"

"Yes."

A smile twisted his lips, and his hand moved up my thigh, parting my legs.

His phone buzzed against my skin. He slipped his hand into his pocket and pulled it out, glancing at the screen. And just like that, my dark lover vanished in front of my eyes, replaced by the cold soldier. He dropped his hand from my thigh.

"We have to go," he said, standing.

I followed him toward the exit, my pulse pounding with unfulfilled need.

"Can you focus?" Nero asked as we stepped outside into the scorching night.

"I'm fine," I assured him. *After I have a cold shower.*

"I can make it snow over you," Nero offered.

He'd read my thoughts again. I scowled at him to let him know what I thought about that.

"I can't really not hear your thoughts when you're broadcasting them to me loud and clear, Pandora."

I wasn't broadcasting anything. Ok, maybe that wasn't true. Back in the restaurant, I'd been broadcasting loud and clear. But whatever. I didn't have time to be self-conscious right now. The message Nero had received was obviously bad news.

"I'm fine," I repeated, this time without the inner

monologue. "What's going on?"

"Valiant and two of the other Pilgrims took one of our trucks and drove onto the Black Plains."

"They're going after the relics," I said.

"And we're going after them," he told me. "Before the monsters get them."

CHAPTER EIGHT
Lost Relics

"THE NIGHT IS dark and full of monsters," I commented as I reloaded my gun.

Beside me in the truck, Drake snickered.

Captain Somerset glanced at us from the driver's seat. "Less joking. More killing monsters."

I shot at the metal, roughly man-shaped giant chasing after our truck. The ground shook beneath its feet with every heavy stride. The fiend looked like a monster born out of the metal debris of the fallen cities and shattered roads of the Black Plains. See, monsters weren't just made of flesh and blood. They could be plants. They could be made of metal or wood, of glass or mud, of water or fire. Of basically anything you could imagine and then a whole lot more.

This metal giant was a whole lot more. Its armor was seamless, as hard as dragon scales and as flexible as steel. The only things we had that worked against the monster were bullets filled with a magical agent that corroded metal, making it rust. We just had to keep hitting it until it had enough holes in its armor for the big cannon on top of the truck to blow it to pieces. That was taking a long time. Even longer than it had taken us to take down the other two metal giants.

"We're going to run out of ammunition," Drake said.

"Just keep shooting," Captain Somerset commanded us.

Morrows didn't need to be told twice. He hadn't stopped shooting since a trio of these metal monsters attacked us outside the Windy Woods, one of the many haunted forests on the Black Plains. Cupcake handed him a new gun whenever he ran out of bullets, so the party never stopped.

"Are you sure you're actually hitting the target?" I asked Morrows.

"Come a little closer and find out for yourself."

"I think I'll pass," I said as one of my corrosive bullets hit the monster in the eye. "There's no space over there."

Since the Pilgrims had taken one of our trucks, we all had to squeeze into this one. Twelve Legion soldiers—eleven right now since Nero was flying ahead to clear our path of monsters—and enough weapons, ammunition, and potions to take out a legion of monsters.

"You can sit on my lap, baby," Morrows offered. "I'll even let you hold my gun."

"No, thank you. I don't want to pet your cannon."

Morrows roared with laughter. "You've got spunk, Pandora. No one can deny that."

"Too much spunk," Lieutenant Lawrence said, each word dripping scathing disapproval. "I cannot fathom what Colonel Windstriker could possibly see in you."

"The fact that she doesn't wear underpants probably helps," Claudia said, snickering.

"I thought I was the only one who'd noticed," Greer

said.

"No." Morrows grinned. "We all noticed."

My cheeks burned. "I'm pretty sure there's some Legion rule about staring at your comrade's ass," I muttered.

"No, just about touching it," Claudia informed me, looking at Morrows.

"I can feel you burning a hole in the back of my head, Sergeant Vance," he said gleefully.

"This is all incredibly asinine," Lieutenant Lawrence said.

She scored a perfect shot in the metal monster's mouth. Bellowing in anger, it hurled a boulder at us. Captain Somerset managed to swerve to the side in time. Barely.

The monster's next step was a misstep. Lieutenant Lawrence's bullet must have hit something important inside of its body. Smoke began to rise from its ears. That was Claudia's signal to let loose with the cannon.

"Beautiful," Morrows said in appreciation as flaming metal chunks fell from the sky.

Another two metal monsters burst out of the woods, throwing trees and rocks at us. They seemed to be spawning from the plains tonight, rising from the broken shards of fallen cities. At least these new fiends were smaller than the previous ones, less than half the size of the giants. Claudia used the cannon to blast a leg off of the first. The corrosive bullet I shot at the second monster melted its feet to the cracked asphalt road.

"Take that, you oversized walking trashcan!" I laughed.

"You know what the Colonel says. If you can laugh, you're not working hard enough." Captain Somerset was laughing too, though.

"I follow a very different philosophy," I replied. "If you

aren't laughing, you're not having nearly enough fun. And you should think about a new line of work. I could see Nero as a male model. Or maybe a driving instructor."

"You're joking," Captain Somerset said, speeding up as another two mini-giants saw us.

"What gave it away?"

"I know you've been in a car with him when he was behind the wheel."

She swerved to the right to avoid a monster, then took a sharp left to avoid the other. The truck spilled over the edge of the road and rolled down the lumpy landscape.

"You're one to talk," I said.

"If my hands weren't busy, I'd slap you for insubordination," she told me, grinning.

"Nero is actually a good driver. He just drives at least a hundred miles per hour too fast. Maybe he should be a race car driver."

The two monsters sank into a bog of bubbling black fluid, and Captain Somerset drove back up onto the road. "I'll be sure to tell him to go to you for career advice."

I looked across the plains. Nero was way ahead of us, a shadow in the sky. I couldn't see what monsters he was fighting, but whatever they were, they weren't faring well. Fire rained down from him like bombs falling out of a plane, exploding on the monsters.

"But I guess you don't need me to talk to Nero," Captain Somerset said. "You two are quite chatty. First on the train, and then your date. How was the date, by the way?"

I wasn't surprised she knew. She must have seen us go off together. Or heard us talking before we left the temple. Supernatural senses could penetrate walls, which was why the walls at the Legion office in New York were so thick.

"It was short," I told her. Too short.

"There won't always be an emergency."

I saw something in her eyes, something I couldn't decipher. Humor? A challenge? A dare?

We continued to drive at top speed across the Black Plains. Maybe Captain Somerset should think about race car driving. She drove the big, top-heavy truck like it was a sports car.

The Lost City loomed in front of us, its ruined walls aglow with moonlight. We parked at the edge of the city, right next to the other truck. At least that meant the Pilgrims had made it across the plains without being eaten. Never underestimate the power of dumb luck. I'd been saved by that special mysterious power more than once in my life.

We moved quickly across the city. Having walked these rickety bridges and decayed buildings just hours ago, the path was familiar. We knew the ups and downs, the craters and missteps. But the Lost City was different at night, just like the Black Plains that surrounded it. We came upon a street frozen over in black ice. No, not ice. It was the road itself that shone with that eerie darkness, as though magic had warped its physical properties. Who knew what else magic had warped around here.

"We'll go around," Captain Somerset decided.

We cut around the black ice street, heading for the chasm that led to the sunken city sections. Nero flew down, and we followed slowly, restricted to ropes. A pair of wings sure would have come in handy.

The voices of battle rang in my ears, growing louder the deeper I descended. Before I'd left New York, Jace had told me the phantoms of the past still lingered in the Lost City, waiting to be released.

I wasn't sure I believed any of that. The voices didn't feel like spirits or phantoms. They felt like memories. The question was whose memories they were. And why I was hearing them when no one else could.

"This place is even creepier at night," Drake said.

"Yeah," I agreed, putting up a mental shield to block the voices in my head.

Passing the Spiral Tower, we walked through the thick carpet of dead snap dragons that covered the street. We traveled deeper into the sunken city. Water dripped down the walls, a hollow, rhythmic echo. It popped over the low hum of distant voices. And these voices weren't just in my head.

"It's Nero," I said, recognizing his voice.

"You can distinguish his voice from here?" Captain Somerset asked.

"Yes."

Her brows drew together. "How about the others?"

"I…" I listened as we continued moving toward the voices. "Nero is ordering them to leave. He sounds mildly annoyed, so I'm guessing he's talking to the Pilgrims, not the man in the hood."

"…can't refuse…gods' orders…isn't up for debate…I am in command here, not you."

I could see Nero now. He stood facing Valiant and the other two missing Pilgrims—and he looked just as happy as he sounded.

"We are not abandoning our search. The hooded bandit is still out there, looking for the Lost Relics." Valiant waved his hand to indicate the underground city.

"You don't know that," Nero told him.

"Why else would he steal my notebook? No, Colonel. We're staying right here. You might as well make yourselves useful since you're here anyway."

Nero looked like he'd just exhausted his supply of patience for the year. "I'm going to make this easy for you. You can either leave willingly, or I can carry you out and tie you all to the top of the trucks. That will give you front row seats to the monster attacks during our return trip to Purgatory."

Valiant's companions paled, but Valiant himself just planted his feet in deeper. "You wouldn't dare treat holy Pilgrims in such a manner. We are the voice of the gods."

"You might be the voice of the gods, but I am the hand of the gods. And I am fully prepared to use that hand to knock you on your ass."

"You're bluffing."

Nero met his defiant stare and was unimpressed. "We are sworn to protect you, and you are making that difficult. You didn't just put yourselves in danger by coming out here. You put my soldiers in danger."

Nero's voice was as cold as ice. I shivered in the balmy air. He sure was scary when he was pissed off. His anger was barely contained, boiling hot below the icy surface of his self-restraint. Gold and silver swirled in his eyes, pulsing with the shifting shades of his anger. Only two hundred years of practice in controlling his temper was keeping him in check.

He spun around, his sword a silver arc of death. For one horrible moment, I thought he'd actually lost it, but then I saw the spasming tentacle hanging from his blade—and the monster he'd severed it from. The creature wasn't a creature at all. It was a curtain of twisting vines sliding down the building behind him. Before my eyes, the severed vine regrew into two new vines.

"Great, just what we needed. A hydra plant," I commented.

Thick fog rose from the ground, moaning. Haunted fog was another thing we didn't need.

More vines poured down the building like a green waterfall. They struck out, snapping like a whip, wrapping their thick coils around us. Nero set a bundle of vine monsters on fire. They swelled fatter, larger. He tried frost next. The monster froze, and Nero cut his blade through the frost-bitten plant. It shattered to pieces.

"Use ice spells," he told us.

I reached for my potions kit. I couldn't cast elemental magic, but I had a few potions that would produce a similar effect. I tossed a snowy powder over a nearby vine beast. Once it was frozen, Drake shot the monster, and it exploded like a shattered mirror.

We were just starting to make progress on the Lost City's weed problem when the sparkling fog showed its true nature. A patch of dew-dripped light shifted in front of me, forming into the shape of a man. Before I could move, the smoke had turned to solid rock. The man-shape slammed its stone fist into my side. Pain exploded in my ribs. The monster had broken two of them. Biting back the agony, I swung my sword at the monster, but my blade passed right through it. It had changed back into smoke.

A cyclone turned inside the sunken city, a whirlwind of magic that sucked the smoke in. Nero stood at the center of the spell, his hands twisting and turning to keep the air spinning—and the fog monster trapped. But how long could he keep it up?

The rest of the team was busy with the vines. Beyond the battlefield, Valiant was retreating deeper into the city. He was going alone, going after the relics. The other two Pilgrims weren't far from me.

"Come," I said, channeling the siren. I knew it had worked when their terrified faces went blank. "Stay with me."

Holding to my side, I ran toward Valiant. Those relics were going to get us all killed long before we even found them.

"Stop!" I called out to him. "You can't go alone, Valiant. There will be more monsters."

"Then come with me. You I can trust." He frowned. "But not that angel who threatened to tie me to his truck."

"Nero is trying to protect you," I told him as the other two Pilgrims came up behind me.

"You can protect me."

I glanced down at my broken ribs. My breaths came out in uneven gulps, each one like a stab from a hot needle. "I can't. We need Nero. We need everyone. And most of all, we need to come back after dawn. It's not safe here."

"No, we can't delay. The hood—"

"Is not here." I held out my hand. "Come on."

Valiant's eyes flickered from me, to his companions, then back to me. I didn't have enough magic left in me to compel him too, so I was just going to have to count on his survival instincts.

It seemed I'd overestimated his will to live. He turned and ran off.

He didn't make it far, though. He slipped on a patch of black asphalt ice and fell, bumping his head on the street.

From the sounds of it, he'd broken something too. Good. The pain would succeed where common sense had failed. It would keep him from running off.

"Gods, I'm thinking like Nero more and more every day," I muttered to myself as I went after him, careful to avoid the black ice.

Valiant stirred, letting out a pained moan. And then my vampiric senses smelled it. Blood. The vines screeched and changed direction, drawn to that same smell. I hurled ice potions at the vines, but that hardly slowed them down. The blood had incited them, bringing out their most primal need: hunger. They crashed through their frozen kindred, shattering and splitting them apart in their need to reach the source of that blood.

I was all that stood between the wave of vines and the three defenseless Pilgrims. Unfortunately, I was out of elemental spells, and my sword did nothing but sprout new baby vine monsters.

"Our chances don't look good," I told the two mesmerized Pilgrims beside me.

They only nodded, watching the monsters with disconnected interest. The vines were so busy fighting one another to get to the blood that it was slowing them down.

Valiant lay on the black ice. He'd fallen on a sharp rock, which had penetrated his arm all the way through. On the plus side, the rock had kept him from sliding too far. He was still close enough for me to reach without having to step onto that black ice. Beyond him, the shimmery black ground slowly dipped...and then disappeared into a chasm. I could work with that. I hoped.

"Valiant, I need you to listen to me, and do exactly as I say," I said. "Can you do that?"

He nodded, his eyes wide with horror.

"Don't look at the monsters. Look at me."

His gaze flickered to me.

"Good. Now I'm going to come get you. When I pull you off the ice, throw yourself on the ground. Got it?"

He nodded. I didn't think he realized he was impaled on a rock or how much it would hurt when I lifted him off of it.

"You two, stay down and out of the way," I told my Pilgrims.

They obeyed, and I stepped up to Valiant. The vines were coming, so it was now or never. I pulled him off the rock. I tried not to jostle him, not completely succeeding. He was bleeding out all over now. I helped him off the ice, quickly cutting his shirt off of him. He dropped to the floor, and I launched the bloody bundle of fabric across the ice.

The vine monsters shrieked, taking the bait. I threw myself over Valiant as the vines shot over me, straight for the blood-stained shirt. They skidded when they hit the black ice, sliding over the edge into the chasm. Rising to my knees, I pulled out a healing potion and poured it into Valiant's mouth.

"Thanks," he coughed.

"You can thank me by promising to listen to me next time."

A burst of magic slammed into my chest, throwing me onto the black ice. The fog monster had broken free of Nero's spell. It was spinning, twirling out of control around me, speeding me along on my way to the edge. I looked for something—anything—to hold onto. There was nothing. My fingers slipping off the glossy lip, I fell into the abyss.

CHAPTER NINE
Order and Chaos

ROCKS RAINED DOWN with me as I fell into the abyss. They were on fire, burning down to the ground like falling stars. A brilliant white light caught my eye, and I turned. My hair. It was rippling in the wind, shining like a beacon of light in the darkness of night. I waited for it to do something more than shine, something magical, something that would save me. After a few moments, the glow on my hair faded out, and I faded into darkness. My hair wasn't going to do anything. It couldn't do anything.

"Nero," I whispered.

Leda.

"I wish we'd had the chance to finish our date."

We will.

A blinding light, a thousand times brighter than the weak glow of my hair, flooded the expanse. The darkness melted away. Black blotches floated in the air in front of my face, suspended in time.

A winged silhouette dove down, displacing the floating rocks. Arms folded around me. I looked up into Nero's face.

"I've got you, Leda." His voice shook with naked vulnerability.

I blinked, my eyes adjusting to the searing light. He was carrying me up. Either I was already dead, or Nero had just saved my life. Based on the throbbing pain from five distinct locations across my body, I was guessing the latter.

"Oh, thank goodness," I said. "I did not want to die down there surrounded by those vine monsters."

"Neither did I. Want you to die," Nero added quickly. He was uncharacteristically flustered. It was adorable.

"Yes, I figured that out when you swooped in heroically to rescue me. How did you do that trick with the rocks?"

"Telekinesis."

"You mean inverse telekinesis," I said.

"Inverse telekinesis?"

"Telekinesis is moving objects with your mind. Inverse telekinesis is making them stand still."

He stared at me for a moment, then declared, "You just made that up."

"I did not. It's a thing. And you just did it. Case in point."

"That's circular logic."

"No, it's not. It's very un-circular logic."

"You can't just assign your own names to things that already have names."

"Of course I can." I smirked at him. "Don't you know me at all?"

"You're throwing the entire world order into chaos."

"And that's different from what I normally do exactly how?"

"You make a valid point," he said as we landed. Rocks littered the ground where the black ice had once been.

"What happened up here?"

"The smoke-and-stone monster broke free of my spell and knocked you over the edge. Then it floated up and turned to stone. I broke through it."

"Wow." I looked around at the rocks. They covered everything. Neo hadn't just broken through; he'd broken the whole monster. "You must have hit it hard."

"I was motivated."

Eleven pairs of eyes were watching us.

"Where are Captain Somerset and Valiant?" I asked Nero.

"Captain Somerset carried Valiant ahead to the truck because he was passing out from the pain."

I hoped Captain Somerset didn't make good on Nero's threat to tie Valiant to the roof of our truck. Sure, he had just nearly gotten us all killed, but there was no reason to return the favor. Besides, we had the same goal. We all wanted to keep the angel-killing weapon safe.

"Nero. Maybe you should put me down," I whispered since everyone was still staring at us.

"Why?"

"Everyone is staring at us."

His arms held me in a protective embrace. "I'm not putting you down, Leda."

Nero backtracked our path out of the city. The others followed, not saying a word.

"They are oddly silent," I commented to Nero.

"Shh. I'm appreciating the silence. Usually, it's impossible to shut them up. Especially you."

"Hey, you should be nice to me in my frail state."

He arched his brows. "I'm carrying you, aren't I?"

"I thought you just wanted to cuddle."

We passed the next few minutes in silence.

"What do you think of my two Pilgrims?" I asked Nero.

"*Your* Pilgrims."

"Yes, *my* Pilgrims. I had them compelled for a solid two minutes." I turned my hand to show him two fingers but dropped it, wincing from the pain.

"Try not to move," he said. "Your injuries aren't life-threatening, so I haven't healed them. There's no time for that now. We need to make getting out of here fast a priority. Before any more monsters come."

Now that the high of surviving that fall was wearing off, the pain was returning with a vengeance. The broken ribs didn't hurt as much as the bump I'd gotten on my head when the fog beast had tossed me onto the black ice.

"It hurts," I admitted.

"But you're tough."

"You bet your ass I am." I cracked a smile, which hurt as much as moving my hand had.

He sighed. "I told you not to move. For once, could you just follow orders?"

"Well, you know me." I kept smiling. It hurt, but it was worth it to see the frustration—and more so, the admiration—in his eyes. He might have been annoyed with me for not listening, but he respected my strength for toughing out the pain.

"I know what you're thinking. And what you're feeling."

I realized I wasn't blocking him from my mind—and that I didn't have the strength to do it now anyway.

"Anyone else would be screaming in agony at that pain you're feeling," he said, his tone reverent.

"If you can read my thoughts, then you know I'm

screaming inside."

"Yes, and I'm very impressed by your creative use of such colorful language. I've never heard anyone swear so well."

I grinned through the pain. "I aim to please."

"We both know that's not true."

"Ok, maybe not." I winced. The pain was growing stronger.

"We're almost there." He glided along, moving so smoothly, not jostling me at all.

I rested my head on Nero's shoulder. The two Pilgrims were walking behind us at a limping gait. Every so often, one of them stole a quick glance up at me.

"Are you all right?" I asked them over Nero's shoulder.

"Our injuries are far less severe than our crime of acting against Colonel Windstriker's orders," one of them said, dipping his chin.

"We await his punishment," said the other.

Nero looked back at him, shaking his head with slow disapproval. But he didn't speak threats, not even to repeat his promise to tie them to the top of the trucks. All he said was, "I am in command of this mission, not Valiant. Not you."

And it was enough. They nodded, lowering their eyes in shame.

"Wow, that was lenient," I whispered to him.

Nero said nothing. I looked back at the Pilgrims again. They quickly averted their eyes from mine.

"What's up with them?" I asked Nero. "Why are they afraid to look at me?"

"Because I went after you back there in the ruins. The fight wasn't over, the monsters weren't neutralized, the

Pilgrims weren't safe—and I went after you."

I'd been so glad to be alive that I hadn't realized what his actions meant. His mission was to protect the Pilgrims, and he'd instead dove into that chasm to save me. The Pilgrims could have died. He'd broadcast to everyone there that saving me was more important than saving them. That was why the Pilgrims were looking at me differently. Anyone important to an angel was important to them.

We'd reached the truck. Nero set me down in the backseat.

"Try not to move during the drive back," he said, putting a small bottle into my hands.

"A healing potion?"

"Yes, one of my own invention," he said. "Take it. I don't have enough magic to heal you gently, and I will need all the magic I have for the drive back. Too many of you are injured. You won't be able to take out all the monsters alone. And the potion will help with your pain."

"I thought what doesn't kill you only makes you stronger," I teased.

"I don't want you to be in pain, Leda." He kissed my forehead. "Stay safe."

Then he shot into the air, a determined gleam in his eyes. He was preparing to clear our path of monsters.

Captain Somerset got into the car. When she looked back at me, I saw a very different expression than the one the Pilgrims had given me. It was a look that warned me I'd gotten in the way of Nero doing his job—and that there would be consequences.

I fell asleep during the drive back. Whatever was in that potion Nero had given me, it had not only dulled my pain, it also knocked me right out. The next thing I knew, I was back in New York, blinking up at the ceiling from one of the beds in the medical ward.

I looked around. I wasn't the only one here. In fact, the medical ward was busier than I'd ever seen it. In addition to my wounded team mates, there were another two dozen soldiers warming the beds in here tonight.

"How are you feeling?"

I turned at the sound of Nero's voice. He was sitting beside my bed, and when I looked at him, he took my hand.

"Fine." I rubbed my head.

His eyes traced my body, cataloging the cuts and bruises. "You aren't lying to me, are you?"

"I thought you liked your soldiers to be tough."

"Yes, but I want you to be healed. And for that, I need you to be honest about your injuries."

"My hands feel like they've had an unfortunate encounter with an angry sandpaper monster, my head feels like it's going to explode, and from where I am, there appear to be two of you sitting next to my bed. And I'm not sure how I feel about that. On the one hand, I'm glad you care enough to stay, but on the other, I'm not sure I have the energy to talk to one of you right now, let alone two of you."

Nero sat there in silence.

"You wanted me to be honest."

"Indeed." He set his hand over my ribs. A warmth

flashed through me, driving out the pain.

"What was in that potion you gave me before?"

"As I told you, something to help you sleep. Its healing effects were minimal. I wanted to heal you like this."

"Why?"

Before he could answer, Dr. Hallows stopped beside my bed.

"Colonel," she said. "We need to look at her injuries."

"I'm taking care of it."

"If you would—"

"I said I'm taking care of it," he said coldly. "Now go check on Valiant. He seems to be on the verge of another panic attack."

Dr. Hallows looked from the cold fire in Nero's eyes, to the warm glow of his healing hand, to the soft touch of his other hand holding mine. Though he sat there perfectly still, I could sense the tension in his body. Everything about him was broadcasting danger, telling everyone to stay back because he was on a short fuse right now. The doctor turned, hurrying toward Valiant, who was screaming about hooded thieves and man-eating plants.

"Will he be all right?" I asked Nero.

"With time."

"Will *you* be all right?"

"I am perfectly fine."

"No, you're not. You're wound up more tightly than I've ever seen you."

"It's been a long day." He gave me a small smile. "I'm fine."

"Nero—"

"I said I'm fine," he said, his voice a low growl. He took a deep breath, then lifted the hand from my ribs. "How do you feel?"

"All healed," I said.

"Leda, stop watching me like I'm going to explode at any moment."

"Then stop looking like you're going to explode at any moment," I countered.

"After your experience, I expected at least a short respite from your insubordination."

"Then you expected wrong," I replied, smirking.

He handed me a bar of chocolate, and my mind flitted back to those two dead cowboy gangsters hanging from the temple chimney, swinging in the wind.

Nero has it bad for you. I thought a little fun could cure him, but it seems he only wants one cure. You. And now he's stringing up dead criminals to let you know. Why couldn't he have gone with chocolate?

Because he's an angel, that's why. And you know chocolate isn't the same. Not at all.

Chocolate is less complicated.

"What's this?" I asked Nero.

"It's chocolate. I thought you'd recognize it," he replied, a hint of irreverence in his voice.

"I meant, why are you giving me chocolate?"

"Your body just healed some very substantial injuries. Chocolate is one of the best substances on Earth for replenishing your magic and energy."

"Oh, good. That gives me yet another reason to love chocolate."

Nero's eyes darted to the door. A man in a bright white tunic stepped inside the room and headed right for us.

"Expecting trouble?" I asked Nero.

"Always."

The man stopped in front of Nero. "Colonel Windstriker, I have a message for you from the First Angel." He handed Nero the envelope, then left.

Nero turned the envelope over in his hand once before opening it. His eyes panned down the page. Then he folded it back into the envelope and looked at me.

"Nyx wishes to speak to us," he said.

"Both of us?"

"Yes."

"Good news or bad news?"

"The First Angel is not in the habit of spoiling the dramatic impact by dropping hints."

"Of course not."

"How are you feeling now?" he asked.

"Almost human again."

"You aren't human anymore. Not entirely," he reminded me.

"It was just an expression."

My head had stopped spinning. I wiggled my fingers and toes. When none of them screamed out in pain, I eased slowly off the bed.

"All good. Now I just need someone to find my clothes. I don't think the First Angel is expecting me in a hospital gown."

When we got to Nyx's office, the door was closed, so we waited outside. There were no chairs. Apparently, soldiers of the Legion didn't need chairs. They sure would have been a nice touch, though. The minutes ticked by, and all the while Nero stared at me, his eyes hard with guilt.

"Do you regret saving me?" I asked him quietly.

"No," was his immediate response.

"But you still feel guilty about it."

"Yes."

"I would have done the same for you," I told him.

"Leda, you shouldn't say such things here. We don't know who's listening."

The door to Nyx's office opened, and a man with cropped blond hair stepped out, dressed in the black leather uniform of the Legion of Angels. He was frozen in time at age twenty, that same physical age so many of the Legion soldiers were. His eyes were older, though. Much older. Clear blue, as bright as a cloudless day, they had a hard, cynical edge to them, especially as they cut right to me and Nero standing across the hall.

As he turned, I caught my first glimpse at the symbol on his uniform. He was a colonel, level nine just like Nero. An angel. He was a tad shorter than Nero, but wider, built like a bodybuilder. He had an iron jaw, and looking at him, I knew it would hurt like hell to punch him.

The two angels looked at each other with professional disdain, as though they'd hated each other for so long that it was routine, another part of the day like brushing their teeth or waking up before dawn. The angel's eyebrows, so light that they blended into his tanned skin, arched, and he shot Nero a smug look.

He had numerous swords and knives strapped to his body, and a high-tech bow on his back, one that looked like it could shoot right through those hard-scaled snap dragons we'd fought earlier. But the weapons were mostly for show. He looked like he tore the heads off of monsters for sport, preferably with his bare hands—or with his teeth.

My eyes shifted to the name on his uniform: Colonel Fireswift. So this was Jace's father. They certainly did look a lot alike, the father a meaner and more powerful version of the son. I bet his wing feathers were blood red. This was a man who had risen from the ashes of pain—his own suffering as much as that of others. And he'd pulled himself up on his own, triumphant. So this was what Colonel Fireswift wanted to mold his son into.

After a final farewell sneer, Colonel Fireswift turned and walked down the hall. We crossed the room to enter Nyx's office. She stood at the center of the room, poised and regal. Her black leather bodysuit fitted perfectly to her slender form, and her high-heeled boots only added to her already impressive height. Her hair, braided and pinned to her head, was as black as her glossy bodysuit, and her eyes were as blue as the ocean.

A full vase of Angel's Breath flowers sat on her massive wood desk, bringing in a touch of spring on this cold day. Snow fell freely beyond the windows, the thick flakes fluttering in the winter wind. Just a few hours ago, I'd been sweating in the scorching heat of the Black Plains, and now I was here, watching snow fall.

Nero and I bowed before the First Angel.

She let us stay like that for a moment, then said, "Rise, Corporal Pierce."

I looked at her in surprise. Nero was an angel. He should have been asked to rise before me.

"Come on, my dear, don't keep me waiting."

I rose out of my bow. Nyx looked down upon Nero for a few more moments, then she lifted her hands in the air.

"All right, Colonel. Stand up." Nyx sighed. "Let's get this over with."

Nero watched her, his face blank.

"Your mission was to protect the Pilgrims during their pilgrimage to the Lost City. Why the blazes did you leave them unprotected?"

"They stole a truck and drove out onto the Black Plains at night, against Nero's explicit commands," I told her.

She held up her index finger, which I was surprised to see tipped with pink fingernail polish. "I'll get to you in a moment." Her gaze slid to Nero. "Under the city, you were attacked by monsters. During the fight, you went diving into a chasm, leaving the Pilgrims unprotected."

Technically, there had been ten Legion soldiers with them. And Nero had blasted apart the last monster before diving into the chasm. Nyx held up her hand, cutting me off before I could point that out, like she'd been reading my thoughts. Damn angels.

"Well, Colonel?" she said. I wondered if she could read his thoughts too. "Why did you leave three valuable Pilgrims at the monsters' mercy to dive into the abyss after your Pandora?"

"You want to make Leda an angel. That makes her valuable, more valuable than three Pilgrims," Nero said without a hint of emotion.

Nyx looked from him to me. "Well, it looks like all the cards are on the table now." Unlike Nero, she was showing emotion, amusement being the predominate one.

Nyx was an interesting angel. She was strict but had a sense of humor. She ensured the rules of the Legion were upheld to the letter, but I could have sworn that half the time she wasn't taking herself seriously at all. She was not arrogant except when it suited the situation, which was basically when she needed to keep people in line.

"A compelling argument, Colonel, except she is not an angel yet," Nyx said. "She must still prove herself, just like everyone else."

"She will."

A smile tugged at the corner of Nyx's mouth. "Colonel, you've had a long and distinguished career at the Legion, so just this once, I'll forego the usual punishments."

The way she said 'usual punishments' made me wish I never found out how the Legion punished misbehaving angels. Angels could take a lot of damage, so the punishments must have been truly horrendous.

"Really, Nero," Nyx continued, her tone lighter now. "You should have just slept with her, not wooed her. Feelings make things messy. Especially when those feelings are for someone under your command."

I resisted the urge to point out that Nyx, as head angel of the Legion, reported to the gods, one of whom was her lover.

Nero shot me a hard look.

"What? I didn't *say* anything. You can't punish me for something I didn't say."

"When angels are involved, I can," he replied. "We can read thoughts. You need to learn to control what you think."

"Sorry, I'm still working on controlling what I say."

"I fear that work will never be done." Nero bowed his head to Nyx. "I apologize for her inappropriate thoughts."

"No, it's quite all right. She is right. Everything just goes out the window when love enters the picture, doesn't it?"

I could have sworn Nyx winked at me, but it had happened so fast.

Nero didn't say anything, and I didn't ask him if that was how he felt. I wasn't even sure what I felt.

"Now, just a few more orders of business. Nero, you're coming with me, at least for a while. I have an important mission for you."

"What about me?"

"Yes, I did say I would get to you, didn't I?" said Nyx. "You will continue your current mission, though it's changed somewhat after recent events. Colonel Fireswift will be overseeing the mission now. It turns out his mission and yours are very much connected."

Colonel Fireswift's mission? I thought back to what Jace had told me before he'd left with his father.

"Colonel Fireswift is tracking down a rogue angel. Osiris Wardbreaker," I said.

Nyx's dark eyebrows arched. "I'm not going to ask how you know about that. Trouble seems to follow you wherever you go, Leda Pierce." Nyx folded her hands together. "Yes, Colonel Fireswift is after Osiris Wardbreaker. I believe you've met him."

I'd only ever met three angels: Nero, Nyx, and as of a few minutes ago, Colonel Fireswift. If you could count exchanging icy glares as 'meeting'. But none of those three angels was Osiris Wardbreaker.

"You know him as the hooded bandit," Nyx told me.

"*That* was a rogue angel?" I asked, remembering how he'd moved. How fast he'd been. How strong.

"Yes, a rogue angel is after the holy relics, and if he gets to them first, no one on Earth will be safe, not even the angels."

CHAPTER TEN
Legion Legacy

NYX FOLLOWED UP her doom-and-gloom warning with a bit of good news.

"For your unwavering determination to protect the Pilgrims and some very resourceful monster extermination technique, as well as your dedication to your continued magical development, I am promoting you, Leda Pierce, to the third level of the Legion. There's just the small matter of surviving the ceremony, and then it will all be official."

That 'small matter' was drinking the Nectar that would boost my magic to the third level—unless it killed me. My body took right to Nectar, so as long as I was ready, everything would be all right. And Nyx thought I was ready. I had to take comfort in that.

"You are ready," Nero assured me when we were standing again outside of Nyx's office. "The way you compelled those Pilgrims proves that. Don't worry." He glanced toward the door. "I have to go back in and speak with Nyx about my new mission."

"Right." I started walking. "So. Have fun."

"Leda."

I stopped and looked back at him.

"It's always more fun with you," he told me.

I winked, then continued walking. My destination: Demeter, the Legion canteen. They were just about to open their doors for dinner, and I was famished. The chocolate bar from Nero hadn't been nearly big enough. And, unfortunately, a girl couldn't live on chocolate alone.

I met up with Drake at the pasta counter. We carried our full trays over to the table where Ivy was already sitting with her boyfriend Captain Soren Diaz.

"So, Soren was just telling me that you guys had an exciting adventure on the Black Plains yesterday," Ivy said as Drake and I slid into the chairs facing them. "Did you really fight a dinosaur?"

"I'm not sure if it was an actual dinosaur, but it did bear a striking resemblance to a tyrannosaurus rex. And there were four of them," I added, impaling a tomato on my fork. I looked at Soren. "How did you know about that?"

"I was talking to Claudia and Basanti earlier, and they told me all about it." He arched his dark brows at me, inviting me to speak. He probably wanted to hear all about how Nero had dove into the chasm after me.

I gave him monster details instead. By the time I'd told him about all the bizarre and terrifying monsters we'd encountered on the Black Plains, we'd all moved on to dessert. My time with my vanilla pudding was cut short, however, when Colonel Fireswift entered the canteen. The room fell silent, and everyone watched in surprise as he crossed the room to the head table and sat down in Nero's chair. Well, that was ominous.

"The First Angel has put me in charge of this office

until further notice." His eyes flashed in triumph as they met mine. I'd never spoken a single word to the guy, and he already hated my guts. And now he was in charge. "Colonel Windstriker has been reassigned." He spoke the words with a sense of finality, as though he never expected Nero to return.

Whispers rose from the crowd, and eyes turned in my direction. It seemed the events of last night's adventure in the Lost City were common knowledge. And now they all thought it was my fault Nero was no longer here.

Colonel Fireswift lifted his hand into the air, and the whispers died out. "Things will be different here from now on. You'll find that I am not as lenient as Colonel Windstriker."

Jace slid into the seat beside me, looking positively ill. If Colonel Fireswift's own son was afraid of him, the rest of us didn't stand a chance.

"The First Angel wants you all to be ready," Colonel Fireswift told us.

No one dared ask what it was we were getting ready for. The hard look on Colonel Fireswift's face made it clear that frivolous questions would not be tolerated.

"Your updated schedules will be arriving shortly."

Hundreds of phones buzzed simultaneously. I looked down at my schedule, which starting tomorrow was blocked off for the mission on the Black Plains. Drake's was the same.

"He neglected to schedule in time for sleep," Ivy said drily, showing us her phone screen.

"That isn't a mistake," Jace said.

For the first time, Ivy looked like she actually felt sorry for him.

I'd lost my appetite. Not that there was time to eat anyway. According to Colonel Fireswift's sadistic schedule, I had training in Hall Five with Jace. And the Colonel himself would be overseeing this session.

An hour later, I had a broken arm and a bloody lip. My face was smeared with blood. My hair, which had started the training session in a ponytail, now fell across my shoulders. It was stained with my own blood too.

Based on my blurred vision and the persistent ringing in my ears—not to mention my complete inability to stand upright without swaying to the side—I was pretty sure I had a concussion. My body was a tapestry of fresh cuts and blossoming bruises. Colonel Fireswift believed in training with real weapons—and in fighting to kill. Jace wasn't really trying to kill me, despite his father's continued commands to do so.

The first five minutes of training had gone ok, up until Jace had knocked my sword from my hands, and I'd retaliated by throwing his metal thermos at his head. Colonel Fireswift had shot me with a telekinetic blast for my impudence and lack of proper decorum—and then promptly removed all such items from the room. Now it was just me, Jace, and the devil himself. Whose name was Colonel Fireswift.

"She's barely standing. Knock her down now!" Colonel Fireswift snapped at Jace.

"There's no honor in that," his son replied.

"What has Windstriker been teaching you?" Colonel Fireswift demanded. "Honor is for fencing matches and ballet recitals. This is the Legion of Angels. We stand between humanity and its destruction, between good and evil. Soldiers of the Legion do not flinch, and they do not hesitate. We act, swiftly and mercilessly, to strike down the fiends. Before they strike down you." He waved Jace aside. "I will show you how it's done."

Colonel Fireswift faced me, but his words were for his son. "The most dangerous monsters are not the beasts beyond the wall. They are the ones who look like us—supernaturals who serve demons, rogues who only serve themselves. Osiris Wardbreaker, what is he?"

"An angel," Jace said.

A blast of telekinetic magic slammed into him, hammering him against the wall, holding him there.

"Try again."

"A rogue."

A knife rose from the floor and shot at Jace, piercing his wrist.

"A traitor."

A second knife nailed his other wrist to the wall. Jace gritted his teeth but didn't make a noise. My stomach turned as I began to realize this wasn't the first time Colonel Fireswift had taught his son a lesson in this manner.

"My enemy."

The third knife took Jace in the stomach.

"You're getting there," Colonel Fireswift said. "But you need to dig deeper. Why is Osiris Wardbreaker your enemy?"

"Because he betrayed the Legion."

The fourth knife sank into Jace's thigh.

"He is your enemy because he is you," Colonel Fireswift

told him. "He represents what you could become. That is the threat he and his rogue kind represent. Not the flashy magic they throw around, but that dirty little truth that we can all fall into darkness."

He waved his hand, and the four knives lodged inside of Jace broke free and dropped to the ground. Jace dropped with them. He peeled himself off the floor, leaving bloody smudges on the smooth surface. I expected Colonel Fireswift to throw him a healing potion. Instead, he threw him a sword.

"You can prevent your fall into darkness by identifying your triggers—your weaknesses—and eliminating them." The Colonel turned toward me again. "And you must do the same for your soldiers. We'll start easy and work our way up. Soldier, why did you join the Legion?" he asked me.

Little did he know, he'd just kicked off his interrogation with the one question I could not truthfully answer. Colonel Fireswift could not find out about my brother. Ever.

"To keep the world safe from rogue supernaturals," I answered, throwing him the line I'd written on my Legion application form.

A hard, cruel smile twisted his lips. "You're lying."

I felt my arm twist back of its own accord. No, not on its own. Somehow Colonel Fireswift was controlling the movements. A sharp surge of pain trailed that unwelcome realization. My body bent at the waist, and my shoulder popped out of its socket. I pressed my lips together and glared up at the sadistic angel.

"Why did you join the Legion of Angels?" he asked me again.

"I heard angels are hot. But it's not true. Not about all of them," I snarled viciously.

His eyes were as hard as blue diamonds. "Nero might have tolerated your insubordination, but as I said before, things are different now. And I don't find your brazen remarks funny, nor do I consider your complete lack of class charming."

My other arm moved, reaching for the knife at my thigh. Before I knew what was happening, I'd stabbed myself in the stomach.

Colonel Fireswift caught my face roughly in his hand, his fingers locking around my jaw. "I will find out what you're hiding."

He squeezed down on my jaw like he was crushing a tin can in his hand. The bone groaned under the pressure, and pain shot up my nerves. Then, just as I thought my jaw would break, he let go, moving away from me. I felt my control over my own body return—and along with it, more pain.

"Jace." He waved his son forward. "What is Leda Pierce?"

"Me."

Colonel Fireswift nodded. "Now fight your inner darkness, ensuring that this will never be your fate."

Jace moved forward, slashing with his sword. I stepped out of the way, putting some distance between us. I popped my dislocated shoulder back into place.

"Move faster. Overwhelm her. Don't give her time to recover," Colonel Fireswift called out.

"I'm sorry," Jace mouthed to me silently, his back to his father. "Go left."

He swung his sword. I went left, avoiding the blade. He

snapped his arm around, slamming the hilt of his sword against my temple. The next thing I knew, Colonel Fireswift was standing over me, that familiar sneer twisting his mouth.

"It would seem you're not so special after all. Nyx has overestimated you. You aren't strong. You're weak. Weak and unworthy. Pathetic," he spat with a dismissive flick of his wrist. "Go to the medical ward and get yourself cleaned up. I don't want to see you, someone so unworthy of the gods' gifts. You are a street urchin, a vagrant, a boor. Soldiers of the Legion represent the gods. You represent everything that is wrong with the world—the sin, the flaws, the rot."

I got to my feet, not saying a word. There was no point to talking to someone like that. I'd thought I'd seen evil. I hadn't seen anything at all until I'd met Colonel Fireswift. My head dizzy, blood dripping down my body, I stumbled down the halls, banging against the walls. Blackness pulsed in front of my eyes, my vision going in and out. I didn't know how I made it to the medical ward in that state. Maybe it was muscle memory.

"Leda!" Ivy called out. She led me to a cot. "Drink this."

I lifted the cold bottle to my mouth and drank. My vision slowly returned, and then I realized I wasn't alone. The medical ward was overcrowded with patients.

"What is this all about?" I asked Ivy. "What happened to all of them. Missions?"

"No. We have our new leader to thank for this."

"Colonel Fireswift?"

"He's ordered the implementation of new methods for all training groups, effective immediately. And this is the result." She waved her hands, indicating the blood and burns and limbs lost in training. "This is his so-called training. Torture is more like it, cruel and brutal torture. I hadn't even imagined some of these injures until I saw them tonight. That man is a devil."

"Don't let him hear you say that," I told her. "I don't want him to put you through this." I pulled out the knife still in my stomach.

Ivy pressed a bandage to the wound as I chugged back what felt like the hundredth healing potion in two days.

"Under Nero, training was tough and it brought us to the breaking point. But it was never about hurting people like this. It was never about destroying them totally. Or stripping us apart, unraveling us layer by layer, leaving nothing of ourselves," I said. "This is what happens when someone who tortures enemy combatants is given power over the Legion's own soldiers. He doesn't care about them as people, about how much he has to hurt them to turn them into what he wants. They are tools to him, weapons."

"Sooner or later, Colonel Fireswift's training is going to kill someone," Ivy declared, angry tears pooling in her eyes.

I wasn't just angry. I was furious. "If I wasn't sure I'd get my ass kicked, I would have marched up to Colonel Fireswift and given him a piece of my mind. But I have to do this carefully. I have to be smart."

"How?"

"I need to talk to Nyx."

"She's already left," Ivy told me.

Awesome. I didn't have her number or any way to contact her. I *did* have Nero's number. I wondered if he'd pass along a message for me, something along the lines of: 'SOS, Colonel Fireswift is a sadistic son of a bitch. Please send a replacement, someone who doesn't staple his own soldiers to the wall. Love, Leda'. Or something like that. I still had to iron out the exact wording.

I got off the cot, leaving it for the next patient. A line was forming, and it already extended into the hallway. I pushed past the curtain that led to the back room, where the Pilgrims were resting in their beds, recovering from their injuries.

"Hi," I said, waving at them. "You're all looking better already."

"You're not." Valiant looked my torn and bloodstained athletic suit up and down, frowning. "What happened? Monsters?"

He had no idea just how right he was. Colonel Fireswift was more a monster than all the monsters combined that we'd faced during the pilgrimage. How ironic that he claimed his methods were designed to rid the world of monsters.

"Colonel Fireswift happened," I said.

"Colonel Fireswift," Valiant repeated, grimacing. Apparently, he wasn't a fan either.

"We've heard the hooded bandit is the rogue angel Osiris Wardbreaker," one of the Pilgrims said.

"Where did you hear that?" I asked him.

"Everyone is talking about it."

So much for Nyx's secrets.

"Valiant wants to go back to the Lost City to find the relics," another Pilgrim said.

"After what happened to you? Really?" I asked Valiant, shocked. Though I really shouldn't have been.

"We can't go," a Pilgrim said. "Colonel Fireswift is in charge of the mission now, and he's not letting any of us out of this building. We had trackers put on us. He claims it's for our protection."

"Colonel Fireswift is an insufferable ass," Valiant declared.

I had to fight not to laugh. It was not proper for a soldier of the Legion to laugh at an angel. I only said, "Colonel Fireswift is right. It is too dangerous out there for you."

"The Legion is using my research to discover the Lost Relics and save them from a rogue angel. All without me," Valiant grumbled. "I won't even be there when my life's work, my legacy, is realized. And all so Colonel Fireswift can steal the glory."

I wasn't sure he was wrong about that. Colonel Fireswift *was* a glory hog. He believed there was a finite amount to go around in the world, and he wanted to save it for him and his. But I still thought the Pilgrims were better off staying here. Protecting them had nearly gotten my team killed.

"You're injured. And you don't heal as fast as we do," I reminded Valiant. "This isn't about glory or who gets to make the great discovery. This is about keeping these powerful relics from those who would use them to hurt lots of people. You can help me save lives."

"Of course, whatever you need," a Pilgrim said.

"Is there anything you know about the Treasury that holds the relics? Anything that might help me?"

"Some say Sierra, the last angel known to wear them, died with the relics on her, but her body was never found," Grace told me. "An old battle hymn tells of her bringing them into the treasury for safekeeping as the city crumbled to the ground. To save them for a day they would be needed again."

"Needed again? That's a pretty romantic view of an angel-killing weapon," I commented.

"It's epic poetry. That's how they are. Romantic," she said.

"How do you know the Treasury even survived the city's destruction?" I asked.

"The Treasury is protected by magic, by great spells. These spells keep it from being crushed. And it keeps thieves out."

"So if the Treasury is protected, how did you plan to get in? And if that protection spell is so powerful, aren't the relics safer left there?"

Valiant looked horrified that I would even suggest such a thing. Academics had their idealistic heads stuck in the clouds.

"Another epic poem says the keepers of the Treasury left behind the clues to unlocking its wonders, so that someday a hero might reclaim these lost treasures."

I lifted my eyebrows. Hero? There was that romantic angle again.

"A hero with a great mind. Someone with the intellect to puzzle it out," Valiant said. " 'For in the midnight hour, the sun and moon will shine, and a new hero will rise, his mind unlocking the secrets within.' "

"That poem was the last piece to the puzzle," Grace said. "Valiant and I found it last month."

"There's supposed to be a picture on the wall of a building in the sunken city. When you reach it, you are at the door," Valiant added.

"What kind of picture?" I asked.

"The text only tells us we'll know it when we see it."

Well, that wasn't cryptic at all.

"Why are you helping me if you don't want the Legion to do this without you?" I asked him.

"Because you're different than soldiers like Colonel Fireswift. You aren't seeking glory or your own advancement," he said. "So if someone in the Legion has to find it, I want it to be you."

The other Pilgrims nodded in agreement, offering their good luck wishes.

As I turned to leave, Valiant said, "The rogue angel who stole my notebook has all of this information and my notes. He knows what you know." He set his hands over mine. "Be careful."

I left the overcrowded medical ward, walking back toward my apartment. I needed to shower and change into something that wasn't stained in my own blood.

"Leda."

I looked back to find Jace hurrying down the hall after me. He wasn't bleeding anymore. Colonel Fireswift must have healed him himself.

"Are you ok?" he asked.

"What do you think?"

He turned his eyes from my bloody clothes. "I'm sorry about my father."

He sounded genuine—and he had helped me in the fight, while putting on a show for his father. At least I thought it had been a show.

"Have you visited the medical ward to see what the victims of Colonel Fireswift's training look like?"

"I haven't, but I can imagine. Angels are different from us," he said, echoing Calli's words. "Especially angels from the early years of the Legion. Times were different. Here, let me show you something." He took my hand, leading me to Nero's office. No, Colonel Fireswift's office. It was his now.

No one was at home, but the door was unlocked. Colonel Fireswift must have believed no one was bold enough to go into his office uninvited. As we walked past the desk, I saw that Jace's father had already made himself at home. Medals and plaques cataloging his triumphs and accomplishments hung on the walls, right beside the pictures of the Legion's angels, past and present. I touched Nero's picture, wishing he were here instead of his evil replacement.

"Look here," Jace said, pointing at a large framed photo of Nyx surrounded by twelve other angels. "Nyx's original angels. There's Osiris Wardbreaker, the rogue we're hunting down. A vicious angel." He pointed at an angel who looked like Colonel Fireswift's twin. "My grandfather." He tapped a couple holding matching swords. "Those are Colonel Windstriker's parents."

The photos of the original angels and their descendants were positioned below this central picture. The photos of other angels not descended from the original angels were on another wall.

"Legacy is important at the Legion," Jace said. "You remember how I told you Legion brats wear the name with pride? That's even more true for those of us who come from one of the original families. We carry our history with us. Our knowledge. Our rich and beautiful traditions." His gaze slid down to the photo of his father. "When Nyx trained the first angels, the world was a different place. It was a time when the gods and demons were at war. There were so few soldiers in the Legion and Nyx needed them to level up fast. She needed an army. Training was harsh and cruel, worse than even my father's training."

He looked at me. "Some of the original angels fell and became the first dark angels, back at a time when the Legion couldn't afford to lose anyone. My grandfather was an original angel. He saw some of his friends turn against him and go to the other side. My grandfather made my father into his image, with all those same fears. My father is his father's son, and he wants to make me in their image too. I'm not saying this to excuse him, Leda. I just want you to understand. Maybe it will help you survive the tyranny that I have for the past twenty years. Goodnight. See you tomorrow."

"Goodnight, Jace," I said, and we parted ways, each of us turning down a different hallway, heading to our apartments.

We would be leaving early. In just a few hours, we would take the train to Purgatory so we could enter the Black Plains as the sun rose. I was exhausted—physically, mentally, and emotionally—but I was not going to bed covered in my own blood. I took a shower, and when I returned to my room, there was a book on my bed that hadn't been there before.

It was called Angels. I opened the cover to find a sticky note stuck to the title page.

Survival training, the note read in Nero's neat handwriting.

He must have given it to me so I could learn my enemy. I sent a silent thank-you out to Nero, wherever he was right now. I would need all the help I could get to survive Colonel Fireswift and his games.

CHAPTER ELEVEN
In the Midnight Hour

WE RODE THE train back to Purgatory. Our team had more than doubled, so we'd had to bring more trucks along. Captain Somerset sat on my right side. She was staring at me like it was my fault that Nero had been reassigned, and she was right. It was because of me. Nyx clearly wanted him to spend time away from me so he could clear his head of the nonsense I'd put there.

"Nero will be back, right?" I asked Captain Somerset, thinking about how comfortable Colonel Fireswift was getting in Nero's office.

"Maybe. Or maybe not. The First Angel might reassign him permanently."

"Did he say what his mission is?"

"Why? You thinking of running out after him?"

"No, he can take care of himself."

Captain Somerset shot me a weird look. For not the first time, I couldn't decide whether she was happy or just plain pissed off at me.

Drake and Jace sat in the seats facing us. Jace was trying to engage Drake in a conversation.

"So, you were a football player," he began.

"Yes."

"I heard you were pretty good."

"They called me the Dragon." That said it all right there.

Jace nodded. "Were you ever tackled down?"

"Yes. It took five guys."

He showed Jace his teeth. It was a dangerous smile. Drake was so friendly with everyone. He must have really hated Jace. Maybe because of the way the brats had treated Ivy. Drake wasn't the sort to blame people for the sins of their fathers. Just for their own sins.

Jace didn't talk after that, and Captain Somerset wasn't feeling very chatty either. The rest of the train voyage passed in silence. It was so completely unlike the last time we'd traveled to Purgatory.

When we arrived in town, Colonel Fireswift was waiting. He'd flown ahead last night, right after he'd finished beating me and Jace bloody. The sun was about to rise, so the Colonel had us drive out immediately onto the Black Plains.

As we parked outside the Lost City, heading into the ruins, I saw Jace step out of the lead truck with Colonel Fireswift. The angel patted his son hard on the back. I couldn't tell if that was supposed to be punishment or praise.

We went into the city in teams, splitting up to explore the lower levels of the sunken districts. Colonel Fireswift put Jace in charge of me and Drake. We walked down the dark streets, looking for the entrance to the Treasury. I hadn't shared what the Pilgrims had told me, but I was looking for these mysterious markings that were supposedly on the building that kept the relics.

"He made me team leader for a reason," Jace said.

"Because you're leadership material. Yes, I heard the speech," I replied.

Beside me, Drake snorted.

"No, the real reason."

"So you can be in charge of me?"

"He put us together because trouble finds you, Leda. And he wants me to be there when it does. He put me in charge, so I could claim credit for defeating the trouble you attracted."

"Clever." Or should I say devious?

"Too clever," said Jace. "With my luck, you'll attract a horde of monsters *and* the rogue angel, and then we find the way into the vault only to be attacked by a horde of the dead."

Skeletons lay in the streets, wearing the armor of a war long since passed. So many people had died here in this battle between heaven and hell. My gaze snagged on a skeleton with wings. The angel's feathers had long since turned to dust, but a purple flower bloomed from one of the wings, right where a feather would have been. I moved in closer to the angel. A golden light fell on the skeleton, as though from a skylight, and the air hummed with an old forgotten hymn. More purple flowers rose out of the ground, wings of petals, every bit as beautiful as feathers.

"Leda," Jace called out. He and Drake were standing across the street, watching me.

"Do you see…"

I blinked, and the blossoming wings were gone. There were no flowers, no golden light, no music. I must have been imagining things again, not just hearing voices but seeing things now. This place—it was saturated with memories, scorched like permanent imprints into the magic that flowed through the city like a river.

Drake and Jace were looking at me like I'd lost my mind. Maybe they were right. I rose from my knees and walked back to them. We continued deeper into the city. We didn't meet any monsters. Where were the monsters?

"There," I said, pointing down a street lined with small houses.

"What's down there?" Jace asked.

Not answering, I moved quickly, drawn to a faint glow. I found it there on one of the houses—the picture. Valiant had been right. I did know it when I saw it. It was a halo with wings, the symbol of the angels. A glow pulsed slowly from the picture.

"A gateway. How did you know it would be here?" Jace asked, amazed.

"I followed the glow."

Jace traced his finger across the picture. "This is the door to the Treasury. The relics have to be beyond this wall."

Drake looked for a way into the building, but the house's doors and windows were sealed shut. "I wonder how we get in."

"There has to be a trick to it." Jace pressed his hand to the stone wall. "Angels protect their treasures with wards."

" 'For in the midnight hour, the sun and moon will shine, and a new hero will rise, his mind unlocking the secrets within,' " I quoted softly.

Jace's head jerked around. "Where did you hear that?"

"From the Pilgrims."

If Jace was surprised that the Pilgrims had shared secret

information with me, he didn't say anything.

"That is the solution," he said. "…in the midnight hour…sun and moon…" I could almost see the gears turning in his head. "I believe this gateway can only be opened at midnight."

"Well," I said, sitting down on a boulder beside the house. "It looks like we'll be here awhile."

By midnight, nearly the whole expedition had gathered around that little house. Maybe I should have kept my mouth shut. The Pilgrims had wanted me to be the one to find the relics, and now Colonel Fireswift was on his way to claim the glory for himself. I didn't give a damn about glory, but I wasn't about to stand by while someone who'd done nothing took it all for himself.

Our collective minds had puzzled out that midnight was the hour the gateway could be opened, and that the sun and moon represented light and darkness. We had to shine some light on the symbol, something to penetrate the darkness.

Captain Somerset cast a small flame in front of the angel mark. When the picture failed to react, she grew the flame. It continued to pulse along in the same, slow way with no signs of change.

"What if the mention of the moon is literal?" Claudia said. "What if the gateway reacts to moonlight?"

Jace looked up. Moonlight streamed through an opening in the rocky ceiling, but the moonbeam didn't come down at the right angle to touch the symbol on the wall. Jace drew his sword, putting it into the moonlit stream, turning the blade. The pale light bounced off the steel. He shifted the angle until the stream hit the angel symbol. Everyone held their breath for one long moment, but nothing happened.

"Well, that was anticlimactic," commented Lieutenant Lawrence.

"I haven't heard you offer any ideas," I told her.

"It's obvious, isn't it?" she said with a derisive smile. "The text says you need the moon *and* the sun. We need sunlight and moonlight together in a single stream."

"You mean an eclipse," I said.

"You know, you're only half as dumb as you look."

I ignored the jab. "Ok, dazzle us. Save the day. Show us the spell that creates an eclipse."

The smile wilted from her lips. Ha! I had her there.

"I take it from your extended silence, that you don't have that kind of magic." I said sweetly at her. "You know, you're only half as powerful as you look."

She stepped forward, but she was cut off from me when the crowd parted, making way for Colonel Fireswift and his team.

"I see we've found the gateway," he said, glancing at the angel symbol on the house. His gaze shifted to Lieutenant Lawrence. "And one of you had the brains to figure out the key to opening it."

"Leda was the one who told us the puzzle that will allow us to open it," Drake said.

Colonel Fireswift shot me a sardonic smile. "Congratulations, you can repeat back something you were told without understanding what it means. You must be so proud."

I calculated how many strikes I could get in before

Colonel Fireswift hit back. I decided the answer was one, if I was lucky. Which meant it wasn't worth the risk. I needed to get faster and stronger, and I didn't care how long I had to train to make that happen. Colonel Fireswift looked down on everyone like they were the muck beneath his boots, and one day I would wipe that superior look off his face. That I swore on everything that was holy and unholy.

"Lieutenant Lawrence had a good idea with the eclipse," Colonel Fireswift said, walking toward the symbol. "Let's explore that."

"He never praises anyone," Claudia whispered to me. "He's only praising her because he's figured out that you two are mortal enemies."

"The whole mortal enemy thing is all on her end," I replied in a whisper.

Colonel Fireswift was so busy listening to himself speak that he hadn't even heard us.

Claudia snickered. "He'll sure be vexed when he realizes that her obsession with Colonel Windstriker is the reason you two don't get along."

Magic rumbled overhead. The rocks of the ceiling began to rearrange themselves. I glanced at Colonel Fireswift, who was directing their movements, shifting the hole in the ceiling so that the moonlight hit the angel symbol directly. Squinting, I watched a blinding light flash to life in front of the moon, as bright as sunlight. The tiny sun spun in the air like a disco ball, moving in front of the moon. I gaped at Colonel Fireswift. He'd just summoned his very own personal sun.

The combined light of the moon and sun streamed down in a single beam, shining against the angel symbol on the wall. The house groaned in the light of the potent magic spell, but no doorway opened up.

The underground city began to rumble and quake, the walls of the buildings exploding under the weight of the falling ceiling. Colonel Fireswift issued a sharp order to retreat, and we all ran as fast as our supernatural powers could carry us. We managed to get out without anyone getting killed, but the entire sunken city section was now buried under several hundred tons of rock.

Colonel Fireswift glanced down at the collapsed entrance, then shot me an irked look. "What have you done? What game are you playing at?"

I wanted to point out that it was his haphazard reorganization of the ceiling that had brought down the roof, but before I could get myself into trouble by talking back, Claudia called out.

"It's Wardbreaker!" she said, pointing up at the cloaked shadow running along the rooftops.

"Get him!" Colonel Fireswift snapped, and we all scrambled up the bridges and buildings that would bring us to the Lost City's upper levels.

But by the time we got there, Wardbreaker was gone, as though he'd vanished into thin air. Colonel Fireswift pushed us aside, dark crimson wings spreading from his back. I'd been right. His feathers were the color of blood. The Colonel flew over the city for over an hour, but he didn't find any sign of the rogue angel. Finally, he called off the search, summoning us down to street level.

"Telekinetic magic will be required to clear the way," he said, looking at the collapsed entrance. "Of all of you, besides me, only Captain Somerset possesses that kind of magic." He gave us all a hard look, as though it was our fault we didn't have enough magic to make his plan work.

"We will return with reinforcements."

CHAPTER TWELVE

Siren's Song

LEGION SOLDIERS LEVEL six and above, those with telekinetic magic, were hard to come by. By the time our train arrived back in New York, Colonel Fireswift had called every Legion office on this side of the Atlantic—and even a few beyond. By tomorrow morning, the Colonel would have his dream team to clear the way to the Treasury of the Lost City. Between all these hotshots and geniuses, surely they'd figure a way past the angel ward.

In the meantime, Colonel Fireswift had called all of us into Hall One because his office was too small to comfortably fit twenty-five people. Not that he cared about our comfort. Quite the contrary, in fact. He'd brought us to this particular hall because the blood hadn't yet been cleaned up from the training group who'd just finished. This was a psychological game. He wanted us to stand amongst the pools of blood. I was one hundred percent certain of that.

"It will take a few hours for the telekinetics to arrive," he said. "A delay caused by the lax standards currently plaguing this office. If Colonel Windstriker had been pushing you harder, more of you would have already reached the higher levels of the Legion. And I wouldn't have had to call in telekinetics from the other offices."

He wouldn't have had to call in telekinetics from the other offices if he hadn't brought down the ceiling of the sunken city.

"Fortunately, I don't believe in coddling my soldiers like Colonel Windstriker does. The Legion needs more strong, high-level soldiers with powerful magic. This is what your training is about. Improving the soldiers, strengthening the Legion. Nyx was wise to bring me in. Your previous leader just wasn't getting the job done."

Drake stomped down on my foot. I choked down my croak of pain—and the comment I'd been ready to dish out to Colonel Fireswift.

"There will be a promotion ceremony in the ballroom in one hour. Change into appropriate clothing for the ceremony. Some of you will be tested." His mean eyes flickered to me. "But only those worthy of a new gift of magic will survive." And on that happy note, he dismissed us.

"That hurt," I said to Drake as we returned to our apartment. "You have a big, heavy foot."

"It would have hurt more if I hadn't stopped you from mouthing off to Colonel Fireswift."

"And who said I was going to do that?" I challenged.

"Your expression was screaming it loud and clear."

"Well, Colonel Fireswift was too busy basking in the spotlight to notice."

Drake laughed, then we entered the apartment.

Ivy and Soren were sitting on the sofa when we came in. They both rose to their feet.

"Did you see this list for the promotion ceremony?" Ivy asked, her voice strangely solemn. "It goes on for pages." She scrolled down the screen of her phone, showing us the endless lines of names.

"There are over fifty names on it," Soren said. "At most ceremonies, there are only a handful of people up for promotion."

"A mass promotion?" I wondered, pulling out my own phone to look at the list.

"You're on it," Ivy told me.

"A promotion? Colonel Fireswift must like you more than you think," Drake teased me.

"No, this is Nyx's doing. She put my name there." My stomach twisted into a hard knot. "And I'm not sure this is the time for congratulations."

"She's right. This is all very unprecedented," Soren said, a crinkle forming between his eyebrows. "I've been at the Legion for over a decade, and I've never seen so many names on the list outside the initiation ceremony."

The initiation ceremony was a culling. It was the Legion's coldhearted way of slamming the door in the faces of those with not enough magical potential. Except it wasn't a door slamming. It was the lid of a coffin. Over half the people had died at my initiation ceremony, and I'd heard other ones were much worse. So much suffering and death. So many lives destroyed. Just thinking about it made me sick to my stomach.

"The Legion is usually so careful about waiting until someone is ready before giving them the gods' next gift," Soren continued. "If a soldier is not ready, the Nectar will kill them. The Legion sees that as a waste."

"Colonel Fireswift has a different philosophy," I said.

"Indeed." Soren frowned. "He is pushing hard. This could be a bloodbath."

Colonel Fireswift had informed everyone that attendance was mandatory at the promotion ceremony, so consequently the ballroom was packed. These ceremonies were always at night. It felt weird to be wearing evening wear and nibbling on dinner appetizers in the morning. I guess the Colonel didn't feel like waiting to get his leveled-up soldiers.

An orchestra was playing a light, uplifting piece, a contrast to the wild snowstorm raging outside. Skirts and tuxedo tails turned and twirled across the dance floor. The dancers' steps were practiced and precise, but their eyes were distracted. Everyone was wondering why so many of us were suddenly up for promotion at once. Anxiety, excitement, and curiosity battled it out for the dominant emotion in the room.

"You look pretty," Ivy told me as we crossed the ballroom arm-in-arm.

I was dressed in a sleek red evening gown with slender spaghetti straps. The dress was cut to fit my curves down to my hips, then it flared out in cascading ruffles, like a flamenco dress. I'd complemented the look with a pair of black strappy heels and by pulling my hair up into a bun adorned with a rose.

This was the outfit I'd bought awhile back hoping Nero would see it when the time came. But he wasn't here. This was all wrong. It felt off—the whole morning, the ceremony. Nero not being here. He'd never not been there for one of my ceremonies. I couldn't shake the feeling that it was a sign, that something bad was going to happen to me.

And it wasn't just me. There were so many people up for promotion. Trying not to wonder which of the faces I passed would not survive the morning, I kept going.

Ivy turned left at a tall urn stuffed with bundles of giant scented decorative sticks that smelled of oranges. "I'm going to talk to Daz. I think he needs a pep talk."

Daz was one of Soren's friends. He was up for level five, and he didn't look like he was sure he'd survive the test. Ivy joined him and Soren beside the cheese table. Within seconds, his tense muscles noticeably relaxed. Ivy had a knack for calming people down. She'd make an excellent counselor. Thanks to Colonel Fireswift, our office had never been more in need of a counselor than right now.

I'd been relieved to find neither Ivy's nor Drake's name on the roster. They'd been promoted recently, so I hoped they were safe from Colonel Fireswift's cullings until Nero returned. I wasn't going to believe the rumors that he wasn't coming back. He had to come back. He couldn't leave us here at Colonel Fireswift's mercy.

Drake and his girlfriend Lucy were standing behind one of the giant urns. She was crouched over, as though she hoped the enormous sticks and the scent of oranges could hide her. Lucy was on the list. She'd been with us from the beginning. She was sweet, friendly, and quiet, and she loved to read romantic tales. She was an all-around nice person. And I feared she didn't stand a chance.

Lucy's hands were shaking, and her pale face was sticky with sweat. A harsh, overly-sweet scent rose from her. Fear. She was scared out of her wits. As Drake wrapped his arm around her back, drawing her against him, she lowered her head to his shoulder and began to sob softly.

She wasn't ready, and she was going to die. I had to do something. I had to help her. But what could I do? Colonel Fireswift had put her name on the list, and no one, least of all me, would be able to convince him to take it off again.

Before coming down to the ballroom, I'd tried to call Nero, but his phone wasn't on. It went straight to voicemail. I'd left him two million messages. But what would he do even if he heard the messages? Nyx had put Colonel Fireswift in charge here. Technically, Nero couldn't do anything, but maybe he would have an idea. Nero always knew all the loopholes to every rule. Gods, I wished I knew the rules as well as he did. Then I would have known the loopholes too. And maybe one of those could have saved Lucy.

But I wasn't Nero. I was just the girl with a million different wild ideas on how to help my friend, but not one of them would work. Even if I got Lucy out of here, then what? The Legion would brand her a traitor and hunt her down. And the same for me. But there had to be a way. There was always a way.

Jace stopped beside me, the expression on his face mirroring exactly how I felt: helpless. "My father's missions just might kill me."

"That angel will be the death of us all," I declared.

"He wants me to be the one to capture Osiris Wardbreaker. He says the First Angel won't be able to ignore such an act, and I might finally come out of your shadow."

"Since when are you in my shadow? You are better than I am at everything."

"Not everything. You're always the one to save the day, a fact my father reminds me of every time I see him."

"No offense, but your father is a psychopath," I told him. "He crucified his own son to the wall to teach him a 'lesson'. I know you say he's just following the old ways, but I think there's something to be said for leaving those old ways in the past."

Jace looked at me and sighed. "He wants to push me to the top of the Legion no matter what it takes, no matter the risks. And he will never forgive me if you become an angel before I do. He sees it as a blow to his honor for a nobody to make it up the ranks before his own son."

"Honor or pride?" I asked.

"Both." Jace took a sip from his drink, and from the smell of it, it was heavily alcoholic. "I have the same problem, you know. The same flaw. I would stab you in the back if it meant a promotion."

"Then it's a good thing I sleep with a knife under my pillow," I quipped.

"I'm not kidding, Leda. I wouldn't stab you in the back literally, but you shouldn't trust me."

"Nero told me the same thing," I said. "But I think the fact that you can admit this to yourself means you won't do it. You are a better person than that."

"No." He shook his head sadly. "I'm not. Do you know what the first thing I thought was when I heard how you'd nearly been blown up on that airship? I was jealous. Jealous that we'd worked on the mission together, but it was you who got to be there on that airship to save the day. It was you who got to be the hero."

"Are you done?"

"Yes."

"Ok, so first of all, you need to just stop feeling guilty. Those evil thoughts and emotions you're tearing yourself up over—you know what? They're normal. It's called being human. And we all get them."

"Not you," he said. "My father thinks you're the personification of sin, but you're not. You're a saint."

I laughed. "Are you sure you want to keep drinking that? You're talking nonsense. I'm definitely not a saint."

"You're never jealous."

"I'm jealous all the time. Jealous of Ivy's boobs. Of Drake's strength. Of your ability to fight with any weapon. Of that stupid pink-haired fairy…"

"What pink-haired fairy?"

I shook my head. "Never mind. My point is I'm jealous all the time. And a bunch of other nasty things too. Human, remember."

"My father says humanity is a weakness."

"Which is why your father is a psychopath who tortures his own soldiers and plays mind games with his own son."

"It's not that simple."

"Maybe not, but I'm going to say it's that simple because I want to, and I'm just a flawed human who holds grudges and is jealous of everyone here for at least something."

"Even Lieutenant Lawrence?" The corner of his mouth twitched.

"Oh, gods, yes. She can set her sword on fire, and she fights like a fiend. Though sooner or later, I am going to have to kick her ass because she is just pissing me off. Oops, did I say that out loud?" I winked at him. "I guess I'm not a saint after all."

He laughed. "Thanks."

"For being inappropriately irreverent?"

"That. And more."

"You can come talk to me any time, and I'll put you right in your place, I promise." I set my hand on his shoulder. "Look, it will all work out for you. You're getting promoted today too, just like me. I'm not winning any race."

"That's for sure."

I turned to face the unwelcome visitors, Mina and a bunch of other Legion brats. They were Jace's friends, and they didn't seem to get that so was I.

"Come on, Jace," Mina said, pulling him away from me. "You need to make sure your aura is pure before the ceremony. You wouldn't want to contaminate it."

The brats led Jace away to cleanse his aura on cupcakes and shots of vodka. I walked over to join Ivy, Drake, and Lucy as Colonel Fireswift took the stage to begin the ceremony.

Colonel Fireswift started with Jace, making a grand speech about his son's heroic deeds and strong constitution. His words were full of more praise than I'd ever heard from him —and they were much nicer than anything he'd ever said to his son when I'd been around.

Jace survived, and then Colonel Fireswift called up the next soldier, someone going to level five. She died a horrible death, poisoned by the Nectar of the gods. Colonel Fireswift gave his hand a dismissive wave, and the dead soldier was taken away.

From there, things only got worse. One-by-one,

soldiers were summoned to the stage, in no particular order. Most did survive, but the deaths in between cast a dark shadow on the ceremony. Those people were dead because of Colonel Fireswift. He was pushing too hard because those losses were acceptable to him. But they weren't acceptable to me. Not at all.

As a soldier spasmed on the floor at Colonel Fireswift's feet, his mouth frothing with acid and blood, someone in the crowd fainted.

"Get her out of my sight," Colonel Fireswift snapped at the man who'd caught her fall. "That is not the behavior I expect from a soldier of the Legion."

Watching the man carry his unconscious friend out of the ballroom, I got an idea. I made my way slowly through the crowd to Dr. Harding.

"Nerissa," I said quietly, stopping beside her.

"Leda." Her voice was dark. She was usually so energetic, so talkative. She couldn't even contain her happiness. But today she couldn't contain a very different emotion: horror.

"This is a bloodbath," I said.

"The First Angel made a mistake when she put that *butcher* in command here," she replied in a scathing whisper. That was the bluntness I had come to expect from her.

"Do you happen to have a sedative with you?" I asked her.

Nerissa lifted her cocktail. "It's called alcohol, Pandora. Drink deeply." She emptied her glass in a single go.

"Actually, I was thinking of something fast-acting and a lot stronger. Something that could knock out a Legion soldier in under a minute."

"Trying to get out of your promotion?"

"It's not for me," I told her, indicating Lucy. "It's for my friend."

"She looks as fragile as a snowflake. That sweet girl has the most extensive library of erotic deity romance novels of anyone I know, so it would be a shame to lose her." Nerissa took my hand, and then I felt the weight of a syringe in my palm. "This should do the trick. Thirty seconds max and she'll be out."

"Thank you," I whispered, moving back across the crowd to stand beside Lucy.

When her name was called, Lucy jumped in alarm.

"It will be ok," I promised, drawing her into a hug.

She stiffened when the hidden needle pierced her skin. "Thank you," she whispered back.

Lucy walked toward the stage, her steps uneven and wobbly. Her hands shook as she prepared to receive the goblet from Colonel Fireswift. I bit down on the inside of my cheek, praying that the drug would take effect in time.

"Sip now of the gods' Nectar," Colonel Fireswift began the lines he'd already spoken so many times today.

Lucy's eyes rolled back, and she fell to the floor.

"How dare you faint in front of me," the Colonel snapped. "I order you to wake up."

"I don't think she can hear you," someone in the crowd said.

Colonel Fireswift searched the crowd for the soldier who'd spoken out of turn. When he didn't find him, his hard voice rang out, "Dr. Harding."

Nerissa navigated the crowd, making her way to the front. "Colonel, how may I be of service?"

"Wake her up."

Nerissa crouched down beside Lucy, wiping back the hair from her forehead. "That would be unwise."

"It would be unwise to disobey me," he replied in a voice that sent cold shivers down my spine. "Wake her so she can face her test."

"It is against regulations to submit sick soldiers to this test."

"Against regulations," he hissed.

"I can quote the passage if you've forgotten, Colonel," Nerissa told him calmly.

A soft snort rose from the crowd.

"She is not ill," Colonel Fireswift said, anger simmering in his voice. "She fainted."

"Which is a symptom of her illness."

"What illness?"

"Dragon Fever."

"Dragon Fever?"

"In layman's terms, the flu, Colonel."

He let out a derisive snort. "That's impossible. Soldiers of the Legion do not catch common illnesses. We are immortal."

"Just because you're immortal, that doesn't mean you can't catch the sniffles," she replied. "Or any number of other ailments. As you should remember from your visit last year when I treated your little…problem."

Colonel Fireswift's face turned as red as hell's inferno. Nerissa watched him with perfect serenity, her mouth drawing up in challenge, like if pushed she would announce to the whole room what he'd had.

"Take her out of here," Colonel Fireswift said, looking away from Nerissa.

Whatever she'd treated him for, he was obviously too

embarrassed to look her in the eye. It seemed the Colonel had a few weaknesses of his own. And I intended to find out what they were.

Nerissa lifted Lucy into her arms and carried her out of the ballroom. I let out a silent shout of victory. My friend was safe—for now at least. But we had to get Nero back.

Drake stomped down on my foot, and I realized everyone in the room was staring at me. From his high perch on the stage, Colonel Fireswift was staring at me with sinister delight. He must have called my name while I was lost in my own thoughts. I tried to look confident as I strode up to the stage.

"The final test of the ceremony," Colonel Fireswift declared to the whole room with a cold, dark smile.

I had a feeling the order of events had been intentional. He'd wanted me to see people die, to make me realize I was mortal after all, that I could die, no matter what level I was. This was just another one of his mind games.

"Coming down with the flu too?" he asked me with a challenging sneer.

I countered with a big smile. "Nope. I'm in perfect health."

I refused to let him get to me. I would make it. I had to save Zane, and I wasn't going to allow some silly Nectar to defeat me. My body was meant to have Nectar. I could do this. No problem.

"Sip now of the gods' Nectar," said Colonel Fireswift. "Consume the magic of their third gift. Let it fill you, making you strong for the days to come.

"For the days to come," everyone repeated.

I took the goblet he offered me and drank it all down, every single drop. The Nectar's sweetness ignited my senses, waking me up. It was the most perfect, most delicious thing I'd ever had. I soared on the euphoria of a magic I was meant to have.

And then I crashed. The sweetness soured in my mouth, turning to acid. Instead of sweet ecstasy, the Nectar tasted like the poison that it was. My throat burning, my blood boiling, I staggered to the side. My head was spinning. I was drowning.

Was this the end? Was this what the others tasted before the Nectar killed them? I collapsed to the ground, convulsing. Agony ravaged my body. I felt like I was being turned inside out. A sudden surge of pain pierced my chest, and then the darkness swallowed me.

CHAPTER THIRTEEN

Of Heaven and Hell

I DREAMT I was an angel, flying on silver wings, my red hair fluttering in the wind. I walked down the streets of the golden city, looking up at the red and orange sky. The ground shook with earthly tremors as another angel landed before me. He dropped to one knee.

"Sierra," he said.

"Why do you bow before me, Calin?" I asked him. He'd been doing it ever since we'd first met, and no matter how many times I pleaded with him to stop, he just kept doing it.

"Because you are the Keeper," he said. "You are our savior."

I didn't feel like a savior. I felt…lost. Like I'd inherited someone else's destiny, like I'd been thrown into a war I didn't even understand, a war that had been raging since the birth of magic.

"Sierra, we must hurry." Calin took my arm, leading me toward the gateway to the Treasury. "They are coming. You need to don the armor and wield the weapons of heaven and hell. You need to save us all."

I woke up in a hospital bed, feeling like I'd been flayed, then left out to burn in the scorching sun. I was alone in a dark room. Outside, a full moon shone brightly over the city, mixing with city lights born from a million different sources.

I managed to sit up, but I had to fight for every inch. A hand brushed across my forehead. I turned my head to find Nero in the chair beside my bed.

"Hey," I said, my voice shaking.

"Hey."

We stared at each other for a few minutes in silence—I because it hurt to talk, Nero because, well, he's Nero.

"I got your message," he finally said.

I managed a smirk—or at least half of one. "Which one?"

"All twenty-two of them. You must have really missed me."

"Well, just look at what happens when you're gone."

Nero clenched his jaw.

"I take it you've heard of the changes Colonel Fireswift has made around here."

"Yes."

"Has Nyx?"

"Yes."

"And? What is she doing to stop him?"

"Nothing." The word sank like a stone between us. "He was following her orders to get her more higher level soldiers. Last night, forty-two were promoted."

"And twelve people died," I growled. "Not initiates,

Nero. Established soldiers of the Legion."

"Nyx didn't specify how he should get her those higher level soldiers. He picked the people he thought most likely to survive, adding them to the promotion roster. And then he added those he saw as weak links."

Lucy.

"Nyx is happy with the results," Nero said.

"Happy?" I gasped, disgust burning in my raw throat. "She's happy with twelve pointless deaths?"

"Colonel Fireswift took a risk, and it paid off for him. Nyx considers those acceptable losses."

"How could she?"

I couldn't help but feel betrayed. Colonel Fireswift was a cruel, toxic angel, but Nyx was supposed to be one of the good ones. At least I'd thought so.

"Never forget that Nyx is not like us," Nero said in response to my unspoken thoughts. "She was born an angel, born with one foot in the world of the gods. And to the gods, those are acceptable losses."

"Does that mean we can expect Colonel Fireswift's 'acceptable losses' to become a regular visitor to this office?"

"I hope to be back here before then."

"So you're not back now?"

"Unfortunately not. I only came to check on you. I heard what happened when you drank the Nectar yesterday morning."

"So it's been nearly two days."

"Yes."

"That explains why I'm starving."

He handed me a bar of chocolate. "Eat this. It will make you feel better."

I bit off a small piece. It melted in my mouth, and I felt

new energy fill me. Maybe after a few more bites, I'd begin to feel alive again."

"What did happen yesterday morning, Nero? When I had Nectar before, it was so different."

"Every time, every level, is different."

"But not like this. I went from getting drunk on Nectar to passing out when I have it. And the Nectar tasted… different."

"How so?"

"At first, it was the same, sweet and delicious. But then it went sour in my mouth, turning acidic. I felt like my whole body was burning in agony. Like I was being boiled alive."

"The first time you had the Nectar, you threw up," he reminded me.

"I remember. But this time was different. The Nectar was wrong. It tasted like there was something inside of it that didn't belong there."

"Poison."

"But the Nectar *is* a kind of poison. How can you poison something that's already a poison?"

"It's not easy, but there are ways," he said. "Ways known to few people."

For some reason, my mind thought back to Captain Somerset's promise that she would kill me if I ruined Nero's life. And I'd been poisoned shortly after Nyx had reassigned Nero. Had Captain Somerset tried to poison me?

"You didn't ruin anything," Nero said, touching my face.

"You're in my head again."

"It hurts for you to speak. I'm just trying to help." His face was perfectly serious, but I caught a flash of wicked delight in his eyes.

"Nero Windstriker, you are so full of shit."

"I've missed your mouth." His finger softly traced my lower lip.

"I wish you'd never left," I said, pulling him down.

He kissed me softly. "When the First Angel commands you to go on a top secret mission for her, you don't refuse."

"What did she want you to do?"

"Top secret, Leda."

"Oh, come on. Are you really going to make me go through all your files?"

"You wouldn't dare."

I held up the phone I'd swiped from his pocket. "I would."

He grabbed his phone, giving me a look of pure disbelief. "You are nearly dead, and you are pickpocketing from angels?"

"Is this the part where you tell me in your deep, foreboding voice that no one steals from angels?"

"We've been through this song and dance many times before. It's never done any good."

"Then let's not do good." I clawed my fingers through his hair, drawing him in closer.

"You're hurt."

I winked at him. "I'm feeling better already. Promise."

He gently caressed my face.

"You're not actually considering taking advantage of the poor girl, are you, Nero? It hasn't even been two days since she almost died."

I watched as Captain Somerset emerged from the shadows.

"What is she doing here?" I demanded.

She frowned at me. "Nice to see you too, Pandora."

"She thinks you were the one to poison her. On account of her ruining my life."

Captain Somerset snorted. "You got yourself into this mess, Nero. Not Leda. Gods, the way you blasted through that stone monster." She whistled low. "Now, that was a sight to behold." She looked at me. "This wasn't my doing."

"You told me you would kill me if I didn't leave him alone," I reminded her.

She rolled her eyes. "And you always do what people tell you to do? I was playing you, Pandora. I was trying to convince you to sleep with Nero. He hasn't gotten laid in ages, and it's making him downright grouchy. If you're up to it, I can stand guard at the door and give you two a few minutes."

"A few minutes?"

"He's not going to last any longer than that today, honey."

I opened my mouth to speak, but no words came out.

"Thank you, Basanti. I'll take things from here."

"Always happy to help," she said, slapping him hard on the back as she took a step back.

"Leda?" Nero asked me.

I blinked.

"You've stunned her to silence," he told Captain Somerset.

"I didn't even know that was possible." She waved her hand in front of my face. "I wonder how long it lasts."

"I'm almost dead, not deaf," I told them.

Captain Somerset looked at me and laughed. "I like you, Pandora. You're not afraid of anybody. Or of asking questions that will probably get you in trouble."

In the next room, the door to the medical ward swung open. Voices spilled in from the hallway. Captain Somerset rose and went to divert the doctors I could hear headed for this room.

"You trust her?" I asked him.

"Yes, I do," he replied. "Basanti was the one who brought me here. She contacted me to tell me what had happened as soon as you collapsed at the ceremony."

I decided to trust his judgment. After all, he'd turned against his other best friend when he'd turned out to be evil. Nero had a clear head, and he wouldn't bullshit me.

"Is she keeping guard?" I asked him as laughter rose up in the front room.

"Yes. No one knows I'm here."

"Why do I get the feeling you aren't supposed to be here?"

"Because I'm not."

I frowned. "I'm getting you into trouble again."

"I am perfectly capable of getting myself into trouble all by myself, thank you."

I couldn't help but laugh. I did it quietly, though. There was movement beyond the closed door. Captain Somerset was talking to the doctors, trying to convince them to go away so I could sleep. Nero watched me, his thumb drawing slow, even circles on my palm.

"What is it?"

"You had me worried. The doctors couldn't do anything to help you after you were poisoned."

My breath stuttered. "How did I survive?"

"Your body did it alone. It must have integrated the poison like it did the Nectar. It's a part of you now." He shot me a look that was part admiration, part concern. "It was Venom, the demons' equivalent of Nectar. That's what was in your Nectar. That's what made you pass out."

"What will the Venom do to me?"

"Soldiers of the Legion of Angels drink Nectar and soldiers of the demons' own legion drink Venom. Like Nectar, Venom will change you," he said. "The question is how much such a small dose will change you. You've already had so much Nectar that the effects might not be big. Maybe you won't even notice any changes."

"There were an awful lot of mights and maybes in those sentences, Nero."

"We don't fully understand the effects of Nectar and Venom. The fact that you survived a mixed dose of Nectar and Venom is remarkable. No one has ever survived both together in a single dose. That combination should have killed you."

"So the demons' poisoned me?"

"That is one theory."

"You don't look convinced."

"I have another theory," he said. "Colonel Fireswift."

"I know he wants to get me out of the way, but to risk poisoning me in front of the entire New York office? That's gutsy."

"He is a gutsy man. And he isn't afraid to use a flamethrower to kill a mosquito."

"Yes, I saw that firsthand when he rearranged the stone ceiling of the underground city."

Nero made a derisive noise. "He always was a showoff."

"Is he more powerful than you?" I asked him.

"He has raw power but no subtlety. It would be hard to kill him in a fair fight."

"If he's so direct, he wouldn't use poison."

"Colonel Fireswift is an angel, a top member of the Legion. There are rules in the Legion, rules even we angels must follow. Colonel Fireswift cannot kill you outright, but if you were to die during battle or be poisoned during the ceremony, then it would look legitimate. Colonel Fireswift doesn't want to lose his place or the place of his son in the Legion."

"In the Legion, do the children pay for the crimes of the parents?"

"Not directly. But one way or the other, you must atone for them. Especially treachery," he added with an almost woeful look. Maybe he was thinking about his own father who'd gone rogue all those years ago.

"What do you know about Osiris Wardbreaker?"

"Not much. He was one of Nyx's original angels."

"Like your parents."

He gave me a surprised look.

"I've taken the photo tour of your office."

"Yes, my parents knew General Wardbreaker well. The originals were a closely-knit group. Wardbreaker has since moved back to Europe, so I've had few dealings with him. But he is an original angel, and that makes him dangerous."

"Has Colonel Fireswift returned to the Lost City?"

"Yes, with a team of thirty telekinetics. They've been working day and night to dig a tunnel to the Treasury so they can secure the holy relics."

"The Lost Relics are not holy."

He gave me a curious look.

"What I meant was, they aren't what the Pilgrims and the Legion think they are. They were not made by only gods. Some of the pieces were forged in the fires of hell. They are relics of both heaven and hell."

"Nyx has had me following whispers of ancient weapons, powerful relics forged in hell but lost on Earth. The demons are trying to reclaim them. She needed my ability to track objects of dark power."

"You're after the same thing as Colonel Fireswift. He is looking for heavenly weapons, you for hellish ones. But they are one and the same," I realized. "Weapons of heaven and hell. And Osiris Wardbreaker is after them all."

"How do you know this?" he asked me.

I told him about the visions I'd had in the city and the dream I'd just woken from. He didn't look at me like I was crazy. He looked intrigued.

"Are you well enough to travel?" he asked.

I pushed off my blanket. "Are we taking a field trip?"

"Yes, back to the Black Plains."

I tried to get out of the bed, but my legs collapsed under the strain of my own weight. Nero's arms flashed out, catching me.

"Maybe you can carry me there?" I joked.

"Your body is healed," he said, drawing a knife as he sat down beside me on the bed. "It's your equilibrium, your magical balance, that's off."

He sliced the blade across his wrist. I immediately felt my body go alert, like every cell in it was drawing me toward him, toward his blood. But I hesitated.

"Hurry," he urged me. "We don't have much time."

I took his hand in mine, bringing his wrist to my mouth, and I drank deeply. His blood tasted like pure, undiluted Nectar—the food of the gods, the song of my soul. It poured down my throat, flashing through my veins like a raging river, cascading, building, burning. Need crashed through me, driving me hard and fast into a dizzying state of raw arousal.

I pulled away suddenly, before I did anything rash. I glanced down at my hand, which was planted on his thigh. So much for not doing anything rash. He chuckled as I removed my hand from his leg.

"Are you feeling better?" he asked me, tapping his finger against the cut at his wrist. The skin sealed together before my eyes.

"Yes. Much better." Well, except for the dark, wanton thoughts flashing through my head, reminding me that Nero and I were alone—and that we were already in bed.

"I like this dress," he said in a silky voice.

Apparently, no one had bothered to change me out of my evening gown. Come to think of it, it had probably been Captain Somerset's idea.

"I bought it because I thought you would like it," I told him.

"That is a dangerous confession."

"I like living dangerously."

"That is an even more dangerous confession." Nero's fingers brushed through my hair, caressing my scalp, even as his mouth dipped to my throat. "You smell so good. I can hardly resist taking a taste."

"Then don't."

"Leda." The word was a plea, a demand.

"Bite me, Nero."

He locked his hand around my waist, tugging me roughly against him as his fangs pierced my skin. "Your blood tastes different." He gasped. "Even more delicious." He drank faster. Pain and pleasure twisted together inside of me, pulsing against my skin. His hold was hard, possessive.

"Nero," I gasped. "I'm getting dizzy."

He held onto me, drinking greedily.

"Nero. Stop."

He didn't stop. His hold was tight. I wasn't sure he was even still here with me. He'd gone somewhere else, somewhere dark and dangerous.

I made a fist and hammered it against the side of his head. His whole body froze for a moment—then he jumped off the bed, backing far away from me.

"Leda." His eyes trailed down my neck, burning with guilt.

"I'm all right."

"I can't drink from you again." He brushed his glowing hand across the punctures in my neck, and they healed. "As much as I want to." He traced his hand up my jaw. "As much as I can think of nothing else." Silver flashed in his green eyes, and then he was on the other side of the room, as far away from me as he could physically be.

"Nero."

"We have to go," he said. "We have a rogue angel to stop."

CHAPTER FOURTEEN
Bringer of Chaos

WE TRAVELED TO Purgatory on board a private airship owned by an old friend of Nero's. As far as I could tell, Dominic was completely human. I hadn't even known Nero knew any humans.

It was a good thing he did, though, because we couldn't trust any supernaturals right now. Technically, this was Colonel Fireswift's mission, so we weren't supposed to interfere. Nor would we ask to join. Nero didn't trust Colonel Fireswift after what he'd done to me, and neither did I. I saw what he'd done with just normal weapons and magic. If he got his hands on the weapons of heaven and hell, he would hurt people. I felt that in my gut, and I'd learned to trust my gut.

Not that Osiris Wardbreaker was any better. The first thing he'd done after defecting from the Legion was butcher an entire town. That meant we couldn't let him get the weapons either. We had to find the relics, stop a rogue angel, and do it all without letting anyone know we were there.

"Why do our plans always sound so impossible?" I

asked Nero.

"Because you come up with them," he replied.

"We'll just have to be stealthy."

I pulled on a black cap, stuffing my pale hair inside of it. The rest of our clothes were black too. We looked more like we were getting ready to rob a bank than save powerful ancient weapons from falling into the wrong hands.

"Captain Somerset is covering for me back in New York, and everyone thinks you're off by yourself on a secret mission," I continued. "No one is expecting us."

"I think you're underestimating the paranoia and viciousness of angels," he told me.

"You realize *you* are an angel, right?"

"So I know all about being paranoid and vicious."

"I prefer your other qualities," I said with a smirk.

"Oh?"

"Yes, I'm especially fond of your smile."

He gave me a hard look.

"That's the one."

Dominic plopped down on the sofa opposite us. A man in his late thirties, he wore a long coat of light brown leather over dark denim pants and a chocolate brown dress shirt. A gun was strapped to one hip, a knife to the other. He looked like he would be right at home at the Frontier— or on a pirate ship.

"Colonel, when were you going to fess up to me that you hang out with swindlers?" I asked with a coy smile.

"I like her, Nero. She's such a sweet-talker," Dominic said with a grin.

"You should hear how nicely I follow orders," I told him.

Dominic burst into laughter. "I'll bet," he said, rising.

"All right. We're coming up on Purgatory. We'll be landing soon."

He went back to the front of the ship, leaving me alone with Nero, who was looking at me like I was dying.

"What's wrong? I guess you don't appreciate my humor as much as your friend does?" I said.

"I'm not feeling much like laughing right now." He paused. "I nearly drained you dry. I couldn't stop."

"But you did stop."

"I lost control. I never do that."

"Around me you do. I can see that perfect control breaking in the twitch of your eyebrows, of your lips—every time I talk back, every time I use a water bottle or car antenna in a fight, every time I don't act like a pompous stiff soldier of the Legion."

Nero's eyebrows crinkled.

"Yes, that. Exactly that. You like my spunk." I shot him a saucy smile. "Admit it."

"You are incorrigible."

"Admit it."

He tucked a loose strand of hair into my hat. "I like your spunk."

"Of course you do," I told him, looking down over Purgatory.

It looked so different from up here. The wall dwarfed the town, casting a dark shadow over the small houses. I could see the districts clearly, like they were pre-cut slices of a pizza pie. A tall, slender tower sat in the middle of each district. That was where the men who called themselves lords looked down upon their territory. Their gangs were not out tonight. Instead, paranormal soldiers patrolled the streets. Hundreds of them, all over the city. I wanted to believe the government had finally made a move to take out the crime lords, but I wasn't feeling delusional tonight.

Nero's phone rang through the silence, like a heavy stone dropping into a tranquil pond. "Basanti, what do you know?"

"They figured out Leda is gone," I heard Captain Somerset say through the speaker. "Sorry, Nero. There was only so long I could hold off the doctors. And since Leda wasn't checked out or cleared for duty, everyone is on the lookout for her."

"Colonel Fireswift?" Nero asked

"He's issued a statement that Leda was weakened by her close call with death and that she probably wandered out while in a state of delirium."

"Delirium, my ass," I ground out.

Captain Somerset continued, "Colonel Fireswift furthermore stated that she is dangerous. He believes she will return to Purgatory on her way to the Lost City, and everyone has been ordered to keep on the lookout for her. For her own safety and for the safety of others."

By now, I was swearing so loudly that Colonel Fireswift could probably hear me all the way in the Lost City.

"All the paranormal soldiers in Purgatory are on the lookout for her, Nero," Captain Somerset said. "Watch your backs. Both of you."

"Thank you, Basanti," Nero said.

"Thank me by giving your girlfriend a kiss."

"I can hear you, you know," I told the phone.

"I know you can, sweetheart." Captain Somerset made a loud kissing noise, then hung up.

Nero tucked his phone back into his pocket.

"The paranormal soldiers should be guarding the wall

from monsters," I said, anger simmering in me. "Or how about keeping the people of the town safe from the crime lords? Instead, all those resources are being put into one of Colonel Fireswift's dominance games."

"These are the games of angels, Leda," Nero said. "If you want to play in our ranks, you need to learn to deal with it. Fast."

"Ok, how do you suggest we win this game?"

"This is your town. You tell me."

Wow. He was leaving it up to me? The fact that he trusted me to come up with the plan meant more to me than he realized. It meant so much, I could have kissed him —if we weren't so busy right now.

"We can't get past the wall as long as they are watching," I said, talking it through. "There's only one gate, and we can't fly out because this ship is too easy to spot in the sky."

"Dominic is crazy, but not crazy enough to fly over the Black Plains anyway," Nero said.

"Hell, no," Dominic called out from the front of the ship. "There are flying monsters out there. And giant monsters that grab things out of the air."

"And you can't fly us out because people would see the angel in the sky and know you're here too," I told Nero. "If Colonel Fireswift knows we're coming, we won't be able to get down underground to those relics. He will be ready. We have to catch him off guard, to sneak in when he's not looking. But first we need to sneak past the paranormal soldiers and make it past the wall. But how..." The idea came to me, one simple, perfect idea. "We have to climb the wall."

"If they turn on the magic barrier, we're dead," Nero

told me.

"Come on, Colonel," I said, grinning. "What's life without taking a risk now and again?"

It was a crazy plan. And to make it work, we would need help.

As it turned out, Dominic was the best kind of pirate: the kind with secret smuggling compartments. The paranormal soldiers who searched the airship walked right over us, none the wiser.

We snuck down the streets, keeping to the shadows, taking shortcuts through houses, cutting through the old underground train tunnels, and hiding under bridges—all those little things I knew about that the paranormal soldiers didn't. I was a town native, and they were just passing through, another stop on the career train. They came here for only weeks or months at a time before going home. And what little time they had here was spent mostly at the wall.

A bunch of them were clustered there now, but the wall's Magitech wasn't on. It burned too much power to keep it on all the time, so there was an alert system to decide when to turn it on, based on the monster attack risk level. Green, yellow, orange, and red were the alert levels. Green meant 'safe', and red was 'apocalypse imminent'. At the moment, the alert board was yellow, which meant monsters had recently been sighted close to the wall but there were none in sight right now.

We wouldn't be getting over that wall as long as the soldiers were standing guard at the bottom. We had to draw them away, and for that, I needed Calli's contacts. She knew people who could be bribed to create a distraction so we could get out. I'd had contacts once too, but it had been too long. I didn't know which people I could trust and which ones would turn around and double-cross us for a payment from the paranormal soldiers. But Calli had people who owed her favors and people she had dirt on. She could make them behave.

The problem was getting to Calli. Paranormal soldiers patrolled the sidewalks, streets, and lawn around my house. Colonel Fireswift must have thought I'd try to go home. The thick curtains were on the windows, so Calli was expecting me too.

"This way," I whispered to Nero, leading him into the abandoned building across the street from my house.

We squeezed into what had once passed for a bathroom. I pulled up a hidden panel in the floor.

"Is it common for people in this town to have secret tunnels?" Nero asked, looking down into the dark hole.

We jumped down. The hole really was just a hole— with a single locked door.

"No, this is a Calli thing," I said, entering the combination on the lock. "My mom dug this passageway herself in case we ever needed to make a quick escape. Or get in secretly like now."

We followed the musty, dirty tunnel to its end, where another locked door awaited us. And then we were in the cellar of my house, surrounded by shelves of canned goods and other long-lasting treats.

"Is your mother preparing for the apocalypse?" Nero asked, looking around.

"Calli says the apocalypse already hit Earth once, so

chances are good it will hit again. And she plans to be ready. It's kind of her motto. She likes to be prepared for everything."

Calli was waiting for us at the top of the stairs, dressed in a flour-dusted apron. "I was expecting you." Her gaze flickered briefly to Nero before returning to me. "I was not expecting him."

"Long story."

"You can tell it to us at dinner. I was just about to put the food on the table. Gin, put two more settings at the table!" she called in the direction of the kitchen. "We have guests."

"Did Leda come like you thought she…" Gin froze halfway through the door, her jaw dropping when she saw Nero. She quickly retreated back into the safety of the kitchen.

"Do you have someone you can bribe to create a big distraction?" I asked Calli.

"How big?"

I slapped a fat wad of money into her hand. "Big enough to distract all the paranormal soldiers in town so Nero and I can climb over the wall onto the Black Plains without anyone spotting us."

Most mothers would have fainted at that statement. Calli didn't even blink. "You ask for miracles, Leda."

I grinned at her. "And you always deliver miracles."

She slipped off her apron, hanging it onto its hook on the wall. "One of these days, I won't have a miracle up my sleeves."

"But not today?"

Calli wrapped her arm around me, leading me toward the dining room. "Don't you worry about a thing. I have just the guy for the job. I'll give him a call. By the time dinner is over, you'll have your 'big distraction'."

Bella gave me a knowing smile as Nero and I sat down opposite each other at the table. Gin didn't even have a look to spare for me. Her wide eyes were glued firmly on the angel who had come to dinner. My little sister looked like she couldn't decide whether to faint or flee, so she just stared.

My other little sister had more than enough to say for the both of them.

"Your picture is being projected all over town with some fancy Magitech machines the Legion dropped off," Tessa told me. "It must be costing a boatload of magic to keep that all running."

I felt my jaw clench up involuntarily. Colonel Fireswift was being such a pain in the ass.

"Are you two on the run from the Legion? Are you going rogue?" Tessa asked me.

"No."

"Then what's going on?"

I scooped potato pancakes onto my plate. "It's classified."

Tessa gave me a hard look. "You really are one of them now, aren't you?"

"One of what?" I asked, spreading applesauce over the pancakes.

"One of *them*. The Legion. A soldier. The old Leda wouldn't keep things from us."

"It's for your own protection."

Tessa pouted out her lips. "I bet you told Calli."

"Calli is an adult, not a seventeen-year-old girl."

"I'll have you know that I'll be eighteen in four months."

"Then we can revisit this topic at that point."

"Not cool, Leda. Not cool."

"Leda is just teasing you," Bella told her.

Tessa gave me a challenging stare.

"Yeah, I am." I snickered. "You are such an easy target."

Tessa was sensitive about her age. She wanted to be an adult—yesterday—and she didn't like being called a kid. You had to know your loved ones' weaknesses so you could tease them properly. And protect them. Especially that.

I told them all why Nero and I were here. When I was done, Bella said, "This Colonel Fireswift doesn't sound like a very nice person."

"What a dingleberry," Tessa declared.

Nero's eyebrow twitched like he'd appreciated the insult. "Indeed."

"I can't believe we have a real-live angel in our house. At our table." Tessa smiled sweetly at him. "How old are you? How many feathers does an angel have? Is it true an angel's wings are an erogenous zone? I read that in Paranormal Teen. Oh my gods, I have so many questions! How many people have you killed? What do angels like to eat? How many lovers have you had? Do angels really mark their lovers? I read that in Paranormal Teen too. And that angels can have sex like twenty times in a row."

"Are *you* writing a piece for Paranormal Teen?" I commented.

She ignored me, her attention firmly on Nero. "Inquiring minds want to know."

Translation: she was going to repeat back everything he said to her friends at school and thereby become even more popular than she already was.

"How many Legion soldiers passed through here yesterday?" I asked Calli, before Tessa could come up with any more crazy questions for Nero.

"Nearly a hundred," Calli replied. "It's the biggest excursion onto the Black Plains that I've ever seen."

"Do you think we could borrow your motorcycle, the one you keep outside in the wall in that shed?"

"The last time you borrowed one of my motorcycles, you almost got killed trying to rescue an angel." She looked at Nero like it was his fault.

Nero responded to the accusation with cool silence. That silence held for a few minutes, while we ate our pancakes and applesauce.

Tessa finally broke it to ask Nero, "Is it true you once fought nearly two hundred monsters all by yourself?"

"No. It was over two hundred."

"Wow." She looked at him in awe. "My sister's boyfriend is a super-hot angel."

"He's not my boyfriend."

"Oh?" Tessa asked with a challenging grin. "Then what is he exactly? Because you have been staring at him all of dinner like you want to jump his bones."

I blushed.

"And?" Tessa persisted. "What is Colonel Stud to you?"

I looked to Calli for support, a silent plea to tell off Tessa for being inappropriate.

But Calli braided her fingers together and said, "I'd like to know the answer to that too, Leda."

"As would I," Nero said.

Tessa latched onto him like a drowning woman holding onto a life raft. "Do you think you and Leda are soulmates? And when you get married, can I plan the wedding? I'm thinking white roses, pale like Leda's hair. Or do you think she'll look washed out all in white?"

"The Legion uses white roses at funerals to honor our soldiers who have fallen in battle," Nero informed her.

Gods, he did *not* just take the bait.

"Red?" Tessa asked.

"The Legion uses red roses for promotions, to signify the blood that was spilled on our path to glory."

Tessa shot him a cute scowl. "You are just making this up."

Nero shook his head once.

"Well, do you have a color chart or something for what wedding-approved colors I can chose from?"

"Golden roses. They signify new beginnings and the gods' will. That is the flower color of weddings."

I had a feeling he was playing along to tease me. Angels had a twisted sense of humor. Kind of like family.

"Only golden roses? That's it? That's the only flower you can use for an angel wedding? What happened to freewill and choice?"

"Dear, I don't think you understand how a military works," Calli said gently. "The Legion of Angels isn't about freewill or choice. It is about rules and regulations, duty and honor."

"Sounds like a dull wedding," Tessa pouted.

Calli had failed me, so I shot Bella a desperate, silent plea for support.

"Speaking of weddings, do you know who's getting married soon?" she said. "Dale and Cindy. Isn't that wonderful?"

"Not as wonderful as an angel wedding," Tessa said, refusing to be derailed. She looked at Nero. "What are they like?"

"Marriages of angels in the Legion are arranged. The goal is to make good magical pairings, which in turn produce offspring with a high magic potential to become angels one day."

"Wait, what? So they tell you who you will marry?" Tessa looked horrified.

"Yes, every angel's magic is tested, and then we are paired with a Legion soldier with a high magical compatibility."

"Another angel?"

"Rarely. For some reason we don't understand, angels generally have a low magical compatibility with other angels, so their spouses are chosen from the greater pool of Legion soldiers."

"So you don't have a choice who you get to marry?" Tessa asked.

"You may choose from the five or six soldiers whose magic is highly compatible with yours."

"What about love?"

"Love doesn't enter the equation," he said.

"That really sucks, you know. So basically every soldier of the Legion doesn't get to fall in love."

"They can. These rules only apply to angels. The offspring of an angel is a hundred times more likely to later become an angel too."

"So what if two people get married, then one of them later becomes an angel. Will the Legion split them up?" Tessa asked.

"It's complicated."

"You're like two hundred years old," she said. "Why aren't you married yet?"

How had I known that question was coming?

"The Legion hasn't found anyone yet who has a high magic compatibility with me."

"I wonder what your and Leda's magic compatibility is." She winked at me.

And I'd known that one was coming too.

Calli's phone chimed. She glanced down at the screen, then said to me, "Your distraction is ready. Ten minutes."

"Saved by the bell." I rose from my chair. "We have to go. Relics to find, villains to thwart."

Nero patted his napkin to his mouth, then set it down, standing. "Thank you for the meal. Mrs. Pierce." He nodded to my sisters. "Ladies."

Tessa and Gin put their heads together. Whispers and giggles rose from them. I thought I caught the word 'wings'. Nero and I walked out of the dining room. Right before he passed through the door, golden swirls of magic slid down his back. Wings appeared where nothing had been the moment before, the full tapestry of black, green, and blue feathers spreading wide so the girls could get a good look. They squealed in delight. Nero tucked his wings against his back, then he followed me into the cellar.

"You shouldn't encourage my sisters' silliness," I told him as we strapped on the weapons we'd brought along. We would need them to survive the monsters who roamed the Black Plains.

Nero's eyes were laughing at me.

"What?"

"It was worth it just to see you so flustered." His wings

vanished. He'd put them away to leave more space for swords and guns. "I've never seen you like this. Well, except maybe that time you marched up to my apartment to confront me after you'd tossed your panties on the floor of my office."

"Well, I'm glad you enjoyed yourself at my expense," I said through clenched teeth.

"It's only fair."

"What do you mean?"

"After all those times you tried to incite me."

"I never do that."

"Purposely forgetting Legion decorum, tossing found objects in a fight…"

"Ok, so maybe I sometimes do that to get a reaction out of you," I admitted. "But mostly I do it because it's just who I am."

"Wearing those skirts," he added.

"Which ones?"

"You know which ones, so don't play coy with me." He cast a long, languid look down my body, and though I was dressed in long sleeves and pants, I suddenly felt very naked. "The ones so short that I can't help but think about what you're wearing under them. Or *not* wearing under them. Leda, do not walk around me with no underwear on if you expect me to behave myself."

"Ah, I hadn't thought you'd noticed," I said coyly, just for him.

"Of course I noticed." He inhaled slowly, deeply. "You knew I would. You are tempting me after making me promise to take this slow. Leda, I cannot take it slow with you."

My back hit the doorframe.

"And then there are these tops you wear. Designed to torment me."

He popped open the buttons of my jacket.

"Oh, you mean my uniform?"

"Yes. That." As soft as an angel feather, his fingers slid below my tank top strap, teasing it aside. "When this mission is over, we are going to have a second date. We will eat dinner and dessert, and then I will bring you back to my apartment."

His mouth dipped to my throat. He drew my hard, throbbing vein between his teeth and sucked. A harsh, unintelligible noise scraped past my lips.

"You don't want to take it slow," he told me.

"Oh, is that so?" I replied, breathless.

His lips came down hard on mine, devouring the inside with insatiable hunger. It was like kissing a lightning storm.

"Leda."

Calli's voice brought me back down to Earth. I ducked under Nero's arm.

"I found what you were asking for on your last visit," Calli said.

My last visit? It took a few moments for my head to clear. And then I remembered. I'd asked Calli if she knew anything about my past.

"What did you find?" I asked her.

Calli's gaze darted to Nero.

"It's fine. We can trust him."

"He's an angel," Calli said.

"An angel who has kept our secret, even from the Legion. An angel who is training me so I can gain the power I need to find Zane. An angel who helped me catch a glimpse of Zane to know he's safe."

Calli sighed. "I hope you know what you're doing, Leda."

So did I.

"Julianna Mather was an alias," Calli said. "Your foster mother's real name was Aradia Redwood."

"I know that name," Nero said.

I looked at him in surprise. "How?"

"Major Redwood was a soldier in the Legion of Angels. She died in battle about twenty years ago."

"Around the time I was born."

Calli showed us a photograph of a red-haired woman in a Legion uniform. Julianna…no, Aradia. That was the woman who'd raised me until she died.

"Why was she hiding her true magic?" I asked, not directing the question to anyone in particular. "And why did she fake her death? Why was she raising me? Who were my parents?"

"I don't know. That's all I could find," Calli said.

"Thank you."

"Be careful, Leda," she said, then walked back upstairs.

She wasn't just talking about being careful out there on the Black Plains. She was telling me to be careful with Nero. And when looking into my past.

I glanced at my watch. "Let's go."

We hurried down the tunnel. Just as we stepped into the old abandoned house on the other side, Calli's distraction went off. Paranormal soldiers ran past the grimy windows, chasing after the loud music playing on the next street. A trashcan exploded, drawing more soldiers. And that was just the beginning.

A woman was dancing naked on the rooftop of the Witch's Watering Hole. The soldiers were *real* quick to check out that disturbance. A few blocks over, a drunk was shouting out profanities. A street fight closed down an entire block. A motorcycle gang drove in front of the wall, singing lewd songs and throwing empty liquid bottles at the soldiers.

Someone with a pale blonde ponytail jogged toward the wall. She saw the paranormal soldiers, then turned back around and ran away. They took the bait.

"Your mother sure knows how to create a distraction," Nero commented.

"She's a pro," I agreed.

This wasn't a distraction; it was a whole freaking symphony of distractions. With the soldiers distracted, and the rest of the town in a state of chaos, no one noticed the two shadows rushing toward the wall.

We climbed, keeping close to the stones. The soldiers in their towers over the wall were watching the gate, as if they expected something to happen there. They didn't see us slip over the edge of the wall and climb down the other side.

Alarms blasted, and the alert screen turned orange. Magic slid across the wall, enveloping it in a golden light, electrifying anything touching it. That included me. I let go quickly, falling the rest of the way down to the ground. Nero landed beside me, also in a low crouch. The guards still hadn't seen us. I unlocked the shed and rolled out Calli's motorcycle.

"Why does your mother keep a motorcycle on this side of the wall?" Nero asked me.

"It's her contingency plan in case we ever need to flee into the Black Plains and disappear."

"She really has planned for everything." He looked impressed.

"Now comes the hard part," I said. "How to turn on the engine without attracting the soldiers' attention."

"Look out there." He pointed across the blackened plains.

An Orange alert meant monsters had been spotted in the distance. I saw them now, a stampede of buffalo-like monsters.

Nero pulled me onto the motorcycle behind him. "We need to direct the monsters here, then when they are all around us, we start up the motorcycle. The monsters are so loud that the soldiers won't hear the engine revving up. And then we ride with the herd out onto the plains."

"How do we get the monsters to surround us?"

"We compel them."

"That works on monsters?" I asked, surprised.

"It works very well on monsters."

"I've never seen that."

"The monsters were made by gods and demons. They were made to be controlled. It's built into them. Their minds are simple," he explained. "Long ago, they changed, evolving. So now we can't control them passively, but as long as you are concentrating on them, you can actively control their movements."

Cool. "How many of them at a time?" I asked him.

"It depends. Together, I believe we can control this entire herd. We should be able to handle simple direction changes when they are in herd mode like right now, but don't try to make them do anything fancy. We have to direct the herd like it is one being. Got it?"

I gave him a thumbs-up.

"Follow my lead. We'll do it together," Nero said, his green eyes glowing greener as he stared across the plains at the approaching herd.

They changed direction like an ocean wave, heading for us. I reached out with my magic, sensing for their minds. They were like one mind, and I could feel Nero controlling that mind. I hitched my wagon to his magic, so we could work together, a link made easier because we'd so recently exchanged blood.

As the beasts surrounded us, engulfing us, Nero turned on the motorcycle. We drove away inside the herd. The beasts were so huge and running so close to one another that I doubted anyone had noticed us hiding in the wave. And Nero drove tightly to them, his reflexes amazing, reacting to every step, quick but never jerky.

Together, Nero and I compelled the herd of monsters, directing them where to go. It felt a bit funny, really cool, and extremely exhausting. We traveled with the beasts until we were out of sight of the wall, then we sent them off in another direction, releasing their minds as we turned down the road toward the Lost City.

I yawned. Compelling the monsters had taxed me.

"Sleep," Nero said. "I'll wake you when we get to the ruins. Or when monsters attack."

"You sure?"

"Would it make you feel better if I made it an order?"

"Nah, I'd probably just disobey it."

"Sometimes I think you are just trying to incite me."

"If I wanted to incite you, angel, I wouldn't be wearing underwear right now."

Nero grunted. "Go to sleep, Pandora, bringer of chaos."

I smiled against his back. "You won't let me fall off?"

I felt a gentle pressure wrap itself around me, holding me to his back. "I've got you. I won't let you fall."

CHAPTER FIFTEEN

The Gateway

I SLEPT MORE soundly than I'd thought possible on the back of a motorcycle. I didn't wake up until we came to a stop at the edge of the Lost City. Nero informed me that no monsters had attacked us along the way. I guess we didn't look like tasty targets.

"I wonder who my parents were," I said as we secured the motorcycle, hiding it from sight. The last thing we needed was a nosy patrol to find our ride and go tattletale back to Colonel Windstriker.

"Were they also in the Legion? Did they know Aradia? Are they really dead, or did Aradia take me from them? I have so many questions." I'd have to look in the Legion's records when we got back to New York. Maybe there was something in Aradia's file that would shed some light on all of this.

"Some of your answers might be closer than you think." Nero tapped his finger on my forehead. "There are memories inside of you, memories that are not your own."

"How did I get them?"

"I'd guess someone buried them there. It's no

coincidence that they are coming out now. I believe they were triggered by the Nectar and maybe by the Venom, by your growing abilities, your growing magic. If I'm right, as your power grows, more memories will surface."

"And whose memories are they?"

"You have memories of this city."

"Yes. From the final battle here." Which happened over two hundred years ago. How could they possibly be linked to my parents?

"Memories from one person or from many?" Nero asked.

I thought about it, sifting through what I remembered from the flashes. "More than one person, but they are all jumbled up. And I can't control them. They just come at random."

"You need more discipline."

"This is hardly the time for a lecture."

"It's not a lecture. It's an offer of help. Let me help you." He set his hands on my cheeks. "We exchanged blood earlier tonight, Leda. We're linked. I can help you."

"How?"

"Just like the last time when I helped you see your brother. Close your eyes," he instructed me. "Is there someone you see more often than the others in your visions?"

"Yes, an angel named Sierra."

"Focus on her."

I pictured the red-haired angel with the silver wings.

"Did she have the relics?"

"Yes," I told him.

"Picture them too."

Her armor was silver just like her wings. I could see it

shimmering in the light of the moon. She held a flaming sword. But it wasn't like other fire swords. Its flame wasn't orange; it was blue.

"Good," Nero said. "I can see it in your mind. Now follow Sierra to the treasury."

Images flickered past, flashes of memories. Faster and faster in dizzying, whirling loops—and then it all stopped.

Sierra walked down the underground city, but it hadn't been under the ground then. Moonlight melted with the city lights, bathing the streets in an almost ethereal glow. Sierra stopped in front of the small house and touched the angel symbol. The wall shifted, the gateway opening.

The memory bled away, and I found myself facedown in the dirt. I pushed myself up, and immediately began pacing, trying to sort through what I had just seen and make sense of it.

"Sierra touched the symbol of the angel, and the gateway just opened. But how? How did she do it? What's the trick?"

"Recite the line for me."

" 'For in the midnight hour, the sun and moon will shine, and a new hero will rise, his mind unlocking the secrets within.' "

"It's a metaphor," Nero said. "This isn't about the sun and the moon. It's about a person. Someone who embodies the balance of darkness and light. Someone like you."

"The angel symbol was pulsing. Light and dark," I realized. "In my dream, Sierra spoke of inheriting someone else's destiny, and the gateway only opens to someone who embodies light and darkness. Sierra wasn't the first keeper of the weapons of heaven and hell. I wonder how many keepers there have been? And where they all are now?"

"I believe I'm looking at one right now."

"I don't know, Nero. Sierra was so…powerful. I'm just some watered-down version. You probably have a better chance of opening that gateway than I do."

"I have darkness and light in me, Leda, but they're not in balance. They're in conflict."

"And that makes a difference?"

"More than how much magic you have, I believe." He touched my face. "You survived Venom mixed with Nectar. If that isn't proof of your light-dark balance, then I don't know what is," he said. "Also, I tested you."

"Tested me? How?"

"With the beasts. What I told you wasn't completely true. Not all Legion soldiers of the third level can compel the beasts. In fact, until today, I'd thought I was the only person who could do it," he said. "You see, the monsters came from gods and demons. Some were beasts of light, and some were beasts of darkness. But that changed quickly. They bred with one another. That weakened the gods' and demons' control over them. Slowly, their hold over the beasts faded, until a few generations later, it was gone."

"Because the monsters are now of mixed magic. Of light and darkness," I realized.

"Gods and demons are just two sides of the same coin. And so are their beasts."

"How do you know all of this?" I asked him. "It doesn't sound like something the Legion would tell its soldiers."

"No, of course not. They would call what I just told you blasphemy. The gods refuse to accept that they and the demons are the same. It was my mother who told me the truth of what happened, of how the gods and demons lost control of the beasts."

Nero continued, "Humans are like gods and demons, like monsters. Our magic can be light or dark. But unlike monsters, there aren't many of us who possess both dark and light magic in large quantities."

"But you do," I said.

"Because I am the child of two angels, one of light and one who turned to darkness. It is an explosive combination." He set his hand on my cheek. "But not in you. In you, the light and dark are balanced. I controlled the beasts with raw power. You controlled them just by being. The Nectar brought out your light magic. And the Venom is now bringing out your dark magic."

"Can all monsters be controlled?"

"Not all. Also, it doesn't work once a battle has started. The beasts need to be calm. And it's best if it's a herd, those who follow by instinct. Top tier predators are almost impossible to control. Practice this power but just don't depend on the ability to save you in a fight."

"Ok. I won't."

"And don't tell anyone that you have the power to control monsters. It is a dangerous gift. If the gods or demons think they have any chance of regaining control over the monsters, they will not hesitate to do whatever they can to make it happen."

Which would probably involve experimenting on, drugging, and torturing us. No, thank you.

Nero turned toward the Lost City. "Ok, let's move in."

I felt like a thief in the night sneaking through the city,

avoiding Legion patrols. But at least I wasn't alone in my delinquency.

"I'm glad you're here," I told Nero. "No matter what Nyx thinks, we make a good team."

"She knows we're a great team. She just wanted to separate us for a time so I could clear my head of you. Obviously, it didn't work."

"If I were Nyx, I'd probably separate us too," I admitted. "I'm a bad influence on you. Just look at what's happening here. You're breaking rules because of me."

"That's not what's happening here. I'm not breaking any rules. And neither are you," he told me.

"Oh?" My lips curled. "How do you figure that?"

"I am here to track a weapon of darkness, the mission Nyx gave me. Our meeting is pure chance. You came here because you figured out the truth that the relics are of heaven and hell, and you puzzled out how to open the door. You were concerned that someone was trying to keep you from saving the relics, someone on the inside who poisoned you. Fearing for your life, not knowing who you could trust, you came here in secret to save the relics from falling into the hands of anyone who would use them for great evil."

"Nice story," I told him.

He inclined his head.

"So, do you really think anyone will buy this load of bullshit?"

"You have to believe it when you tell the story," he told me. "You have to sell it. You have the gods' third gift, Siren's Song, the power to persuade, to make others believe. And besides, you were already a siren anyway." He was looking at me like I would be the death of him yet.

"Ok, convincing. Serious. I can do this."

"You practice your story. I'm going to scout out ahead and make sure the way is clear."

With that said, Nero left me alone with my thoughts. And my head was bursting with them right now. As the minutes passed, I thought about Nero, about my past, my magic, and about how it didn't all add up because I was still missing too many pieces. All I knew—and I was somehow certain of this—was that everything going on was linked. The rogue angel, the relics of heaven and hell, my being poisoned, my past, these memories, my light-dark balance: it was all part of the same picture. But how was it all connected? What did it mean?

A tall man with dark, spiky hair and pale blue eyes came running down the street, and he was headed right for my hiding spot. I didn't recognize his face. Maybe he was from the Legion, but then why wasn't he wearing a Legion uniform?

I crouched down lower. I could have sworn he looked straight at me. This was bad. Really bad. If he wasn't from the Legion, then he was most likely a thief come to rob the Lost City of its treasures. He'd see me as competition and attack, at which point Colonel Fireswift's men would close in around us. I had to strike first and take him down before he could fight back. I reached for my gun.

But I hesitated. There was something about him, something familiar. His scent. Yes, that was it. His scent. His scent was Nero's scent. The moment I made the connection, the man's face blurred, a visual hiccup rippling across his skin before the spell resettled.

"Nero?" I whispered.

He crouched down beside me behind the rusted old

truck. "How did you know? How did you see through that spell?"

"I'm not sure exactly." I took his hand in mine, lifting it to my nose. "It had something to do with your scent. It reminded me of your blood and how much I crave it. How it sings to me. How my pulse syncs to yours whenever you're near."

He brushed the hair back from my face. "That is the most beautiful thing anyone has ever said to me."

I caught his hand as it brushed through my hair. "When I recognized your scent, your face blurred for a moment." It was so weird to watch someone with a stranger's face touch me like that. "How are you doing this?"

"It's shifting magic," he told me. "Glamour, one branch of shifting. It's a mental shift, not a physical one."

"Meaning you didn't actually change your appearance? You're projecting it into my mind?"

"Right."

"Will others be able to see through the glamour?" I asked.

"It depends on how strong their magic is. Up close, other angels and high-level Legion soldiers will be able to see through it. From afar, it should fool most people, though. If we keep our distance, our disguises will hold. We should be able to get past them."

"*Our* disguises?"

He drew his sword, showing me my reflection to the blade. An unfamiliar face stared back at me, a woman with hair as black as obsidian and dark skin as smooth as honey. I puckered up my full, red lips and blew myself a kiss.

"Couldn't you have made me taller? Or given me bigger

boobs?" I teased him.

"Changing larger dimensions is tricky."

I sighed. "Too bad." I gazed at my new face in the sword. Even though I knew it was fake, I had a hard time seeing through my own glamour.

"Why can't I see through it, knowing it's fake? If this is a mental spell, shouldn't that knowledge be enough? Why do I have to squint my eyes and concentrate really hard to see the blurry mask?"

"Because I am an angel with high-level magic."

"I thought modesty is a virtue," I teased.

"Not in angels."

I snickered.

"Your ability to see through glamours will grow with practice and as you level up your magic. For now, you should just know that not everyone is what they appear. So always make sure someone is who they look like before spilling secrets. Even if you see me, it might not be me."

"Things were so much simpler when people had only one face."

"We all have many faces, Leda."

Colonel Fireswift had at least a dozen—all of them cruel.

We snuck through the city ruins, avoiding Legion teams, avoiding Colonel Fireswift most of all. Nero said his disguise probably wouldn't work against him, not even from a distance.

"How long have you known him?" I asked.

"We were in the same initiation group. We entered the Legion together, both of us Legion brats, both shooting high."

"So he saw you as his greatest competition?"

"He still does." Nero pulled me into a building as a patrol passed by. "You need to be careful with him. He didn't get to be an angel by being just a dumb brute. He knows how to play the game. He will find your weaknesses and exploit them. And you make that easy. Your enemies can see everything because you put it all out there. They will use it against you, including Fireswift's son, your friend. Everything you share with him he will use against you when push comes to shove, when it's a choice between you and himself. I've seen it before. His father did the same to me."

"Jace is not his father, nor does he want to be. And that's what really matters in the end. I have faith that he will find the right path."

"You can't save everyone."

"No, but I think I know who can be saved." I smiled at him.

We emerged from the building, continuing toward the entrance to the underground levels."

"You mean me," Nero said. "You think I can be saved."

"From the moment you walked into that back room holding my Legion application, I knew that was an angel who was screaming for someone to kill that bug stuck up his ass."

"And you figured yourself equal to the job?"

"Of course. I excel at lost causes. You're already much more agreeable than you used to be. If only you would stop giving me pushups."

"Pushups build muscle and character," he said seriously.

"I'm pretty strong, and I think we can both agree I have more than enough character to go around."

We slowed, growing silent as we crouched down and

looked at the piles of rocks that littered the street from here to the entrance into the underground city. Every patch of ground that wasn't occupied by rocks was occupied by Legion soldiers moving rocks, either by hand or by magic. There were too many of them. We'd never be able to sneak in unnoticed, not without a pretty sizable distraction.

The Lost City delivered, as though it had heard my prayer. Wolflike monsters streamed across the ruined city, flooding down the streets, pouring down the buildings. The Legion soldiers stopped moving rocks and turned to fight the monsters. Even Colonel Fireswift moved off his spot beside the growing hole to attack the swarm of monsters.

With the Legion soldiers busy, Nero and I slipped around behind them and jumped unseen into the hole. We ran down streets and tunnels not yet completely cleared of debris. The whole place looked about as stable as a tissue paper house, and it might come down at any moment.

We came up on the little house. I touched the pulsing angel mark. And just like in my vision, the wall split to reveal the gateway. Warm streams of magic rippled across my skin, drawing me forward.

Magic slammed into me from behind, hurling me through the opening. I landed in a pool of gold coins. Nero shot over my head and hit the back wall. He jumped up, magic exploding out of him. The telekinetic wave shot toward a hooded figure, but it dissipated before it ever made it there, absorbed by the dome of magic that had blossomed out to protect him. Nero stood frozen, as though he couldn't believe his eyes, as though he'd never seen anything like it before.

That moment of surprise cost him. The hooded angel's telekinetic blast was bigger than Nero's. It hammered into

Nero, throwing him against a stone column so hard that the column snapped. The ceiling caved in and collapsed on top of him.

I ran toward the rocky waterfall burying Nero. I could feel him in there, being slowly crushed under the weight. Panic surged in me. I had to get him out.

"Leda," a cold voice bit at my skin, chilling me to the bone. "I've been waiting for you for two hundred years."

A cold phantom hand of magic closed around my throat, squeezing. Something hard slammed into the side of my head, and the world went black.

CHAPTER SIXTEEN

Rogue Angel

I WOKE TO a slow, steady drip in my head. Water? Blood? Everything was blurry. I blinked, trying to clear my eyes. My whole body hurt, especially my head. Someone had hit me hard there. My balance was off, distorted. Sickness churned in my stomach, and I felt cold. My skin shivered against the icy breath of the rocks I was lying on. These thin clothes definitely weren't suited to the cold darkness of the underground ruins.

I looked around, but my eyes could barely focus behind the throbbing swell of my head injury. Everything looked distorted, like the ground was moving, tipping like on a boat caught in a tempest. Sitting up made me feel like I was going to throw up.

I wasn't alone. The angel was there, speaking to two men. He was wearing a dark brown leather suit. He wore a sword, a bow, and two guns—which was more than a little overkill, especially considering the deadly duo of the magic spells he'd been throwing around coupled with his enormous size. His hood was down, revealing a face framed by messy dark hair. The shadow of a beard covered his face, just enough to make him look rugged. I recognized the rogue angel from the picture in Nero's office, the recently fallen angel.

"Osiris Wardbreaker," I said, my voice croaking. "We've been looking for you."

A smile twisted his lips. "And I've been looking for you, the one who can open the door." He lifted his hand, and lights flared up across the chamber.

I blinked, shielding my eyes against the blinding twinkle of treasure. It was everywhere—sparkling, glistening, glittering. Gold. Tapestries. Weapons. Armor. Urns. Jewels. Treasure boxes. It was like a pirate's dream. The treasure in this treasury must have been worth millions.

"If I'd known you were coming, I would have slammed the door in your face," I said to the angel.

Osiris laughed and looked at the two minions beside him, men dressed in high-tech armor. "She's cheeky, isn't she?"

"Just get what we need from her," one of the armored men said gruffly.

It seemed the balance of power wasn't what I'd thought. This angel was working with them? Or for them? They sure weren't his minions, and not only that, they weren't even afraid of him. What was the matter with them? Even I had the sense to be afraid of him.

"All in good time," the angel told him.

Osiris looked relaxed, unrushed. Immortality, and being one of the oldest angels in the world, must have done that to you. He was comfortably confident, like he always got what he wanted.

"We will get results," he assured the two men. "And

you're going to help us, aren't you, pretty?" His hand caught my face, clamping down on my jaw much as Colonel Fireswift had once done.

The relics of heaven and hell were too dangerous to be in the hands of a powerful, corrupt angel like this one. I was almost choking from the darkness dripping off of him. I had to escape from here. I had to stop these fiends.

In my delirium, I must have muttered some of that aloud because Osiris laughed and said, "You need to worry about helping yourself."

I realized I was chained to the floor. The chains were long enough that I could stand, but I wouldn't get far. And then there was the small matter of the very big bump on my head. I still couldn't focus my eyes properly.

I squinted, looking in the mirror on the wall. My glamour had faded away. I looked like myself again, albeit a really awful version of myself. Maybe it was a good thing that I couldn't see very well. The crimson stain on my head looked bad enough with blurry vision. I did not need to see it in crisp detail.

If I had my own face back, that meant Nero could no longer maintain the spell. I hoped he was ok. I could still sense him. Somewhere. The feeling was unfocused, muffled. Was he still unconscious? I wondered how long I'd been out.

"Your angel won't be coming for you," he told me in a cruel voice.

I was dizzy and a little delirious, but I *definitely* hadn't spoken that time. Which meant he was reading my mind. Mind-reading, what was only mildly annoying when Nero did it, was about to get very problematic.

I tried to put up a mental barrier. I knew it had holes in

it the size of New York City, but it was the best I could do right now. My headache was reaching epic proportions.

"Then I will come for Nero," I told the angel defiantly.

He laughed. "Will you?"

"Yes. Right after I kick your ass."

The angel laughed again. Apparently, I was really funny.

"I'm serious," I said to him, glaring.

"Oh, I know you are, snowflake. But you'll forgive me if I don't panic. I'm rather busy at the moment. And so are you. I need your help to get us into the Treasury."

I looked at the sizable pile of gold beside him. "You're already in."

My eyes panned past the gold, snagging on the pile of rocks. My stomach knotted up. Nero was buried under all of that. I didn't see the way out of the house, so the gateway must have closed. There were two hundred Legion soldiers in the city, but they didn't even know Nero and I were here. And even if they had, they couldn't get into this chamber. Only I could open the gateway. My heart surged with hope. That meant the rogue angel and his allies couldn't kill me, not if they wanted to ever get out of here again. That hope died as soon as it had come. One look into the angel's cold eyes reminded me that there were fates far worse than death —and that he was intimately aware of all of them.

"We're not in the real Treasury. This is just the foyer. These worthless trinkets are not the real treasure." He gave the gold and gems a dismissive wave. "The real valuable things are beyond there."

His hands clamped around my throat, and he lifted me up like I weighed nothing. He dragged me over to the gold-framed door, my chains scraping against the floor. The gateway had been sealed by a single angel symbol. A grid of thirty distinct symbols was etched into this door.

"Open it," Osiris said, his voice snapping with a harsh strike of the command.

I tried to hide my hands behind my back.

"Putting your hands on the door is the first thing we tried," he said, his voice almost bored. "It didn't work. Your blood didn't work either. I think this is a door that requires a spell."

"Then cast away," I snapped. "You're an angel. I'm sure you can figure it out. You know a lot of spells."

"Oh, but *I* can't do that spell. Only a child of darkness and light can. You."

I looked at the door. "I don't know how to open it."

He tapped his finger on my forehead. "It's inside of you, that memory. Just waiting to be unlocked. And I'm going to help you remember."

Black magic sparked on the angels' hands, but it was the inhuman abyss of his dark eyes that chilled me to my core.

CHAPTER SEVENTEEN

Memory

I COULDN'T BELIEVE my luck when my restraints popped open, freeing my hands and legs. I backed up slowly, not knowing where I was going but just glad to be able to go somewhere.

"Wardbreaker, what are you doing?" one of the men protested. "This isn't a game."

It was then that my foggy mind snagged on the realization that the angel had been the one to open my restraints. His companion was wrong. This *was* a game, that deadly mind game angels played.

"I know what I'm doing," Osiris declared. "If you want results, then leave me to my work."

The men grumbled but left the chamber to go down a narrow tunnel. Where did it lead to? Nowhere useful, I feared. The only doors the angel seemed to care about were the gateway to the outside, now buried under rock, and that gold-framed door that led to the real treasure, the weapons of heaven and hell.

I realized that while I might be unchained, right now I was in even more danger than when I'd been nailed to the wall. I looked away from the angel's dark, unyielding eyes, trying to find a way out, but there wasn't one. The angel stood in the doorway to the blocked tunnel. There was no way in or out of this nightmare. Maybe—just maybe—I could get to Nero, but Osiris would catch up to me long before I could dig him out. I didn't have telekinetic powers, and I wasn't that strong, not strong enough to move boulders. And right now I could barely lift my own head, let alone a pile of rocks. I couldn't see straight, couldn't walk straight.

Osiris watched me with cool patience, with that confident air that he would eventually get exactly what he wanted. I wouldn't be able to frustrate him, to make him emotional. He was clearly prepared for the long game.

So what could I do? He was a powerful angel, more powerful than even Nero. I'd seen his power for myself. I couldn't even beat Nero, so how did I have any chance of beating this original angel, hardened by centuries of training and killing. He was faster, stronger, and more powerful than I was. I didn't have a move he hadn't seen.

Or didn't I? Maybe I couldn't win the way Legion soldiers fought, but I wasn't like them. I wasn't disciplined. I was chaotic, rough, dirty. Uncivilized. And maybe that unpredictability would be just what I needed to catch this well-trained angel off guard. It was a long shot, but it was my only hope.

"Why did you leave the Legion?" I asked.

"We are not here to discuss me. We're here to discuss you. And what you have in your head."

"I have nothing in my head," I quipped.

He laughed. "I've caught glimpses of those memories, those visions you're afraid to talk about. Seeing things doesn't make you crazy, Leda. It makes you special. You can help me save the Earth, save countless lives, prevent a war that would tear the world apart."

"By giving you a weapon that will make you invincible, that will give you the power to kill angels? To kill thousands. Or even millions. Are you taking it for yourself or for your demon masters?"

"There is so much you don't understand, Leda. The gods are not the saviors of the world. They were the ones who brought this destruction upon us."

"I know what happened. I know that both gods and demons released the monsters and that they lost control of them."

"And yet you serve those false gods." He looked at me as though he could drill through to the core of my soul. "You need something from them."

I locked down my mind.

"Nectar. Power." He laughed. "You don't seem like the sort, but it always comes down to power, doesn't it?"

"You don't know anything about me."

"I know what I've seen in your delightfully manic mind. Until you blocked me. Impressive. It takes a lot of mental fortitude to do that."

"Mental fortitude is just another word for stubbornness, and I've got stubbornness to spare." I smirked at him.

"It won't last, you know."

"I can hold you off." I tried to make my words ring with strength, but they clanged weakly in my ears. My head felt like it was splitting open from the burden of being alive.

"I wasn't talking about blocking me," he said. "I meant

your honeymoon with the Legion. You will come to wish you'd never joined their ranks, that you'd never cast your lot in with the gods."

I didn't fail to register the threat laced into the pleasant tone of his voice. He was going to torture me. Nice.

"Threatening me won't convince me to help you," I told him.

"It wasn't a threat. It was a truth. People like you, they can't be happy in the Legion. You don't fit in there."

"Is this the part where you confess to me how you never felt like you fit in? The part where you say how alike we really are? Cut the crap and save me your lies. You're an angel. You managed to fit in well enough, I'd say. Maybe *too* well. What happened? Did you get restless? Did you want more power, more magic? More than they would give you?"

"I told you we aren't here to talk about me. We're here to talk about you. What you can do for me. And what I can do for you."

"I have nothing for you. I want nothing from you."

He let out a resigned sigh. "I didn't think you'd want to do this the easy way."

"With angels, there is no easy way."

He laughed. "Indeed."

I didn't even see him move. One moment I was mouthing off to him and the next I was hitting the ground hard. Telekinesis. If only I could block that power like I could the mind-reading. I got up groggily, slowly. He could have hit me twenty times over in the time it took for me to stand, but he was just watching me. He was probably someone who liked to draw out his brutality, torturing his victims. That's what I had heard about him. Osiris Wardbreaker. Osiris the Black-hearted.

I patted down my body, surprised to find I still had all of my weapons and potions. He really was arrogant. He thought I was no threat. Maybe he was right. Maybe I wasn't a threat. But sometimes you didn't need to be a threat. Sometimes being an annoyance was good enough. He wouldn't be the first to underestimate me. I was used to it.

He watched with amusement as I pulled out some potions from the pouches at my belt, mixing them. I tossed them, sprinkling them all over the treasure chest behind him. The lid burst open. Gold coins and jewels and other sparkling things shot up like a geyser, raining down on him.

He gave me a bored look. "Pretty but ineffective."

Behind him, the chest was growing larger, thanks to the growing spell I'd put on it. He was too busy judging my inadequate magic to notice.

I tossed another potion. A stream of sparkles hit him, a wind spell. He stood there, his hair rippling in the wind, his feet planted firmly on the ground. He didn't slide an inch.

"You're going to have to do better than that," he told me.

The wind spell slammed into the big empty treasure chest behind him, tossing it up in the air. It fell over him, trapping him beneath. I sprinkled a sticky potion at the box, sealing it to the ground. And not a second too soon. The box was rumbling, like he was trying to hurl it off of him.

But he couldn't do that now. Even an angel wasn't strong enough to break *that* seal. The glue moved with you, absorbing the force of your movements, using them to power the sticky spell. All that potion-studying was coming in handy. Now if I could just figure out how to get around that big box and make my way out of here.

The box exploded in my path, wood shards flying everywhere. He'd broken through. I gaped as I saw the bottom of the box was still glued to the ground. The glue had held, just not the rest of the box.

"Cute magic trick, but the time for games is over," he told me.

He whirled an air spell like a lasso, wrapping it around me. A band of cold air pinned my arms to my sides. I couldn't even wiggle my little finger. Fire poured down the magic ropes, igniting the air spell. As it burned through my skin, I screamed out in agony. Osiris swung his hand across my face, hitting me hard. Pain bloomed up beneath my raw, wind-cut, fire-blistered skin.

Time bled away. Osiris's spell squeezed harder, sucking the air out of my lungs. Delirious, I started to see things, things that weren't there.

A red-haired angel putting on the silver armor. She lifted the shield. She slashed out with the sword, warming up her arm. Instead of air, her blade met flesh. A monster, lured into the city from the wilds. Its jaws snapped at her. She cut across its body, ending it swiftly. It was not the enemy. The enemy lay further on. They had invaded her city.

The cries and calls of the battlefield melted into me, mixing inside my mind, pulling me under.

I snapped out of the memory of the city's destruction to find I was fighting Osiris again. Or was that *still* fighting him? Time was bleeding together here too. I didn't know which was worse: the memory that always had the same inevitable end, playing out over and over again—or the real-life torture right now, tearing through my body with unbearable pain. My throat was so cracked that I couldn't even scream anymore.

"Move past the final battle," Osiris commanded me. "I need you to go deeper."

I didn't want to go deeper. I no longer had the strength to keep him out of my mind, so I was screaming profanities at him inside my head, looping those curses again and again.

He looked into my eyes and said cooly, "You really are stubborn."

"I did warn you about that," I rasped.

The magic holding me up dissipated, leaving me with burns and cuts and bruises and broken things. My feet slipped on the gold coins that covered the ground, and I fell. Osiris stood back, watching me pretend that it didn't hurt as much as we both knew it did.

He'd left the doorway open. I could make a run for it. I knew he was baiting me, that he would throw me back. Not that he needed to bait me to have an excuse to hurt me. I needed a plan, some way to counter him, but the only way to hurt an angel was to overwhelm him with sheer numbers, or with the super weapon behind the gold-framed door. I didn't have sheer numbers, and even if I could open that door, he would plow me down long before I made it to the weapon, assuming it was even in there.

"Wardbreaker," one of the angel's comrades said as the two armored men entered the chamber.

"Just a moment, precious. I'll be right back," he told me

with a sick smile, then looked at the men. "I told you never to bother me while I'm working."

"You promised progress. We don't see progress."

"Unlocking imprinted memories takes time. Patience," Osiris said.

"You should just kill her."

"She is the only one who has any memory of how to open that door," the angel explained with cold patience. "The others have been dead for a long time. So unless either of you knows how to raise the dead, leave me be."

"Raising the dead would be faster," one of the men quipped.

"How do you even know that she's the one?"

"The spell doesn't lie. It showed us the one the Guardians entrusted these memories to," said Osiris.

"What spell?" I asked.

Osiris turned to give me a smile. "The one I cast the first time you came to the Lost City, the one that unlocked the treasure trove of memories inside that precious little head of yours."

Who were these Guardians, and why did they give me memories that were not my own? What did they want? How did they give me these memories if they've been dead for so long? And did this have anything to do with my strange reaction to the Nectar?

As I watched the angel and his companions, these thoughts buzzing in my head, an odd flicker danced in front of my eyes. Osiris's face blurred. I blinked to clear my vision, but it was still there. I recognized that effect. Someone with glamour.

"You aren't who you appear to be," I said, laughing at the angel. It hurt to laugh, but I didn't care. "Where is the real Osiris Wardbreaker?"

He snapped his hand to the side, hitting me with a hot lash of magic. The pain catapulted me back into my own mind, what should have been a sanctuary but was nothing short of a nightmare.

I didn't see the battle this time. I saw a wedding, a union bound in secrecy. The doors of the temple burst open, and Legion soldiers stormed inside. A different battle in a different time and place than the Lost City—and yet it played out the same. They always began and ended the same. With death.

I saw a pale-haired angel walk across the Black Plains, her wings drooped, her wingtips drawing a trail of blood across the ruins of the Lost City. She set her hands on the angel symbol to open the gateway, passing through it. Then she went to the gold-framed door. Her head bowed, she leaned against the door. A tear of pure despair fell from her eye, splashing against the panel of symbols. They pulsed once, and the door opened. The symbols weren't a puzzle; they were a poem, written in a dead language. And it was tears that opened the door.

Wiping her wet face, she put on the armor. The pieces fit to her body, adjusting to her like magic, sliding over every dip and curve until they were like a second skin. She clasped her locket, kissing it. Then she tucked the necklace into her armor, over her heart, and prepared to meet her end.

The memory faded away, and as my eyes adjusted to the real world, I realized I was standing in front of an open doorway. The weapons of heaven and hell lay inside the small room, just as I remembered them.

"How…"

"It's an old magic. A magic to make you go through the motions of your memory, like you're in it," Osiris explained, setting his hand on my shoulder.

I tried to take a step toward the relics, but my body didn't move. I pushed against the spell holding me in place, but my mind slammed against a wall it couldn't break.

Frozen, helpless, I watched Osiris and his companions go for the relics at the same time. Magic flashed, steel clashed, and then the two men hit the ground.

The rocky wall barring the way to the Gateway exploded, and Nero rushed through, a storm of magic swirling around him. A dozen armored men were hot on his heels, but they weren't from the Legion. They looked like they belonged with the two men now lying at Osiris's feet. The angel turned to Nero, his eyes sparkling with the first hint of impatience I'd seen from him.

"It's about time," he declared. "You're late. I thought you'd be through that last layer of rock five minutes ago. What took you so long?"

"You're working together?" I asked Nero, shocked. I only realized after I'd spoken the words that I had control of my body again.

"No," Nero said.

Osiris slid his hand across his face, peeling back the glamour. The illusion faded away to reveal an angel I recognized from the picture of the original twelve hanging in Nero's office.

Nero blinked back surprise. "Father."

CHAPTER EIGHTEEN
Dragonsire

THE ARMORED MEN, who must have also been working with the angel, paused in surprise when they saw his real face. I was pretty surprised myself. This was Damiel Dragonsire, Nero's father. This was the angel Nero's mother had tracked down and killed because he went rogue. His mother had died too, wounded in that angelic battle. It had all played out centuries ago, and yet here Damiel was.

"How can you be alive?" Nero said slowly, cautiously, as though he couldn't believe what his eyes were telling him.

"Not now. We have more important problems."

Damiel indicated the armored men, who were moving toward the angels, surrounding them. They must have been trapped behind the rocks that had fallen on Nero.

One of the men stepped to the front, looking between Nero and this angel who looked a lot like Nero. He had the same hair as Nero, if not a bit more bronze than caramel, and his eyes were blue instead of green, but other than that, they might have been twins.

"Where is Wardbreaker?" the man demanded.

"Still buried where I left him, I presume," Damiel said

darkly.

"You took his place."

Damiel met the man's angry eyes with indifference. "There's no need to feel all torn up about his death. You never even met him."

The man's hand waved the others forward. "You played us. Angel or not, you will come to regret that."

"Take care of these men," Damiel ordered Nero, moving toward the relics.

Nero stepped into his path. "If it was you the whole time, then Osiris Wardbreaker never turned rogue?"

"We'll discuss this later, after the battle."

Nero gave his wrist a sharp flick, and a psychic blast cut through the room, slamming the twelve men against the wall. I heard the sharp, sickening snap of their necks breaking all at once.

"Battle's over," he said as the men slid to the ground behind him. "We'll talk about this *now*. Did Osiris Wardbreaker go rogue?"

"Yes," Damiel said in a tone that showed he was only humoring his son. His eyes passed over the men on the ground, and he looked mildly impressed. "I caught up with him about a week after his defection." His gaze slid to me. "He was kidnapping young supernatural children and feasting on their blood. He enjoyed hearing their screams. And watching them die.

I choked on the image. Acid rose in my throat, and I barely kept it down. Damiel wasn't even looking at his son. He was looking only at me.

"So trust me, I was doing the world a favor," he finished.

He was probably right. Killing children, feeding on

their blood and pain, was a crime I could not forgive. The world was better off without monsters like that in it.

"Trust you?" Nero shot his father a look of pure, undiluted loathing. "I don't trust you. Not your words and definitely not with objects of power. I will not allow you to have them."

"Insubordination does not suit you, soldier."

"Insubordination? You're the one who turned dark and betrayed the Legion," Nero said. "I am not your soldier. You don't give orders anymore."

Damiel looked at me. "Make him see reason."

"Don't talk to her like you're old friends." Nero's words bit like a whip. "You tortured her."

"A means to an end."

"Everything is always just a means to an end with you."

Anger flashed in Nero's eyes, splitting the final strands of his self-control. He rushed forward in a flash of supernatural speed, hammering his fist into his father's jaw. He followed that up with another punch. Flames burst to life across his entire body. He'd lost it, truly and completely lost it.

Damiel struck back, throwing Nero across the room. Solid rock split and fissures formed where Nero's back had hit the wall, but he rolled himself around and kept going like he hadn't felt a thing. He wasn't feeling anything but his own anger. The angels fought without mercy or pause, their terrible, beautiful battle threatening to bring down the whole room.

Five armored men climbed through the fallen rocks in the entrance and rushed into the chamber. They ignored the angels fighting above and ran straight for the relics. One of them made it, grabbing the closest relic, a gun, from its stand. I threw a rock at him, hitting him in the forehead. He fell to the floor, his head bleeding out. His four comrades moved around him, trying to reach the relics.

I tossed magic powder on the gold coins that lay across the floor. The gold glowed orange, and smoke rose from the men's shoes. The men hopped in alarm, scrambling away from the gold. In their hurried retreat, one of them stumbled into the middle of the firefight between Nero and Damiel. He didn't last a second.

The others hopped and skipped between the glowing coins, trying to get to the relics. I grabbed hold of one guy's arm, holding him there.

I stared into his eyes. "Shoot your comrades."

The man nodded, taking a shiny silver gun from the floor He aimed at the other men and fired. The bullets cut right through their armor like they weren't wearing any. After he'd shot them down, he froze for a moment, shaking his head. I could feel my control slipping away from his mind. I'd been through too much. I didn't have enough power left in me. I lifted my hand to knock his gun away, but I was too slow. He shot me in the stomach.

Pain seared through me like wildfire, exploding in my blood. I fell to my knees. Through blurry eyes, I saw him walk toward the relics. I pushed agains the weight of the impending blackout, struggling to my feet. I had to get to him. I had to stop him. He already had a piece of the silver armor in his hand.

A glowing sword tip broke through his chest, piercing him from behind. He dropped dead to the ground. My eyes panned up, expecting to see Nero. But it wasn't Nero. He and Damiel were still fighting up above.

Seconds passed. Pain pulsed by every beat of my heart. My mind struggled to stay conscious. Blood dripped down my body. I blinked.

"How did you get down here?" I asked, blinking again.

My mind was slow, failing to process what I was seeing. He wore the weapons of heaven and hell. The silver armor fitted his wide, masculine body as perfectly as it had fitted Sierra's feminine curves. He held a shield in one hand, a sword in the other.

"I wasn't going to let anything stand between me and my relics," Valiant said.

Flames flickered on the sword. Hatred burned in his eyes.

"Thank you, Leda," he said. "I couldn't have done it without you."

Then he swung the sword, blasting the angel-killing flames at the two angels.

CHAPTER NINETEEN
Powerless

HIS AIM WAS shit. The flames didn't hit the angels, but they did get their attention. Nero and Damiel stopped fighting. Nero snapped out of whatever trance he'd been in, and when he saw Valiant donning the weapons of heaven and hell, he grew dangerously still.

Valiant didn't bother with banter. He went straight for the killing blow. He swung the sword, shooting the blue flames at the angels again. Damiel used magic to block. Surprisingly, his spell dissolved the blue flames. Wasn't the sword's magic supposed to be stronger than an angel's?

Valiant was clearly wondering the same thing. "Why aren't you working properly?" he demanded, shaking the sword. "Maybe it needs to warm up."

Nero and Damiel weren't giving him a chance to test that theory. They blasted magic at him, trying to knock the sword out of his hand. Their psychic spells slid uselessly against the silver armor. *That* seemed to be working. It was supposed to nullify enemy magic.

Encouraged by the armor's success, Valiant blasted more blue fireballs at the angels, but Damiel's super-shield held.

"I think you're doing it wrong," I commented.

"Shut up." He shook the sword again.

He was focusing on the sword. His eyes weren't on the angels. Damiel motioned to Nero to go right, and Nero nodded.

I wasn't in any condition to fight right now, especially not against the relics of heaven and hell. I knew I had to distract Valiant so the angels could move in unnoticed. I could do that. I could talk. At least talking would help me stay conscious, help me fight the warm wave of lethargy consuming my body one muscle at a time.

"You were the one who hired these armored men, who hired Osiris, to find the relics. And the Legion never suspected a thing?"

It was an invitation for him to talk about how clever he was. Villains liked doing that. This particular villain had done a lot of planning and plotting. He'd fooled the entire Legion, and he was dying for a chance to toot his horn.

He took it. "You make good soldiers at the Legion. Powerful, forceful brutes. But you are not thinkers. You're not clever. The other Legion soldiers are blinded by duty and honor and ambition. But you, Leda. You are just naive. Fooling you was easy. Maneuvering you right where I wanted you was easy."

I glared at him.

"I told you right what I needed you to know, piece by piece, to make you do what I wanted you to do. Or did you think it was an accident that I shared that piece of poetry with you, the key to the puzzle? It had to be you to open the door. I've heard about you, Leda Pierce. What you've done. Your magic."

"Light and dark."

"Yes, light and dark, the perfect vessel for the memories of the relics of heaven and hell," he said. "The Legion is arrogant, so used to everything being something they understand, something they can control. Black and white. They can't see past their well-established hierarchy, their tired view of the world. They can't read between the lines. They can't see how special you are. But I knew from the moment I heard about you. And when I read that poem, I knew I would need you to open the way. To lead me to the relics."

"Your hired guns were talking about a spell that unlocked my memories?"

"Another useful bit of knowledge I found in my research." He smiled like he was in awe of his own genius. "They performed the spell when we first came to the ruins. That unlocked your memories, memories the Nectar had already brought to the surface of your mind." He smiled at the sword. "Finally, after all these years, it's mine."

Valiant spun around, slashing. Magic lapped on the blade, powering his strike. He drew blood from both angels, and they fell back against the wall, clenching their teeth against the pain. Two angels, top of the Legion, as tough as they came, each one barely keeping themselves from screaming out in agony.

"Perhaps it's working after all. This sword can kill an immortal," Valiant taunted them. "It's made me powerful, more powerful than an angel. I am a god. And I will destroy the gods and demons with their own weapons."

"What happened all those years ago?" I asked him, drawing his attention back to me. I wanted nothing more than to go to Nero, to make sure he was all right, but I had to keep the Pilgrim talking. I had to give the angels a chance to heal.

"I can see the pain in your eyes, Valiant," I said. "And the hatred. Why do you hate them so much? You serve the gods."

"Those who serve the gods suffer most of all. My wife and my sister died in my service of the gods, two pointless deaths in the war of titans, victims of the monsters the gods and demons unleashed on this Earth. We all went out there, drawing the monsters away from the town. Only I returned."

"You feel guilty that you were the one to survive," I realized.

"No," he denied it. "I don't feel guilty. I feel fury."

But I could see it in his eyes. He couldn't stand that he'd survived and those he'd loved had died. I almost felt sorry for him—if not for the fact that he wanted to go out and kill a bunch of people.

"I was powerless to save them," he said. "But I'm not powerless now. Not now, not ever again. I will tear through the armies of heaven and hell. I will pluck the gods and demons from their thrones. I will defeat the monsters and return the Earth to humanity."

I didn't think anyone would survive his kind of war. A war built on vengeance was just a self-perpetuating cycle. It would keep going until everyone was dead.

Nero and Damiel came at Valiant from either side, not allowing him to use the sword against both at once. After feeling the mortal bite of the blade, they were more cautious now. They were evading his strikes, but the relics' magic had made him as strong and fast as an angel. It was only a matter of time before he drew blood again.

A memory crashed against me. *An angel cut at her with her own sword.*

Valiant cut across Nero's chest, slicing through the leather. I screamed out.

She looked up, seeing her own death in the angel's eyes. The sword came down—and then just stopped, frozen. It was fighting him. It was fighting for its true master. It turned around in his hand and stabbed him in the chest.

I ran forward, calling out to the sword in Valiant's hand, a stolen weapon that had never been meant for him. It flew out of his hand.

"What's going on?" he demanded.

I kept moving forward, a flash of adrenaline burying my pain. "They're not yours."

The shield sank to the ground. Valiant pulled on it, but it didn't budge.

"They see the hatred in your heart," I said.

The armor shifted, constricting. Crushing.

"And they want no part of it."

Valiant's hands darted to the armor clasps, trying to open them. The silver metal began to glow.

"What are you doing to me?!" he howled at me, pounding at his chest, desperately trying to get out of the armor.

The sword lifted into the air, then plunged through his neck. The armor split open, and Valiant's body fell to the floor.

Damiel's eyes darted from me, to the dead Pilgrim, to the pile of weapons and armor beside him. "Spectacular." He reached for the relics.

Nero got to them first. Damiel didn't try to stop his son as he lifted the relics off the floor.

"You have a big mess to explain," Damiel observed.

"Osiris Wardbreaker and Valiant were after the relics. Their forces clashed. Valiant died," Nero told me.

"And what about Osiris?"

Nero gave his father a hard look, then said, "The rogue angel died too. The armor's magic overloaded and killed him after he killed the Pilgrim."

"Perhaps you do understand loyalty to your family after all," said Damiel.

"Stop talking," Nero told his father, then tossed me a roll of tape. "Bind him in that tape. It's strong enough to hold an angel. The more he struggles, the more his magic is drained."

Damiel watched in silent amusement as I bound his hands.

"The relics of heaven and hell were destroyed," I told Nero. If the Legion got those weapons, the power would destroy them from the inside, turning angel against angel.

"Agreed," Nero said, putting them into a bag.

The room chose that moment to lurch. Nero caught me before I fell. His mouth hardened when he saw the bullet wound in my stomach. The rest of me probably didn't look so great either.

He set his hand on my stomach and magic flowed from him to me. "Hold on, Leda."

Everything went black. I was blind.

"…is not healing."

"Gunshot…she…shot by an immortal weapon."

"You're not dying," Nero told me.

My body felt numb.

"You still have to save Zane. I order you not to die."

I held onto that thought, drawing myself back into the

pain.

"Bossy," I muttered.

He kissed me with lips wet with his own blood. A drop fell onto my tongue, jolting me awake like a shot of pure caffeine. I opened my eyes, and looked up at him.

"I can see again," I said.

"Can you walk too?"

I rose to my feet, swaying but not falling. "We have to get your father and the relics out of the city without Colonel Fireswift seeing them."

"His forces are outside the gateway."

"There's a secret passage."

It was all coming back to me now, the fragmented memories solidifying. I pressed my hand to the wall, one without even a symbol to adorn it. I led them down the passage that Sierra had taken many times before. I hoped it hadn't collapsed since then.

The passage was clear. It brought us to the edge of the city. Later, as we rode Calli's motorcycle across the Black Plains, I realized that was one of the only things to go right all week.

Pressed between Nero and Damiel on the seat of the motorcycle, I drifted in and out of consciousness. I vaguely recalled entering my house, but I had no clue how we'd gotten past the soldiers on the wall.

I heard Calli shouting at Nero for getting me nearly killed. I wanted to tell her that it wasn't his fault, but I couldn't seem to move my tongue. My eyes grew heavy, and I sank into dreamless sleep.

CHAPTER TWENTY
Revelation

BELLA WAS SITTING beside me, wrapping my bandages, when I woke up in my own bed. My body felt a little better, but my mind and magic felt like they'd been put through the blender.

"He can't stay here," Calli's voice streamed in through the partially-open bedroom door. "He's too dangerous."

"I will be moving him," Nero replied. "It's just for now, until Leda can travel again."

"We can take care of our own."

"I will not leave her side. The last two times we were separated, she almost died."

"That won't happen here," Calli said.

"I'm staying. I take care of my own too."

"She's not your soldier anymore."

"She is so much more than a soldier."

Bella brushed a washcloth over my forehead. "Just rest. You're safe," she said in soothing tones.

I closed my eyes. The next time I woke up, it was Nero at my bedside. He looked like he hadn't slept in days.

"How are you feeling?"

"Fine." I looked at my bloody bandages. "Why hasn't it healed?"

"You were shot by an immortal weapon."

I remembered the armored man in the Treasury, the silver gun in his hand. He must have picked up the relic that his comrade had dropped. That explained why the bullets had gone right through armor—and why the wound in my stomach hadn't healed.

"Am I going to die?" I asked him.

"No, the wound will just heal slowly," he said. "And, besides, I forbid you to die."

I grunted. "Nice to know."

"She's tough," Damiel called out from another chair.

"I'm sorry he's here," Nero told me. "I have to keep an eye on him in case he tries anything."

"What am I going to try with these restraints blocking my magic and restricting my movements?" Damiel asked. "I have an itch I haven't been able to scratch for over an hour."

"You think this is funny?" Nero snarled. "She is in this state because of you. She almost died."

"I wasn't the one to shoot her with an immortal weapon." Damiel looked at Leda. "I'm glad you survived. You make my son actually feel something. He's been closed off for so long."

"You don't get to speak to her like that, like she's some old friend. You tortured her, you sadistic swine."

"You don't talk to me like that. I am still your father."

"No, you're not. You're nothing. You're dead. You died two hundred years ago. I wish you'd just stayed that way."

"I did what I had to do. Back then and now. And not everything is as simple as you think," Damiel said. "Stop being melodramatic, Nero. What I did was not torture. I know you know what real torture looks like because I brought you along to witness it when you were five."

Ew. Talk about take-your-son-to-work day, Legion of Angels style. That was twisted. No wonder the Legion brats had issues.

"What I did was unlock the memories in her," Damiel continued. "That meant breaking her physically. You've done that to her, to countless initiates, over the years. You broke them so they could find something inside of themselves. A special power. This is no different."

"This is completely different," Nero countered. "Because you enjoyed it."

"Stop trying to make me fit into that evil image you have of me in your head," Damiel said. "It was a job that had to be done. Nothing more." He looked at me, as though I could confirm that he hadn't enjoyed hurting me.

"You were pretty convincing when you were kicking my ass," I told him.

"I had to be convincing. You had to believe it."

"Well, I did. And so did Valiant's men," I said.

"You should have just killed them," Nero told his father.

"I was saving them. I wasn't sure if the door required a human sacrifice to open the way to the relics, or to unlock them. Some of the old magic does. And I didn't think you wanted me using your girl for that."

"So I should be thanking you now?"

"Yes, that would be appropriate. And while you're at it, how about untying me?" He showed Nero his bound hands. "This is completely undignified."

Nero gave him a look that said hell would freeze over

before he untied him.

"Is it true what you said about human sacrifices? That they activate magic?" I asked Damiel.

"For some kinds of magic, usually objects of power. Magic always has a price, but it's often not very picky about who pays it." He paused. "But the relics are made from a whole other kind of magic altogether. That crazy Pilgrim stained his blade with angel blood, and it didn't activate the magic. But you only had to look at them, and they obeyed your commands."

I didn't really want to think about it. Those weapons were too dangerous for anyone to wield. We had to hide them—or destroy them. Part of me screamed in protest at the thought of destroying them. It was probably the same part that had made the weapons turn on Valiant and kill him.

The door creaked open and Calli peeked inside. "The First Angel is coming across the lawn now."

Nero rose. "Stay here and keep quiet," he said to his father.

I slowly pushed myself up. Before I could get very far, Nero leaned down and swooped me up into his arms. The front door opened as he set me onto one of the sofas in the living room.

"Stay outside," Nyx commanded her guards, then shut the door. She followed Calli into the living room.

"First Angel," Nero said, bowing.

Nyx's eyes flitted from him to me, bundled up in blankets on the sofa.

"I would bow, but I think I might open my wounds and pass out at your feet," I said with a small smile.

"It's quite all right, dear," she replied. "Rise, Nero. We

don't have time for silly pleasantries." She sat down on the sofa opposite mine, watching him take a seat next to me. "Have you forgotten how to heal people, Colonel?"

"No. She was shot by an immortal weapon. The wound is not healing as fast as it should."

"Immortal weapon, you say? Well, Colonel, that's what we're here to discuss." She folded her hands together on her lap. "I got your report. And Colonel Fireswift's report." Her mouth thinned into a hard line. "They vary greatly."

"With all due respect, Colonel Fireswift likes to blow hot air." He paused, dipping his head. "First Angel."

Nyx took a cookie from the dish on the table, laughing. It was a genuine laugh. This was the side of Nyx that I liked.

"Ok, let's hear it."

So we told her Nero's carefully crafted story. She listened in silence.

When we were finished, she brushed the cookie crumbs from her hands and said bluntly, "I don't believe it. Though Wardbreaker's and Valiant's remains do seem to confirm that at least part of your story is true. Remind me again why Wardbreaker is only ashes."

"The relics burned him to ashes," Nero said.

"Right." Nyx paused. "And where are these relics?"

"Destroyed during the fight."

"So you expect me to believe that weapons forged in heaven and hell could be destroyed just like that?"

Nero said nothing. Neither did I. We'd both agreed that it was best. My being a smart ass would just get us into trouble.

Nyx sighed. "Well, I suppose it's for the best. I just hope those weapons don't resurface." She shot us a hard look. "Ok, now, we come to the fun part."

That sounded ominous.

"I trust you both remember our last conversation together, so this shouldn't come as a surprise," she said. "The two of you cause trouble. Nonstop." She glanced at me. "You are a bad influence on him."

"Actually, he's a bad influence on me, I think," I joked.

Nero's hand closed around my wrist.

Nyx's eyes dipped to that gesture. "Going to throw yourself in front of her to protect her from my wrath?" she asked, amused.

"Thankfully, that doesn't seem necessary."

"Indeed not." She looked from me to him, shaking her head in slow disbelief. "What am I going to do with you two?"

I wasn't sure if that was a rhetorical question or an actual question. I went with the safe option and chose to keep my mouth shut.

"Nero, you should have just let Colonel Fireswift deal with her," Nyx said.

"He certainly tried to deal with her."

"What do you mean?"

"She nearly died under his command. From the Nectar."

"A lot of people died or almost died that night," Nyx pointed out.

"Because they weren't ready for the Nectar. Not because their Nectar was laced with Venom."

Surprise flashed in Nyx's eyes. "Are you sure?"

"I tested her blood. Someone tried to poison Leda." He arched a single brow, allowing the rest to go unspoken.

"It wasn't Colonel Fireswift," Nyx said, picking up on

the implication. "That's ridiculous. You are letting your feelings cloud your judgment. Colonel Fireswift is a loyal soldier of the Legion."

"You know as well as I that his ambition defines him. It guides his actions. He would do whatever it took to secure his legacy, his family's legacy."

"Enough, Nero. You two have never liked each other, but even he wouldn't go that far."

"I will be keeping my eye on him. And especially on her," he said, intertwining his fingers with mine.

"That will soon be difficult," replied Nyx. "Look, unofficially, off the record, you two did a great job. You kept the relics out of enemy hands, stopped a rogue angel, and stopped a misguided pilgrim who had the power to destroy everything we're working for. If you two hadn't acted fast like you had, we might very well be at war right now. You did the right thing. You are strong, true, and resourceful. A bit too resourceful if what I hear from the paranormal soldiers stationed in town is true." The corner of her mouth quirked up. "The Legion is lucky to have you."

She paused, giving us a hard look. "But officially, I can't say any of that. You went out on your own, knowing that if you'd come to me, I would have told you to let Colonel Fireswift handle it. You two are trouble together. Explosive. I can't have you at the same office together. I can't have her under your command, Nero. So I'm doing the only thing I can."

"I'm being moved," I said glumly.

"No, you're staying right where you are," Nyx said to my surprise. She turned to Nero. "*You* are being moved. And I know just where to put you." She gave him a long, hard look. "You're being promoted. Congratulations, General." She winked at him.

"Now," she said, rising. "I expect to see you in my office in LA tonight, Nero, so we can discuss your next post."

Then she rose and walked out of the house. As soon as she was gone, my bedroom door creaked open and Damiel stepped into the living room.

"I couldn't help but overhear," he said.

"I have half a mind to kill him," Nero muttered. "Or turn him over to Nyx."

"You can't bribe the First Angel into letting you stay in New York," Damiel said.

"I can certainly try." He looked at me. "I should have seen this coming, her promoting me to solve her problem."

"Stop being cynical."

"Such an attitude is necessary at the Legion."

"Nyx is promoting you because she needs you," I told him.

"I know. But she's also getting rid of a problem."

Damiel grabbed one of the cookies Nyx had been enjoying so much. "He's right. By having you not under his command, she is allowing this lovely relationship to blossom." He looked at Nero. "Assuming you can behave yourself and not try to save her at every opportunity. And assuming you survive the ceremony. Level ten is brutal."

"As always, you give the best pep talks."

"I can help you prepare," Damiel offered.

"I don't need your help."

I made a note to get tips from Damiel. I was not going to lose Nero because he was too stubborn to accept his father's help.

"Nyx is right, you know." Damiel's eyes shifted between

me and Nero.

"About what?" Nero asked impatiently.

"It wasn't Fireswift who poisoned Leda. He couldn't have. Angels can't get the Venom. But gods can."

Nero's expression changed. He no longer looked angry. He looked scared. I'd never seen that expression on his face before.

"What is it?" I asked him.

"He's realized that I'm right. And what it means," Damiel said.

I looked at Nero for clarification, but he didn't say anything. So I turned to Damiel instead. "What does it mean?"

"Best case scenario, one of the gods wants you dead."

"That is the *best* case scenario?"

"Yes. When it comes to the gods, if you gain their attention, death is the best you can hope for. The other reason a god might have poisoned you is to test you."

"Test me how?"

Damiel shrugged. "Maybe to see how resilient you are. Or the god thinks you're special and wants to figure out how—and then turn you into a weapon or a guinea pig. That happens all the time."

"Stop talking now," Nero said to his father, his voice dangerously quiet.

"You sure are on edge, Nero. Are you sure there isn't something you want to get off your chest?" He glanced at me.

"I told you to stop."

"I'm just trying to help."

"No, you're not."

They stared at each other for what seemed like an

eternity. I felt like they were having a silent discussion, excluding me. Maybe they were speaking telepathically.

"Careful, old man. I can still throw you to the wolves," Nero said finally.

Ok, now I was *sure* they'd been talking telepathically.

"You're a terrible liar, Nero. If you were going to turn me in, you would have done it already. I think you have a soft spot for me."

Nero's eyes flashed with indignation. "Did you hit your head when you fell from heaven?"

Damiel chuckled. "Nyx was wrong," he told me. "You're not a bad influence on my son. You are a fantastic influence."

"I'm not sure about that, but thanks. I think."

His eyes took on a nostalgic glow. "This is just like it was with Nero's mother. Except I was the bad influence. We used to stay up late—"

A knife shot across the room. Damiel caught it between his bound hands, twisting them expertly to compensate. He set the knife calmly down on the coffee table.

"Nero, do not throw knives indoors," he said in that same patient tone he'd used back at the Lost City, the tone of an immortal with all the time in the world, the tone of someone unbothered by anything. "Especially not when we're guests in someone else's home. It's simply not appropriate."

I was starting to realize that was the tone he reserved for the times he was really emotional, like it was his counter to strong feelings.

"Do not speak of my mother," Nero said, his eyes burning with rage.

"I loved her."

"You killed her," he spat. His lip quivered, his shoulders shaking with angry tremors.

"No." He paused. "It's time you heard what really happened. I didn't really go crazy. I was always a bit dark, but your mother countered that. She balanced me."

His eyes shone with naked vulnerability. Looking into those eyes, I knew he'd loved her—that he *still* loved her. Nero must have seen it too because he didn't argue with his father. He just listened in silence, waiting for Damiel to continue.

"Those were different times, Nero," he said. "After a few angels defected, the Legion grew paranoid. They began striking preemptively, trying to stomp out darkness. We heard they were coming for me—and that they were going to assign your mother to hunt me down out of some kind of twisted sense of poetic justice."

My heart clenched in sympathy. "That is cruel."

"The Legion is cruel," Damiel told me. "And they are cunning. So we decided to preempt them. We staged a confrontation. Everything you saw was an act." He looked at Nero. "For you. So you would not be forever barred from joining the Legion because of our treachery. As long as the Legion thought your mother died doing her duty, you would be assured entry."

"But why would you want him to join an organization that would force his mother to kill his father?" I asked.

"The gods control the Nectar," Nero said, his eyes meeting his father's. "Without Nectar, you cannot become an angel. This is about power."

"It's about who you are," Damiel replied. "Who you were always meant to be: an angel."

Nero said nothing.

"She's alive."

Nero's eyes lit up.

"Your mother is alive, and we are going to find her. That's why I tracked down the weapons of heaven and hell. They belong to a group called the Guardians. I was going to use the weapons to get their attention so I could find her. After our staged battle, we were wounded and separated. I learned the Guardians had taken her in, but no one knows where they are. I've been searching for her, Nero, for two hundred years."

CHAPTER TWENTY-ONE

Angels

CALLI CAME IN on the tail of Damiel's revelation to announce that dinner was ready.

Damiel patted Nero's shoulder. "Come on, son."

We walked to the dining room in a solemn line. Nero still hadn't said anything. His mind must have been overloaded rewriting two hundred years of history.

"Mrs. Pierce, this all looks delicious," Damiel said as he sat down.

"You put out the fancy plates?" I said to Calli.

"Of course she did. We have two angels over for dinner. *Two*," Tessa repeated with unfettered glee. "My friends will never believe it."

"And you won't tell them," Calli said.

Tessa shot her a pouty face. "It's still cool," Tessa said, recovering quickly. "Even though one of the angels has handcuffs on."

The handcuffs weren't affecting Damiel's ability to eat. He could twist his arms in just the right way.

"Way cool." Tessa watched him cut a carrot neatly in half. "What level are you?"

"Level ten."

"Wow. That's like as high as it gets."

"Not quite. There's the First Angel."

"Yeah, but she's like in a class all her own." Tessa's gaze slid across to Gin. "Did you see her hair?"

"Yeah, it was flowing like it was underwater, like it was caught in some magic field or something." Gin stole a quick look at the angels, then looked down shyly.

"What is your favorite ability?" Tessa asked Damiel.

"What is this, Supernatural Teen magazine article part two?" I demanded.

"Shush, don't interrupt while I'm interviewing your future father-in-law."

"Father-in-law?" Damiel's brows lifted.

I dropped my face into my hands.

"There, there. She means well," Bella said, patting my back.

"I don't have a favorite ability. They are all tools, weapons in my arsenal. They all work together," Damiel told Tessa, bringing them back to her question—and away from dangerous waters.

Thank you, I thought to him, sure he would hear my mental message.

"Would you sign my bellybutton?" Tessa asked Damiel with a coy wink.

"Don't flirt with him," I told her.

"Why not?"

I smirked at her. "Because I'll tell your boyfriend."

"You don't even know who he is."

"I'll find out," I promised her.

"You'd better be nice to me, Leda." She gave Damiel a demure smile. "Someday I might be your mother-in-law."

ELLA SUMMERS

I turned to Bella. "Kill me now."

"What kills an immortal?"

"Seventeen-year-old girls."

Bella laughed.

"I'd love to see your wings," Tessa told Damiel, biting her lip playfully.

"And you thought *I* was bad," I said to Nero.

"When you've had Nectar, you're even worse than your sister."

The mischievous spark in his eyes reminded me of what had happened on our date—and in the library.

"Oh. That's certainly vivid," Damiel commented. "I didn't know the shelves bent that way."

I put up my mental barrier. "Mind-reading angels," I grumbled, my cheeks burning.

"Young man," Calli said.

"*Young* man?" Nero asked.

Calli gave her hand a dismissive wave. "Don't ruin it. I had a whole speech ready."

"Then by all means."

"Are your intentions honorable?" she asked bluntly.

"What would you say if I said no?"

"I'd say that at least you're honest." Her eyes hardened. "And that I have a grenade launcher in the back that will shred more than a few of your feathers, immortal or not."

They stared at one another, ice versus fire. Finally, they both laughed.

Calli took a bite of her roll. "I like you."

Nero dipped his chin. "I like you too."

They'd apparently sized each other up and decided they didn't need to go to war.

After dinner, Nero and I sat outside, gazing up at the stars —and at the complete lack of soldiers watching the house.

"I have to leave now to meet with Nyx," he told me.

"I'll stay here tonight, then go back to New York tomorrow." I paused. "Will I ever see you again?"

"Of course. I made you a promise." He leaned in and kissed me softly. "And I never go back on my word."

With a final brush of his lips against mine, he pulled away. His wings spread out from his back, and he shot into the air. A dark feather fluttered down from the sky, landing in my lap.

"He does love a dramatic exit," I commented as Calli sat down beside me.

Her gaze flickered to the feather I was holding between my fingers. "He's an angel. Of course he loves a dramatic exit. And so do you."

"Yeah. I guess we really are a lot alike," I laughed.

"Are you being careful, Leda?" she asked seriously.

"You know me. What do you think?"

"That you jump into things headfirst with good intentions but not a whole lot else."

I brushed my fingertip across Nero's feather. It was as soft as silk. "Sounds about right."

"I'm worried about you. You've thrown yourself into a dangerous world this time, kid. A world you don't fully understand. A world of gods and demons. And angels." She paused, then added, "That angel is determined."

"To make me his lover, I know."

"You don't understand. The way he acts. The way he looks at you. He won't let anyone else heal you or take care of you. He has to do it himself. He is protective. Possessive. Downright murderous if you're threatened."

I snorted. "Typical angel behavior. They are so bossy."

"Yes and no," Calli said. "I won't pretend that I understand everything about angels, but I did read through the book you had in your bag, Leda. The one about angels."

"Hey!"

She gave me a sheepish smile. "The book had a great cover. And I'm a sucker for a good cover. I couldn't resist."

"I will forgive you if you make me some cookies before I leave tomorrow."

"Deal," she said. "Back to the book. And back to angels. The way Nero Windstriker is acting is classic angel mating behavior. He doesn't just want you to be his lover. He wants you to be his mate."

Calli kissed my forehead and then went back inside the house, leaving me with the weight of her words. Was she right?

Nero had given me the book about angels. I'd thought it was research material so I could deal with Osiris Wardbreaker and understand how to survive Colonel Fireswift's games. But had the gift been more personal? Was he trying to help me understand the ways of angels so that I could understand him, so that I would know what his actions meant?

I looked up at Nero, so high in the sky. He was almost to the train station now. So he had intentions. Well, I had intentions of my own.

"This is far from over, angel," I promised him.

Author's Note

If you want to be notified when I have a new release, head on over to my website to sign up for my mailing list at http://www.ellasummers.com/newsletter. Your e-mail address will never be shared, and you can unsubscribe at any time.

If you enjoyed *Siren's Song*, I'd really appreciate if you could spread the word. One of the best ways of doing that is by leaving a review wherever you purchased this book. Thank you for your invaluable support!

The fourth book in the *Legion of Angels* series will be coming soon.

About the Author

Ella Summers has been writing stories for as long as she could read; she's been coming up with tall tales even longer than that. One of her early year masterpieces was a story about a pigtailed princess and her dragon sidekick. Nowadays, she still writes fantasy. She likes books with lots of action, adventure, and romance. When she is not busy writing or spending time with her two young children, she makes the world safe by fighting robots.

Ella is the international bestselling author of the paranormal and fantasy series *Legion of Angels*, *Dragon Born*, and *Sorcery and Science*.

www.ellasummers.com

49537029R20167

Made in the USA
San Bernardino, CA
27 May 2017